A(

Chandler: ***'Had me stressed and excited ... Top job!'***

Pete: ***'If it was a track I would have it on repeat!'***

Jojo: ***'Loved all the cool 80s nostalgia.'***

James: ***'A great story.'***

Tess_A: ***'Made me want to go back in time!'***

Josh: ***'A great read.'***

London_Mike007: ***'Action packed ... debauchery!'***

Paris: ***'It's all right!'***

dmannonymous: ***'An enjoyable read.'***

Doug: ***'Lively!'***

L.P. STANTON

ACID GLITTER

ROCKING HIPPO

Rocking Hippo
2 Woodside Cottages,
Chacewater, Truro
TR4 8LP

First published in Great Britain in 2021 by Hippo Books

This edition published in Great Britain in 2022 by Rocking Hippo

www.rockinghippo.co.uk

A CIP catalogue record for this book is available from the British Library

ISBN 9798358606067

Printed and bound by amazon.com

Rocking Hippo is committed to a sustainable future for our planet.
This book was printed on demand to reduce waste.

Also available digitally as an eBook

Cover designs courtesy of Rushmore.
www.traxcouture.com

Scan for author pages
and more at
www.rockinghippo.co.uk

ACID GLITTER

01 / *Break and Enter* (Intro)	(00.01)
02 / *All Back To Mine*	(00.12)
03 / *Glitter's Ball*	(00.26)
04 / *White Noise*	(00.40)
05 / *Rehab* (Interlude)	(00.55)
06 / *Decks and F.X.*	(00.70)
07 / *V. I. P.*	(00.85)
08 / *Rock The Night*	(01.04)
09 / *After Parties*	(01.15)
10 / *Chill Out* (Interlude)	(01.33)
11 / *Acid House*	(01.46)
12 / *Their Law*	(01.62)
13 / *Ride On Time*	(01.77)
14 / *Sinister Strings*	(01.93)
15 / *Underground*	(02.12)
16 / *Promotions*	(02.33)
17 / *3 a.m. Eternal*	(02.44)
18 / *Paradise* (Outro)	(02.69)

01 / *Break and Enter*

Saturday night, Will Frances was out to crack a warehouse.

That was the plan.

Part of him was already there. Him and the boys. Their bodies drenched in sweat amidst a haze of smoke and flashing coloured lights. The place turned into wonderland.

The music stopped.

A motorbike shrieked past at a hundred miles an hour. Will found himself squashed between Adam and the passenger door, resenting the Transit van's cramped interior. Tinny speakers, dirty trim, and a ton of litter scrapped for floor space. Will spotted a dead glowstick among the debris and decided his new hi-tops were on the world's worst dance floor.

Beyond Adam, Rob flipped the cassette. 'Check this next one.'

Anticipation roused Will. He just wanted to drop in a stack, light it up, and feel the beat pounding through his chest, a sea of happy people all around him.

A four-to-the-floor beat pattern punched from the speakers, drowning out the diesel engine's dull chug. Electronic effects and string harmonies floated over the top before the track cut into swift piano chords and a stripped-down vocal saying, You Are, every few bars.

'"Rich In Paradise",' muttered Rob as the full arrangement kicked in.

'Wicked!' The track fizzed along, and Will returned to wonderland, the crowd around him, letting loose in their own secret corner of the world. The music taking them somewhere they'd never been before.

Shooting through residential streets, they hit the main road and up onto the flyover. Rising above the urban sprawl, a dazzling light show of pinks and gold stretched along the horizon. Distant silhouettes of cranes towered above squat buildings and disused office blocks where those in the know once partied.

Descending to the junction, austere interiors glowed in the approaching dusk. Convenience stores jutted out to the roadside. Fresh-faced students hauled booze from an off-licence. A group of drunk lads were getting unruly beneath a bus shelter. Outside the bookmakers, misfits eyed them all suspiciously. Into the night, thought Will.

Earlier, at Stuart's rented lock-up, they stripped the work gear from the back of the van. Swapping all the paint tins, dirty sheets and grubby ladders for sixteen loudspeakers, cramming them in up to the roof. At Rob's house, they filled the remaining space with two turntables, a mixer and a dozen boxes stuffed with lights and other bits of kit. Tonight would be their biggest gig yet. An empty warehouse all to themselves.

Buzzing along the dual carriageway, rows of sixties housing gave way to plots of warehouses and small industrial facilities. They were the first to take this journey. A magical mystery tour hundreds of others would take in the coming hours.

Once the event was set up, they'd remove the van from the site and find a phone box to set the answerphone message confirming the party's location. The routine was necessary to keep the whereabouts secret—fallout from the underground scene, which exploded from small, disused spaces in town centres to all-nighters littering Britain's countryside. They'd been promoting the phone number to call for over a month, distributing flyers outside bars and clubs. Tonight had to be a success.

They journeyed through the lifeless industrial sector, past a row of articulated trailers parked along one side of the road. Beyond Adam's nodding head, Stuart focussed on the road. Will imagined Rob was planning tonight's set list, one to rival any they'd witnessed at previous parties. A selection of sounds at the absolute cutting edge of music. As a crew, they formed a vanguard whose electronic drum beat led the party on a merry waltz out of town.

They'd first met a year ago, the breaking hours of a day, early summer, a warehouse party called Hedonism. Curved drapes hung from the low ceiling, and colourful graffiti covered the walls. Keeping the euphoria intense, a John Dean sound system punched out crisp acid house. When the music stopped at seven a.m., desire remained unquelled and, as dawn broke through the skylights, almost an hour passed with the crowd cheering and chanting, clapping and stamping for more. Will watched with fascination as the sound system, its lease expired, was carried out, and Soul II Soul set up theirs in its place. With no lull in the crowd's demands, they were rewarded when the first bar of music looped out, and the whole room rejoiced in dance. When the kick drum's thump returned, pumping over and over, everyone ascended into a state of rapturous pandemonium, sheer euphoria that continued long into the day until no one cared to remember when.

Will lurched against his seatbelt. Stuart had stamped on the brakes to make the turning onto the industrial estate. He changed down, yanked the wheel hard right, and flung his passengers in the opposite direction.

'Bouncing,' laughed Adam, reaching out to steady himself.

Will suspected Adam was high and shoved him back into his seat, mimicking his old school friend's mangled expression.

Cruising the industrial estate, dozens of business units stood behind low hedgerows or trampled strips of grass. All four of them were on the lookout for warehouse sixty, their sense of anticipation palpable.

A regular at one of their previous gigs had tipped them off. The guy, too flaky to be with them now, knew a security guard who knew the address of a warehouse that would be empty for a few weeks. He wanted half upfront with the remaining two hundred squids on the night. Will could tell the guy wasn't lying when Stuart lent his imposing frame to the discussion. He confirmed the offer with a meek nod, Will paid up, and this afternoon they got the call confirming the address. They were good to go.

Coming to a stop in front of their venue, its breezeblock walls and high metal roof as inconspicuous as all the others, Stuart switched off and climbed out, keen as you like. Will lingered a moment longer, imagining the audio carnage about to be unleashed.

Adam elbowed him in the ribs, hustling, 'Cha, cha, cha.'

Pacing around the bright-yellow van, Adam loped behind, adjusting the elastic waistband of his shell suit trousers. From the rear compartment, metal clattered.

Stuart's bald head peered into the hold. He clutched two crowbars and struggled to free a set of bolt cutters from a canvas bag. Rob offered no help, watching on with his hood up; he was the main man after all.

Will envisaged Stuart's clumsiness punching a hole in one of the subs. 'Watch the speakers.'

'It's fine,' insisted Stuart, pulling the bolt cutters out.

Will took the crowbars off Stuart. 'Come on,' he hissed, an absolute blinder about to get underway. He wanted to get in there more than ever. Get it set up. Feel the warmth once the place was packed out. Track after track blasting through the room. Their very own Hedonism.

At the loading bay doors, Will passed one of the crowbars to

Rob, and they made room for Stuart to break the padlock. He positioned the cutters around the bar and, with a grunt, snapped through the steel. The lock clunked to the floor.

Adam did a celebratory jig and pointed to the sky. 'Let's take the roof off.'

Stuart stalked off towards the van.

Will shoved his crowbar between the doors. Rob joined in, and they heaved at their gateway, scraping the floor until the gap grew big enough for Adam to sneak through, singing, 'Party time.'

A wave of excitement passed through Will, and he bounced inside. 'Come on!'

In the dark, they fumbled for the panel that controlled the lighting while Stuart backed the van inside. With the loading bay doors closed, all four stood on the concrete floor, assessing their venue. Fifty feet above, roof lights hummed while the murky industrial glow slowly brightened.

The room was exactly as the guy who tipped them off said it would be, apart from a stack of boxes abandoned on a pallet in the middle of the room. The rest of the floor was clear, and flanked either side by industrial shelves made of scaffolding. Against the far wall was a Portakabin with a barred window.

'We could have turned that cabin into an igloo.' Adam's jaw settled at an unnatural angle. 'To chill out, you know?'

'Visionary,' remarked Rob.

Adam nodded, sure of himself. 'If we had the stuff,' he said before his concentration waned and he looked elsewhere.

Will shared a wry grin with Rob. Adam was oblivious. 'I reckon we put the decks in the cabin,' said Will. 'Right in front of that window.'

'Like it.' Rob pointed his crowbar at the far wall. 'Stack on front two points.'

Will imagined the view. The white glow from the cabin,

speakers both sides, netting draped in front with smoke billowing through. He indicated each flank. 'Party lights on the second row.'

'Perfect,' agreed Rob.

Stuart moved off. 'Let's get cracking.'

☺

In the back of the Transit, a wall of speakers waited ominously. Will removed a sack trolley and snapped open the base. They had four subs, eight midrange and four high-end to play with. Five thousand watts. The punch would hook the crowd before they were even inside.

They wheeled the first two subs beside the cabin and laid them end-to-end on their sides. Four midrange speakers were placed on these, and two tweeters topped the lot. With Adam's high stealing his concentration, he abandoned the task, choosing to root through the equipment, and left the rest of them to build the second stack on the opposite side.

Being a handyman by trade, Stuart used his electrical skills to wire up the system. Will, Rob and Adam organised ancillaries and fixed the trestle table the main setup would sit on.

Will left Rob to organise the decks. After throwing a lead to Stuart, he carried the smoke machine to the side and, with a bike lock, secured it to a pole so no one could pinch it.

They'd used the smoke machine at every one of their parties except the first. Hosted in the function room of a pub called the Red Lion, the night was great, but Will disappointed the landlord with a meagre nine pounds twenty pence payment. Twenty percent of the two-pound entrance fee twenty-three people were willing to pay. The landlord told Will he'd need at least twenty-five quid to make the arrangement worth his while, especially as the punters mainly drank water. Will agreed so long as the landlord let them use a smoke machine. The landlord was fine with it, so Will bought one and advertised it on the next flyer in capital letters: NOW WITH SMOKE MACHINE!!! Will liked to think the addition encouraged one hundred and thirty-seven people to pay three pounds at the next gig. Rob insisted his DJing skills were the real reason, but Will refused to agree in case he had to pay him a bigger cut.

They thought they'd be millionaires in weeks. Unfortunately, enthusiasm was short-lived. The landlord wanted out because of a ruined carpet and the neighbours complaining about repetitive beats banging all night. Will couldn't do anything about the banging and offered to pay for a new carpet, but the landlord refused.

Once Rob finished connecting the monitor speakers to the decks, they retrieved the folded netting and struggled to carry it to the foot of the industrial shelving, in line with the DJ cabin.

Securing his belt diagonally across his chest, the netting tied to it, Will held the bare metal structure's upright and stepped onto the lowest section. Further across, part way up the metal frame, connecting cables to the lighting units Adam passed up, Stuart shouted, 'Watch your trousers don't fall down, matey.'

'They won't.'

Spurred on, Will climbed twenty-five feet up the metal structure, twice as high as Stuart. He wrapped the loose cord, extending from the netting's corner, several times around the metal pole, and knotted it tightly. He wanted to get the job done, get on with the night.

Rob unfurled the netting that hung against the frame, secured at the point Will tied it. He found the opposite corner and carried it to the cabin where, standing on a box, he fastened it to the roof.

Will descended the frame, taking a moment to catch his breath, his limbs trembling from the exertion. Stuart boxed up the leftover cable and dumped it in the van. Rows of party lights were ready to flash and spin. One of the nets was already in place, stretching out like a giant wing, the stack of speakers positioned ten feet behind it so as not to deafen those at the front.

Heaving open the loading bay door, Stuart announced, 'I'll make the call.'

'Lights done?' asked Will.

'Done,' said Stuart, climbing into the van.

'You've tested them?'

'Yes, matey.' Stuart slammed the driver's door and started the engine, leaving a puff of blue smoke as he motored off into the night. Rob closed the loading bay doors behind him.

Disappointed he wouldn't have the kudos of leaving the answerphone message, Will turned his attention to the abandoned boxes. Inside, folded carrier bags packed together seemed solid enough. He removed the loose cellophane from around the sides and covered the platform with a load of Stuart's gaffer tape, sealing it tight. Will climbed on top to test the sturdiness and found it secure enough. He punched the air. The party had a podium.

☺

Stuart whizzed through the industrial estate, amped up and raring to make the call. He wound down the window and blasted Rob's mixtape into the summer night. Best of all, he'd stolen a march on Will, who always wanted to leave the answerphone message. Stuart knew he'd chew everyone's ear off, bragging about it later when he was mashed. First, he needed to ship the hundred and fifty pills he'd scored. Then the party could really get started. Acid house was a mental scene. Mental. Hedonism blew his mind. One of the firm heard about it, and they went over after Brentford away. Stuart hadn't seen anything like it. It was a derelict warehouse in the middle of nowhere. Inside, everyone danced like loons to a pumping, beat-heavy soundtrack. Then he came up, and he was too. Off he went, bobbing through the carnage, smiling his chops off, and talking to anyone who'd listen. He lost the boys; he didn't care. He was on mission, exploring the different rooms until he rested at a spray-painted wall feeling its cool, damp surface on his back. That's when it happened, his epiphany. At that moment, he couldn't figure why he'd ever bothered with football. All the aggression. The violence. And for what? There was no money in it. He decided his future lay in Ecstasy. Look how many people were doing it. He knew the top boys could probably get hold of it. Daz, most likely. Not that Daz was strictly a top boy, he just knew them somehow. Stuart decided he'd make enquiries and see how he went. He felt a tug on his leg and found a scrawny lad wearing the happiest, most contented grin he'd ever seen. Stuart knew exactly where this kid was coming from, and he sluiced down to tell him his plan. Not a brilliant idea, he realised the next day when sober, but no one cared. Soon, this kid, Adam, and his buddy, Will, were onboard. Will had shown up with Rob, a DJ, and the four of them were all of a sudden best friends. Everything made sense. They'd put on parties and make millions. Stuart didn't expect that. Organising a party sounded like effort. But at the time, he couldn't do anything but agree under the influence of the pill buzzing through him.

They arranged another night out soon after. Will had been to Ibiza the previous summer and met some guys who promoted a club night. Stuart didn't have a clue but went with it. After missioning all the way to London, they couldn't get in. Stuart began to stress he'd blown his cash on fifty pills for nothing. The venue, some disused gym, with dry ice wafting out everywhere, was rammed, and the chick working the door was having none of it. Then one of those New Romantic popstars sauntered past with his entourage, straight inside like no one's business. There you are, sir, in you go. It wasn't even a real nightclub. Will wasn't happy. He reckoned they were meant to have a no celebs policy, but that sounded like bollocks; Will was just pissed off he'd arranged the night then couldn't get them in. In the end, they laughed it off and found another place that played the same sort of stuff, around the corner on Clink Street called RIP. It was a warren of rooms, full of all sorts, and Stuart had no problem shifting the pills. Some he could tell were from other firms, but there were hippy wannabes as well, yuppies in suits, cool kids, hard-looking black guys, and posh ones, gays too. All sorts. He'd never seen so many different types, let alone socialised with them. And they were all on it too. Mental. People were literally trying to shake the place down they were so off their nut. No aggro, though. All good fun. The four of them ended up regulars.

Stuart laughed to himself. He remembered thinking the firm would mug him off if they knew he now preferred dancing to fighting. But it didn't take him long to realise the rest of them had discovered E too.

Exiting the roundabout, Stuart parked up before the slip road wound right towards a brightly lit petrol station. From the crest of the rise, Stuart could see the distant lorry trailers parked in a long line. A maze of street lights marked the industrial estate further to the right, their warehouse party buried somewhere within. He'd drive part way back and leave the van among the trailers. From there, the walk to the warehouse would take twenty minutes tops.

Stuart wondered how many from RIP would turn up tonight. Look at me now, he thought, no longer a punter but a promoter. Tonight's gig was massive compared to RIP's joint, but he wouldn't give them the big I am. It was a shame their run came to an end, to be honest.

With no one around except a bored attendant propped at the petrol station's night kiosk, Stuart left the driver's door open and marched along the slip road to the solitary phone box. At the other end of a forecourt was a scrapyard, locked up behind graffitied wooden boards. The phone box stood on a gritty lay-by and, beyond it, a rusted wire fence cordoned off rugged marshland, which descended to the muddy river beyond.

Stepping inside, Stuart found the sticker advertising the number to call, the ☺898 number clearly visible. Dropping the ten pence into the slot, Stuart's gaze lingered on the smiley-face drawn in the phone number's initial nought. He read the phone number and dialled, waiting for Will's phoney answerphone message, a cover story about school tuition, to begin.

Will wanted the phone lines to be associated with their parties for as short a time as possible to not blow their cover. Stuart didn't think it mattered given they were registered to a PO Box, but the little sneak insisted. Stuart went with it to keep the peace.

Bored of hearing Will list prices for non-existent educational classes, Stuart pressed hash and entered the security PIN. Will's spiel was interrupted by an automated female voice announcing menu options. Stuart cleared his throat and selected number three, which instructed him to leave a new message.

At the tone, sounding like a fairground announcer, Stuart cheered, 'Yes yes party people,' his voice ringing with excitement, 'tonight is Dominator. Saturday seventeenth of June, warehouse sixty, Northfield Industrial Estate.' For effect, he added, 'Be there. Light it up. Bring your game and dance for time. Smiley's here. You'll be feeling fine.'

02 / *All Back To Mine*

Setting up the warehouse seemed like minutes ago. But it was hours. So much had happened since. Now the night was over; Will couldn't believe it, trapped amongst the crowd, being ordered out to the car park, where their night started. Maybe ten hours ago. The beats no longer guided him. High up, along the rows of industrial shelves, stretching the length of the warehouse, the disco lights still whizzed and flashed. But their multitude of colours was diluted by the warehouse's main lights. The rancid yellow light revealed dank breeze block walls sodden with hours of dance-fuelled condensation.

For the best part of the night, the warehouse dazzled. A theatre of acid house. Loud, bright and unrelenting. The smoke and lights formed a hazy wall of flashing primary colours, permeating throughout the hot room and dancing amongst the graphic prints on people's loose, damp clothes. Some glowed from fluorescent bracelets or waved glowsticks.

Back then, on the makeshift podium, the heat and the energy rushed through Will like an extension of his body. Now he was at a loss. Man, time flies when you're having fun!

Will thought he could remember it all. Stuart returning. The anxious wait for the first arrivals. Pacing the tarmac outside. A group emerged from the shadows, their dungarees and baggy tees confirming they posed no threat. Stuart flipped the house lights off, and the first beats pounded through the cavernous chamber. Will had seen over a thousand people through the door at five pounds a pop. New faces mixed with those who attended their previous parties. Group after group arrived, leaving a mass of cars on the tarmacked enclosure. The space between the two warehouses full, drivers parked along the road, the line of cars disappearing out of sight. The guy arrived, the one who tipped them off about the warehouse, walking straight to the front of the upbeat queue with the security guard he knew. Talking to Will like he ran the show, waiting for Will to slip him his two hundred. Will going with it until the guy was inside, then telling those in the queue he was a cheeky prick. The ones at the front laughed. No one hassled him. They paid up and danced inside, straight into their routine, admiring the space. The room looked great. Billows of smoke cut through the netting while spots of colour flashed all around. Packing out the front, all the barmies danced amidst a cloud that settled around the cabin, where Rob blended a mix of deep grooves and piano chords that danced around squelchy acid bass and a relentless beat. The podium was rammed too. A permanent ring of dancers blockaded those lucky enough to find space atop the boxes, the attention seducing them as much as the music. Stuart worked his way through the crowd selling pills at fifteens. Adam danced in the middle like he was the only one there. The space between the cabin and the podium gradually filled, and the dancing masses spread backwards to conquer the warehouse's quieter recesses. Will watched all this from the side door. Then Stuart appeared at Will's side, offering one of his few remaining pills. The room already in overdrive, Will couldn't resist. He just wanted to be one of them. As promoters, they were on a roll, and it was time to celebrate. The cardboard cash box laden with coin, Will carried it to the Portakabin with Stuart acting as security. Rob was having fun on the decks, too distracted by his track selections to join the conversation. Half an hour later, Will danced with Stuart and Adam on the podium, the music setting them free. Their long, loose T-shirts drenched in sweat like everyone else. Below them, the sea of revellers rippled in all directions. Spots of coloured light swept through the smoke. Track after track punched from the speakers as Rob took them on a musical journey. Way off, framed in the cabin's window, Will could see Rob working the decks. Over a fading bassline, a tribal beat skipped into the mix accompanied by a high-end acid riff with metallic stabs of mid. The crowd went wild, raising their arms to greet the new sounds. Their energy and noise, all aimed at Rob, sparked a sense of pride mixed with euphoria Will had never experienced before. This was History. The night they'd promoted for weeks was finally here. Their endeavours coming to fruition in front of Will's wide eyes. The tribal beats faded out, replaced by a pulsing acid riff repeating over and over. Rob pitched the tempo up, swinging it between channels, left and right, until a constant stream of high-pitched sound, like a buzzsaw scything across the dance floor, ruled them all. Cheers and shouts joined the chorus while Rob rapidly cut the channel, staccato style, at the same time, letting it wind down, slower, distorting the tones, the crowd's appreciation growing even louder until it became a solid rumble of bass, fading to silence … Then, as the crowd waited, and in perfect time, Rob let the next track drop. The deep, heavy rhythm boomed, beats bounced through the room, piano chords rose, lifting the crowd towards the stratosphere. The dance floor was going crazy, with everyone succumbing to their wildest and freest dance moves. Will was too. The energy in there was insane. He'd never come down. At his feet, the crowd rippled under flashing, coloured lights. Others were still coming in, moving from the side door into the crowd, where others watched the mayhem from the far wall. They'd get in for free, but that didn't matter. Nothing did. You got out what you put in. How many friends could the new arrivals spread the word to? Their presence would add to the atmosphere for those already here. The memory of Dominator burnt on all their minds. *The* dance event of 1989.

But now, shuffling towards the exit, Will realised that was when he should have spotted the cops: up on the podium. Instead, he'd presumed the flashing blue light was a broken one of theirs, which was no problem to fix, and his attention returned to luxuriate on the scene below him. The party he helped to create. Feeling the collective body heat drifting over his skin made the hair on his neck stand up. Focussing on specific groups, he spotted some girls he knew, Charlotte and Michaela, Michaela a total hippy and Charlotte so cool she didn't realise it. He remembered chatting to Charlotte tonight, on the way in, and when he first saw her at one of their early gigs. He thought she was a leader, the way she danced, twisting her slinky hips and pumping her arms to the hypnotic house beat. Tomorrow he'd find her number and call her. They used to have great chats before he got carried away organising this warehouse gig. Maybe he'd go meet her in Glitter if he could persuade the boys. Next to Charlotte, a couple kissed. Nearby, a girl in tie-dye sat on her friend's shoulders. Beside her, two guys were arm-in-arm, punching the air. Further along, a guy and a girl cheered a policeman, with someone else offering a high five. He turned to Stuart, who pumped his arms to the beat, cheering heartily.

'Stu?' Will called, scanning again for the cop. He was still there. The guy and the girl were trying to decorate his helmet with a flower necklace. That was okay, but there were others behind him. About fifteen, hemmed against the rear wall by the sea of people. The cops that worked their way through the dancing bodies struggled to find a clear path, with revellers cheering them at every opportunity and the music obscuring their calls. That was the flashing blue light Will had seen. The cops were outside. He'd been too caught up in the party to realise.

A shot of fear cleared his head. It was time to go. 'Stu,' Will shouted, his eyes wide, a tight grip on his water bottle.

Beneath the flashing, coloured lights, Stuart's sweaty face was ecstatic as it swung Will's way. 'Matey,' he rejoiced, pulling Will close. 'I love it.'

Squished against Stuart's damp chest Will tried to shout, but Stuart squeezed tighter, cackling with laughter. Will waited to be released, reeling at the thought of cops, about what they were going to do.

'The cops,' Will shouted.

Stuart laughed, revelling in the party's vibes. 'Matey, I couldn't be happier if I won a speedboat on Bullseye.' He swung his arms to the beat, his face contorting with sheer joy.

Wide-eyed, Will searched for the cops, unscrewing his bottle and taking a quick swig. The cops continued to push through the crowd. 'We've got to go,' yelled Will.

'You're coming down, matey,' yelled Stuart, 'You want another pill?'

'The cops are here,' yelled Will, and waited a tense moment while Stuart's dancing faltered. On his face, confusion reigned supreme. The music continued without him.

'We need to get down,' shouted Will, feeling like time had slowed. He looked over the dance floor at all the smiling faces.

Stuart used Will to steady himself and rose to his tiptoes, peering across the sea of dancers. 'Bloody hell,' he yelled, 'the cops are here.'

'I know,' shouted Will, running a hand through his damp hair, 'That's what I've been trying to say.' He puffed his cheeks. 'Gatecrashers.'

'I thought you were getting paranoid,' laughed Stuart, taking a swig of water. 'You want me to sort them some pills? It might loosen them up.' Stuart laughed again, screwing his bottle closed and bobbing to the music. 'Oi oi,' he cheered, kicking out a foot.

Will's energy levels were on the floor. The party had turned Jekyll. 'We've got to get out of here,' he yelled. What else could he do but accept the situation?

'They don't know it's us. Keep dancing. Everything will be all right, matey.'

'Yeah, but we've got to get the money, you know, from the cabin,' Will shrugged, waiting for Stuart to realise.

Stuart danced up to Will, his eyes wide. 'We've got to get the money.'

'I know, buddy.' Will checked for the cops.

'Let's go.' Stuart's tense face belied his body, which bobbed and weaved to the music. 'Let's go and get the money from in the DJ cabin with Rob.'

'That's what I think.' Will surveyed the floor below. 'We need to get down.'

Before Will knew it, Stuart yanked him towards the dance floor, the motion disorientating with the heat and the noise and the spinning lights. 'I'm coming,' shouted Will, shaking himself free, waiting for Stuart to land before jolting uncomfortably against the unyielding, concrete floor.

All around, a frantic rush for a spot on the podium began. Dancers swarmed past, and Will remembered Adam still up there, facing skywards with his eyes closed, his head swaying side-to-side. Amidst the clamour, Will flung an arm back, grabbing Adam's leg to alert him. Adam looked down in sheer panic.

'The cops are here,' shouted Will, trying to reassure Adam but instead freaking himself out.

'What you on, man?' Adam shook his leg free, readjusted his trousers and continued dancing. Bending at the knees, he threw out his arms, his face puckered with joy.

With all the people around him, Will just wanted to dance. His inclination floated in the void between the music and what to do. He envied the delirious crowd who partied unaware. Then Stuart was upon him, his face blank, his eyes wide, as serious as he could be under the circumstances. Will knew they needed to get going. His throat dry, he swigged his water and spilt some down his chin.

Nearing the DJ cabin, the heat and the energy at maximum, the bass rumbled through them, and accompanied the bumps from the hot, sweaty limbs they hustled past. Through the cabin's window, Will could see Rob wipe the sweat from his brow. Will wiped his too, watching Rob take a record in each hand, deciding which to play. Will wanted to tell Rob what an amazing set he was playing. It would be cool to reassure Rob how well things were going.

'Bunch of party poopers,' yelled Adam, lagging behind, belatedly getting to grips with the situation. 'Jekyll as anything, man.'

Will yammered, 'How do they know it's not all above board? It's not like the owner gave us a certificate or something. To tell them otherwise. We should have, though. Made one ourselves. Next time, buddy. We'll do that. And I won't get so high either.' Will flung an arm around Adam and kissed the side of his head.

There was a tremendous thump, amidst the music. Will whipped towards the noise to see Stuart rebound off the Portakabin's plywood door. Through the window, Rob stiffened, alert to intruders. Will waited in anticipation as Stuart lunged again. The latch snapped, and he fell inside, causing Rob to jump out of his skin.

Will followed Stuart through. A rush of warm air swept over them. Adam closed the door, and the melodies muted. The bassline pulsed through the cabin's walls. They were in a different world now, with space to move. The DJ cabin's white light bright to their wide eyes. Rob looked at the three of them in disbelief, the turntables spinning beside him.

'What's going on?' Rob yelled. 'The lock broke?'

'All right, matey?' shouted Stuart, scanning the floor for the cash box, not a second thought for Rob's dismayed expression.

'We got cops,' Will blurted and felt another shot of fear as he said it.

'No way,' shouted Rob, snapping round to peer through the window.

'We know,' yelled Will, swigging water to calm himself. 'That's why we're here.'

'I'm going to put the banknotes in my socks,' announced Stuart, dropping to the floor and grimacing as he pulled at a trainer.

'Why are you taking your trainers off?' asked Will, throwing his empty bottle into the corner.

'Because my pockets are full of Ecstasy money.' The trainer jerked loose, and he fell backwards. 'Boys, I'm wrecked,' he cackled, pushing himself upright again.

'Don't do that here,' yelled Rob searching through the window.

'Are you going to play on?' asked Will.

'Yeah,' yelled Rob, remembering his job and clumsily laying a vinyl on the turntable. 'You take the cash. I'll stall the cops.'

'Awesome,' yelled Will. 'What'll you say?'

Rob hunched over the decks, efficiently working the vinyl to match the speeds. 'I'll tell them some old guy booked me, and I ain't seen him since I arrived.'

'Yeah? Cool,' yelled Will raising a thumb. Rob was the only one with difficulty denying involvement. A classically trained musician, he'd swapped his guitar for a set of decks after visiting Paradise Garage. That alone made Rob a total legend.

'Hey,' shouted Stuart looking lost, a pile of banknotes between his outstretched legs, 'you want to wake up and give me a hand?'

'Sorry, buddy,' Will turned to Adam, 'Can you see the cops?' he yelled, trying to keep a fix on the situation. Will delved into the cash box, swirling the coins around to take a scoop. They were heavy, their coldness and texture intense. Will picked them up. 'Why are there so many coppers? I swear I didn't take that many.'

'I can't see them,' yelled Adam, peeking through a narrow gap. 'Hey, do you think we could get lasers for the next gig? They're totally cool.'

'Get out of here,' yelled Rob, adjusting the crossfader to gradually introduce the next record. 'Pocket the cash out there.'

'Good idea,' yelled Will, adding, 'I'm on one, buddy.'

'I'm properly mashed,' yelled Stuart, rolling over to get to his feet, his backside poking in the air.

'A cop's on the podium,' yelled Rob, peering through the window. He cut into the next track for a bar then out again. Outside, the crowd cheered the new beats.

Adam folded his arms, his face tense. 'Boys, I'm crapping it.'

Stuart removed his T-shirt.

'Hey, why you taking your T-shirt off?'

'To cover the cash box.' Stuart grew unsure of himself. 'Does that make sense? I'm proper mashed.' He rubbed his bald head.

'Quick,' shouted Rob, cutting the track in and removing the other record from the turntable. The new track vibrated through the cabin's walls. 'Get out of here. Are you mental?'

'All right,' shouted Will, accepting Stuart's explanation and Rob's instruction.

Stuart made a concerted effort to drape his T-shirt neatly over the cashbox. He staggered towards the exit, unable to control the movement of his jaw. 'Come on,' he yelled, flapping an arm behind him. 'Duck down. We gotta ruuuunnn!'

Will and Adam bumbled over to Stuart. Rob slipped the penultimate vinyl in the case and clicked it shut before joining them.

'I thought you were playing on?' Will asked.

'The cops are nearly here,' shouted Rob. 'Go!'

'Oh,' said Will.

Stuart opened the door and the music burst into the cabin. Rob feverishly ushered them onwards.

'Can you see them?' shouted Will, the energy of the dance floor bearing down on him.

Amongst the crowd, the music loud, flashing lights and movement all around, Will expected the cops to nab him any second. Desperate to run, he stood straight, searching wild-eyed for the law, about to leg it before he realised there were none nearby. Scanning the crowd, he could see some about ten metres away, trying to get a view into the cabin through all the revelry. Will crouched down and scurried after the others.

They were deep into the crowd, distributing the money amongst themselves, when the music stopped. It sounded like the copper impatiently pulled the needle off the record. A brief scratching noise followed by silence caused everyone to stop and groan. Then, gradually, over the boos and the jeers and the repeated chant of 'one more track', the police officers' demands became clear. They wanted everyone to leave.

At first, no one moved. Confused by the abrupt change, they stayed where they were, hoping the mistake would soon be resolved. Some still danced to the non-existent music, an involuntary reaction after having the heavy beats and lively rhythms playing solidly for hours. But slowly, as the police officers worked their way into the crowd, the revellers began to comply.

The cops' requests for the crowd to keep moving were relentless. Being herded towards the unwelcoming dawn, the once united party split into tribes, each allied to an exit. The pathways between groups were littered with crushed beer cans and water bottles, empty fag packets and discarded drugs bags, casually ignored by everyone. Occasionally there was the enthusiastic 'Oi-oi' of a lone nutter with his top off, wandering around, too high to care about anything, not least the cops. No one, not even the police, wanted to take responsibility for those loons.

Despite Will's disappointment at the termination of his biggest gig, the vibe was no different to nights in central London, with everyone too lively to go home. No doubt there would be a party or two in the car park. One night, with everyone mingling on Charing Cross Road after Trip closed, police blipped their sirens to get people moving. In defiance, someone shouted, 'Ch-ch-check this out,' to knowing laughs. The sirens blipped again, and soon afterwards, a small crowd were bopping around the cops singing "Can You Party?" by Royal House. Another night, closing time outside Spectrum, some guy arrived in a Mini with tracks blasting on a decent system. Everyone went mental, leaving the handful of cops with nothing to do but watch a thousand people party in the street.

Hoping a guy in a Mini was speeding to the warehouse right now, Will nudged Stuart, who leaned on him for support. 'Come on, bud, wakey wakey.' Will let go of Stuart's heavy frame. Stuart straightened, taking his full weight on his feet. His eyes barely open, Stuart was wasted, with no idea where he was.

Stumbling forward, the crowd were losing enthusiasm the nearer they got to the exit. Lively chatter towards the back became silent cooperation as each individual stepped through the door like they were attending a police line-up—they pretty much were. The growing, unwavering light of morning reached into the warehouse, preparing them for reality.

Will should have taken the cash to the van, but he'd been seduced by the atmosphere. Right now, he could be leading the charge, arranging an after party or keeping everyone going with banter. Not leaving because they were told to do so. Will felt like he'd lost concentration for a moment, and now the night was over. It really did only seem seconds ago that Stuart left to set the answerphone message.

Rob turned to Will, full of apprehension. He set the record case down, shaking his head. 'I can't take it. We'll get full-on grief.'

Will seized the case. 'They can stop our music, but they ain't taking it,' he proclaimed full of righteousness. Rob decided against a reply, shook his head, and turned away. Who cares, thought Will, things always worked out when you were off your biscuit.

Peering outside, Will could see a row of Austin Metro cop cars behind a line of waiting rozzers. Meat wagons were parked further back. The wrath of authority reminded him of the time he tried to arrange a second party in a local church hall. Such was the carnage of the first event, the red-faced chaplain lambasted Will the second he arrived. The chaplain's complaints of unholy and immoral were nothing to do with the police, so Will felt confident he could wriggle out of this one.

The cardboard cash box discarded, Adam's jacket was tied around Will's waist, concealing the coins in his pockets. Stuart's T-shirt, wrapped around his waist, hid bulges of cash there. With his socks pulled over their ends, Adam's baggy shell suit trousers sufficed to store the remaining coins poured down each leg. Will thought they'd be okay, no one knew what they were carrying, and too many folk were loved-up for any aggro.

Stepping through the pedestrian door, the fresh air brought lucidity. Will saw more clearly the line of cops beyond Rob. Immediately, a senior looking cop pointed in Will's direction. With a worried expression, Rob checked behind. 'What's up?' asked Will, but Rob didn't reply. They werc back in the car park, where their night began. Was it really ten hours ago? Behind Will, Stuart stumbled through the door with Adam supporting him.

'What you got there, son?' asked the approaching copper, another following behind.

'I don't know,' chirped Will cheerfully. He genuinely had forgotten until he followed the cop's determined view and remembered the record case.

The frowning officer considered this. 'Are you giving me lip?'

Why did the copper ask that? 'No,' said Will carefully, thinking it best to get along.

'So, you have no idea what you're carrying …? Riiiight,' said the officer as though he'd been practising his sarcasm.

'I found it just now.' He kind of did. 'Shall we have a look?'

The officer put hands on hips. Will knelt to unclip the two latches. Sensing pressure, he sought support. But Stuart's expression was so muddled, Will thought he had no idea why the coppers, and everyone else piled behind, were so concerned by the metal case. Feeling the officer's persistent stare, Will opened the case.

'Wow,' he cooed timidly, his eyes wide with amazement.

'You can't take them with you,' insisted the copper.

'Why not?' asked Will, genuinely upset at the thought.

'It's evidence.'

'Of what?' asked Will.

Rob sputtered and coughed, and it stopped the lead copper replying.

The supporting cop turned to Rob, asked, 'Are you okay?'

Flustered, Rob nodded, wiping his mouth. 'Cough,' he gasped, staring at the floor and folding his arms.

What was that about? thought Will. Was Rob trying not to laugh?

The lead cop, who'd been made to wait by the distraction,

returned to Will. 'Don't be silly, son.'

'I'm not.' Will fastened the lid and stood with the case. 'It's not illegal me being stood here, is it?'

'Get a move on,' shouted someone behind, 'I'm getting fidgety here.'

Someone else shouted, 'I'm a fidgety fidget.' Laughter rang out among the watching crowd. It disorientated Will, and he grounded himself by focussing on the copper's hat. Slowly, the laughs stopped, and the comments behind quietened to whispers.

The officer, doing his best to muster a sense of severity, finally replied, 'We suspect it probably is illegal for you to be here.'

Confused, Will asked for clarity, 'You suspect it probably is?'

When the frowning copper didn't respond, Will said, 'I'm very, very sorry?' Carefully, he looked to Stuart and stepped aside.

Stuart swayed on his feet, his bare chest shimmering with sweat. Transfixed by the metal case, he looked to the lawmen, completely befuddled by the new development. 'Hiya, maties,' he gurned. 'You all all right?'

The copper assessed Stuart's swinging jaw and swaying hips; the sweaty crowd behind; at the back, some people impatiently slipped away. Annoyed, the copper stuck a thumb over his shoulder, 'Do yourself a favour and get out of here,' he insisted, trying to retain a degree of authority.

03 / *Glitter's Ball*

Ten p.m. Sunday, Will, Stuart and Adam strolled towards Glitter nightclub, located at the far corner of a large, blue-bricked arts centre. Rob, ever the dutiful boyfriend, left Stuart's before the three of them awoke.

Glitter's queue was busy. Along the street, loud groups prowled between bars. Some aimed for friends waiting amongst the jostle. Others lost patience and retreated across the road without a care for traffic. All around, drunken shouts replaced the ringing in Will's ears until he heard Glitter's music blasting onto the street.

Waking in Stuart's living room, his head cleared, and he saw the pile of loose coins and crumpled notes scattered over the low coffee table. That took the edge off the police confiscating their equipment. It was an event beyond concern at six a.m., living in the moment, his pockets full of cash, and the fleeting remnants of the party buzzing through him.

The same lack of concern had carried them to Stuart's house after an hour partying outside the warehouse, bubbling between car boot sound systems and chatting idly to anyone and everyone. They remained upbeat as an absence of taxis became clear. With the law's watchful eye upon them, and a lack of willing drivers, the slow march towards civilisation began. They joined the string of departees peeling away like a column of ants returning to their nest. Around every corner, staggered groups stretched along the road to the next turning. Occasionally they'd pass a lone couple, engrossed in a heart-to-heart over a cigarette, which, whenever enquired about, turned out to be their last. The service station they later encountered was like a utopian paradise. Alive with the promise of excitement, the forecourt was jam-packed with dishevelled revellers sitting around the pumps or dancing within earshot of a car boot sound system. Like a sequel to the antics outside the warehouse, a matching collection of baggy tees, DMs, dungarees and wedge haircuts stretched the remains of the night to the limit. A long queue led from the night kiosk where craving revellers would eventually raid all supplies of fags and water. The four of them did the same, then joined the endless chatter, apologetically retreating off the forecourt to finish their cigarette every time a bewildered staff member approached. Soon the police arrived and waded into the well-meaning mayhem to say hi. Shortly after, Will found himself in a taxi, stubbornly counting one and two pence pieces. Ready to pay the fare until the driver noticed his low-denomination hoard and an argument ensued. Will protested his right to pay however he wished. The driver stopped a couple of miles short of Stuart's house and ordered them out. Will refused to leave, insisting he could pay and got threatened with a baseball bat from the boot. Stuart, still too mashed to do anything about the riled driver, tried nonetheless, stumbling grumpily at the roadside with Rob managing to keep him at bay. Cursing the departed taxi driver, they plodded on until a passing milkman and his float got urgently but pleasantly accosted. The amused milkman, an ex-punk rocker, took pity and carried them to their intended destination where, amidst warmth, comfort and a choice of music, the after party could finally begin. Aided by a stack of booze and some of Adam's weed, they had a private riot in Stuart's pad, chatting about tracks Rob played or events they remembered from the warehouse. Adam got the biggest laugh, using his fingers to count the number of hours he'd been awake and having to start again every time he got to ten. They kept him going for half an hour on that one. The other favourite was the miffed copper and Rob literally pissing himself with laughter when Will tried to deny the rammed-out warehouse party directly behind him. Only a drop, insisted Rob whenever it was mentioned, and got a laugh every time. Things fizzled out around three in the afternoon when Stuart went for a pee and never returned.

It was the end of the latest in a series of events that made Will feel like he belonged to a movement. A revolution in music, as free in its sound as in its spirit. Where dress codes were as fluid as the beats, and neither was ruled by precedence or construct. Everyone who belonged was part of something only they understood. To join was to take a leap of faith into the unknown, glimpse the future and believe anything possible.

☺

GLITTER hung above the club's main doors in swirling neon tubes, its pink glow covering the queue in a veil of faux glam. Crammed with students and local casuals, the night didn't have the best reputation. To Will, to join the sequins and silk shirts was to take a backwards step. Evidently, the majority of the crowd at Sunday's bastion of facile pop anthems were unconcerned by their appearance, in both senses.

He wondered how Charlotte fared, attending tonight's leaving do for Michaela. When he called earlier, she sounded harassed by festivities but didn't let the whoops and whistles distract her too much. Their conversation was brief but positive; she had a good time last night and wanted to hear all about his escape from the law. It was all the motivation he needed to dust off his suit jacket, which he thought looked good over a white tee.

Craning at the neck, he couldn't spot the girls in the queue and imagined Charlotte's group lording over those who waited alongside them.

'Talk about weird,' blurted Adam, 'I'm buzzing. But at the same time, I can see the cops. I want to shout to them 'cause … I loved them, man. You ever felt like that …? About cops?'

'Always,' muttered Stuart, swigging from the bottle of vodka he'd brought along to ease his hangover.

Arriving at the back of the queue, Will reached for the vodka and Stuart reluctantly relinquished his grip. Will hated being stuck in a queue; it meant you were a nobody. He took a quick sip before passing it on to Adam.

'Here, matey,' Stuart sneered, 'Why don't you get Mummy and Daddy to buy us a new system?'

'Get lost,' said Will, 'Hurry up and nick a new one.' He wondered how irritable Stuart would become once the drinks were flowing.

'On a session in Glitter.' Adam passed the bottle to Stuart. 'Mental.'

A disturbance at the club's front doors interrupted Stuart's contemptuous laugh. The three of them peered over the queue to see the doormen being accosted by a slim guy in a shell suit. Before the doormen could respond, the guy retreated, storming alongside the stunned queue.

Then Will realised he recognised the guy. He'd only met him once, at Stuart's.

'Daz,' called Stuart.

Daz's scowl was unmistakable, even behind his round, red-tinted shades. 'All right, stranger,' he muttered without stopping.

☺

From a circular booth on the corner of Glitter's dance floor, the DJ, in his polished DJ voice, advertised the club's drinks promotions: half-priced house spirits and only forty pence a pint. Then he announced the next record that he dutifully cued on time.

On the opposite corner of the dance floor, Charlotte Dean led four equally well-dressed girlfriends up some steps towards a free table. A group of sporty students kept a casual interest in them. Charlotte's smile was mischievous. Not because it was an accompaniment the put-on strut demanded, but because the homemade cocktails were taking effect. It was the last week of term and the weekend had been a big one. The previous night, she and her bestest Michaela had attended Ravisbourne's largest ever warehouse party. Even with the drama of the police appearing, it finished late, and the pair of them were dragged out of bed mid-afternoon by their eager-to-get-ready housemates.

Weaving through the diner-style seating area, they ignored the lustful attention of local roughs and ageing hangers-on among the night's student crowd. Did they really think they'd want to hook up with complete strangers? It reminded Charlotte of the first weeks at university where, for some, the race to find a partner got underway. Charlotte wasn't even sure she wanted a man. She was attracted to them but didn't see herself being tied down.

Charlotte took a seat and her housemates slid alongside, tucking their dresses neatly beneath them. Charlotte smiled dreamily at Michaela, who returned a wild grin in reply. They enjoyed an uproarious friendship, first living in London and then moving back to Charlotte's home town to save on rent. No problem with only four hours of lectures a week. She'd miss Michaela over the coming months. Tomorrow afternoon, Michaela was leaving to spend the summer travelling Europe. As a parting gift, Charlotte suggested, rather studiously, that they made Michaela a travel guide covering all the important historical sites she should visit. Charlotte was impressed with the sketches the arty one, Sophie, doodled one evening, over two bottles of red, with Emma making smutty comments at her side. In typical fashion, Emma tried to hijack the presentation, pointing out her contribution to the sketch of Michelangelo's David. Michaela loved it and was amazed by its accuracy. Charlotte was more amazed to learn old Dave was circumcised. She studied art history, yet she didn't know. The others were appalled at her stupidity and told her to get back to her textbooks right away.

Reacting to a Sophie-ism, Michaela stretched out an arm and declared, 'I'll paint the town red, darling.'

Charlotte loved the way Michaela's enthusiasm could make you feel magnificent while doing the most mundane of things. 'That doorstopper's a showstopper,' she exclaimed the other morning upon entering the kitchen at breakfast. Charlotte felt so proud to be eating the thick slice of burnt toast, she responded by telling Michaela precisely that.

Charlotte vaguely followed their rapid-fire suggestions about how Michaela should fill her summer travels, diligently contributing, 'Shall I prepare a list?' No one appeared to notice her zoning out.

☺

Will slipped the crumpled tenner beneath the metal grille and told the pierced-up, gum-chewing girl he wanted it to cover three. Framed by the ticket booth's window, the space behind her the size of a cupboard, she plucked the change from the plastic cash float and slid the coins across the metal drawer without saying a word. Will put away his wallet, deciding not to leave his suit jacket in the cloakroom next door.

Will cast a critical eye over the venue. With its rundown interior and lack of pretence, Glitter was very similar to the places he found for their parties. He'd once contacted management about hiring it but received short shrift. The guy on the phone had never heard of house music and wasn't interested.

Stuart and Adam were part way down the stairs that led into the club. Adam pointed to black and white photos of pop artists lining the wall and made a snide remark. Will was wary of Adam stepping backwards but played along, acknowledging the images by poking his thumbs down and booing.

The bar was rammed. Will sent Stuart and Adam to find a table while he waited for a harassed barman to serve three pints and a rack of shots. Tray in hand, Will hustled out of the thirsty scrum, shouting excuses and apologies as he went.

Adam had said he'd find a place near their old spot, the seating area styled like an American diner. It was where they used to go in their teens. The club hadn't changed much since. Only that the owners appeared happy to let the decor deteriorate in favour of profit. The current crop didn't seem to mind, downing their booze with youthful exuberance.

It looked like Adam had lucked out and found a two-berth table against the far wall. He and Stuart greedily eyed the tray while Will worked his way through. Will raised his voice to be heard above the cheesy pop din, 'Imagine a decent beat in here.'

'Mental,' said Adam, taking his pint before Will could sit.

Stuart took his too. 'Can't see it happening.'

'You hear about that promoter who turned a barn into paradise?' Adam paused while Will shuffled him along the bench. 'The cops arrive, get told it's a private gig. By the time they find Farmer Giles to check, it's the next day. The party's finished. Farmer Giles gets cheered up by a load of cash, and he lets them use it the following weekend. All sorted. Everyone's happy.'

'They hire tractors to shuttle everyone out there?' Stuart grinned.

Adam said, 'This man might,' reaching over to Will.

Before Will knew it, Adam had pulled him into a headlock, twisting his outfit in the ensuing struggle. Both Adam and Stuart had a habit of doing this to him, and the joke was wearing thin. 'Get off,' said Will, breaking free. They were making him look like a berk.

Adam began larking about. 'Jek, jek, jek.' Adam fluttered his elbows and pecked like a chicken.

'Scatty,' said Will tidying his outfit and trying not to laugh. 'A party in here would be better than a barn or a warehouse.'

'We ain't giving bills to snide club owners.'

Stuart always made that complaint. His working man's cynicism telling him club owners tipped off police about their parties. Will didn't think they had the gumption. He gulped at his pint. After last night's shenanigans, Will needed a way to prove Stuart's cynicism wrong.

It bothered Will that they couldn't get their music into traditional venues. The scene was exploding, but no one wanted to take a chance on it. He'd spent considerable time contacting Ravisbourne's nightclubs, but none were willing to divert from their neatly packaged pop nights.

Will scanned the tables, imagining them filled with the warehouse crowd, brightening the diner in their tie-dye tees, and clocked Charlotte sitting with her friends. Keen to go over, he felt a flutter of excitement.

Stuart waved a shot glass under Will's nose and told him to neck it. Will threw it back, thinking a bit of a courage boost wouldn't go amiss. After a few more, Stuart and Adam wouldn't notice him gone. He could go to the toilet and make a detour to say hi to Charlotte on the way back.

Will thought he had a good chance. She and Michaela always made a fuss over him. If he ran a night at a club, he'd only go up in their estimation. Nightclubs had it all. The smoke, the lights, a permanent sound system—not having to lug one of those around would be a godsend. Punters would have all the amenities they took for granted on regular nights out, and there'd be multiple rooms to listen to different styles of music.

Adam and Stuart downed another round of shots. Will decided he'd leave them to fight over his. He got up to go see how Charlotte was enjoying part two of her big weekend.

Among the group of girls, several conversations were going on when Will interrupted: 'Where's Michaela?'

Charlotte's face showed surprise for a brief moment before her grin was there, welcoming him to proceedings. 'The bar—still!'

She shuffled up for him to join them. The two girls on the other side of the bench, who Will didn't recognise, gave him a quick appraisal before returning to each other.

'What happened then?'

'Where to start,' Will laughed.

Sitting down, he noticed, Adam and Stuart already on their way over. Assuming the role of jolly entertainers, fooling around next to the table, they bemused Charlotte's friends with drunken high jinks.

Charlotte was more interested in Will so he left them to dig their own graves.

'So, what did the cops say?'

'We got told to do one, I think.'

'Hilarious, when's the next party?'

'You know the number to call, don't you?'

'*I* have to call *you*? Aren't I an insider?' Put out, Charlotte's attention drifted over the lively surroundings.

When she came back to him looking aggrieved, Will attempted to redeem himself. 'It's need to know, but I'll put you top of my list.' He smiled.

'You do that.' She wagged a finger. 'Because I need to know.'

Will laughed at her playful scorn, and she squeezed his arm. Her gaze wandered the drunken crowd. 'What a blast,' she said absent-mindedly.

Will's natural response to her touch was to affectionately squeeze her thigh. She came back to him with a warm smile before being distracted by her friend.

Will surveyed the dance floor. Compared to last night, the scene was pathetic. Out-of-touch suburban wannabees stepped neatly in their well-polished shoes. The girls, all high-heeled dollies, swayed under shoulder-padded suit jackets. They must have heard every track a million times before tonight.

The music's volume lowered slightly. 'Any of you girls fancy some S'Express at mine?' announced the DJ, disguising his shoddy mixing with dumb innuendo. He introduced a crossover track, the best of the night by far. A small group cheered, but it was a lame effort from the rest of them.

The tacky club grated on Will more than he anticipated. Charlotte seemed oblivious, nattering to her girlfriends, who were about to retreat to the bar to find Michaela. Stuart and Adam unashamedly hovered nearby, keen to claim the vacated seats.

When Charlotte's attention returned to him, he asked, 'Want to dance?'

She offered him a mixture of surprise and suspicion. 'Here?'

Will shrugged. 'Why not?'

Charlotte watched the girls retreat. Stuart and Adam took their place.

'Sounds like a plan.' She took his hand. 'Tell no one.'

Squeezing between frilly dresses and buttoned-up shirts, Charlotte's confidence shone, returning the affection of those they passed. They were being judged as a couple, and Will was happy to let everyone think that.

She found a spot beneath the glitterball and got into her dance routine, compelling Will to perform to music he wasn't fond of. As though highlighting her awareness of this, she said, 'You wanted it.'

'I know.'

She didn't hold back, making Will feel like his routine was floundering the whole time. Then he recognised a song coming in. A guitar riff reverberated over choppy beats, a simple chord repeating over and over. The lack of bass made the track unmistakable, and with his enjoyment, his limbs loosened.

'"When Doves Cry",' he said.

She smiled knowingly and raised her arms and twisted her hips.

While the track played, they danced freely, enjoying the song. They were within themselves, but the experience was shared. The way they held eye contact, taking coordinated steps towards each other before backing off, each measuring their approach to the other.

Will admired her neat, shoulder-length hair as it swung to the music. Her slender neck and bold collarbones were irresistible, framed above the green off-the-shoulder top. Its loose fit complementing the tight grey pencil skirt, which revealed toned legs all the way to her stiletto ankle boots. Gone was her usual choice of stonewash jeans and graphic tee. Tonight, she had classic style.

The DJ cut out before the extended guitar riff, but Charlotte perked Will up with an alluring, 'Am I any good?'

With the lights dancing over them, Will studied her complexion. There wasn't much makeup covering delicate cheekbones and bow lips he wanted to kiss. 'You're amazing.'

'Am I?' Charlotte enquired invitingly, stepping closer.

Her lips were parted slightly, and Will leaned in to kiss her, relieved when she pulled him towards her.

Their kiss lingered on their lips before tongues got involved. When they separated, neither said a word, swaying to the music before they began again. With the second kiss, Will felt like they relaxed into it, the movement of their mouths natural.

They stopped and Will said, 'Hot.'

So was her raised eyebrow.

Will moved to kiss her again, but she pulled away. Will was confused until she grinned and planted a long kiss plumb on his lips. Wrapping her arms around his neck, she let him have her tongue once more.

When she loosened their embrace, he looked for another kiss and got a quick peck.

'Home,' he said.

Charlotte led him from the dance floor. They glided through the dancers, and it seemed to take seconds to reach the corridor off the main room. There was an open toilet door to one side and, when Charlotte glanced back with a radiant smile, Will acted on a mischievous impulse and pulled her through. The detour caused her to gasp in surprise, but once they were inside, faint lines of amusement assessed him and the private space. She locked the door to the disabled toilet, set down her purse, and came up to kiss him. This time their embrace was more profound than on the dance floor. With no one around, their wanton tongues twisted together without constraint, their hands wandering over their bodies.

Pawing eagerly at each other's clothes, they settled against the wall. Will ran his hands up her sides to gently hold her face. Her hands came up beneath his T-shirt and stroked his sides before one came to rest on his belt.

He caressed her breasts and felt her hand between his legs, making him want her more. He reached for her behind and squeezed the firm muscles underneath her skirt. He hitched it up and found her lace knickers and smooth flesh.

Their eagerness slowed. The embrace tightened when she hooked a leg around his waist and held his neck. He supported her, holding the back of her thigh.

While they kissed, Will's length swelled. Charlotte unfastened the top button of his jeans and slid her hand beneath. Will found the dainty band of her knickers and eased it down. Feeling a patch of fur before finding the folds of flesh between her legs.

The wet pool of skin made him rigid. She removed her hand to push down both waistbands. Bringing his length into the open. She stroked him with a tight, clumsy grip until she found a soft, steady rhythm. He explored her deeper, causing her to groan and suck his lower lip.

Each taken by the other's pleasure, their kissing stopped while their bodies convulsed. Desire softened her face as she looked for more.

She backed to the sink. While he helped her onto the edge, her hand returned to the stiff muscle at his centre, holding it lightly. Will looked to her spread thighs and the gaping slit of pink flesh. He took hold of her raised knees, and she helped him enter her.

Charlotte wrapped her arms around him, pulling him close. Moving together, they began to kiss. Her legs squeezed his waist, Will ran his hands over her body, stroking her from the tip of her boots to her pert breasts. Getting lost in the moment, he pulled away from kissing her neck to be smothered by her warm breath.

Charlotte released him to take hold of the sink's edge. She raised her body up, supporting herself while moving with him. Will took hold of her hips, and they collided in unison, both of them going with it, bucking together until Will felt himself suddenly overcome. Charlotte gyrated around his rapidly draining muscle, and he groaned with pleasure.

Knowing it was done, Charlotte opened her eyes. Their

movements slowed, and they remained together with nothing to say. Will withdrew. He became aware of their dishevelled clothes.

Watching Will zip himself up, Charlotte dropped from the sink to pull up her knickers. She looked at him like he was a different person. Her pupils were wide and dark, her gaze firm.

'You want a drink?' he asked.

'Whoever said romance was dead?' She straightened her skirt.

Will couldn't help but laugh and turned to the sink to wash his hands. She joined him, and he passed her the thin piece of soap.

'Back to normal, eh?' she said.

'What's normal?' asked Will, flicking water off his hands.

Charlotte studied him thoroughly in the mirror then looked for paper to dry her hands. There wasn't any. Her gaze returned to linger on him. Then, without warning, she wiped her wet hands down his T-shirt and laughed.

'Hey,' he complained, stepping back.

She looked at him like he deserved it but couldn't hide the amusement in her eyes.

Retreating to the door, she shook the remaining the water on her skirt, said, 'I'll be at the bar.' Her hand on the latch, she glanced back. 'Give it two.'

Charlotte slipped out, leaving Will alone with his reflection and a damp patch across his front.

04 / *White Noise*

Alone in the toilet, Will re-locked the door and took the opportunity to pee. The whole time his thoughts were on Charlotte, the girl he would soon get to know a lot more about. He was looking forward to it. He fastened a button on his suit jacket to hide the damp patch and stepped out.

The empty corridor reverberated to the music channelling through it. At the far end, two lads argued in the glow of the cigarette machine. Will left them to it.

Returning to the main room, he kept an eye out for Charlotte. Through the outskirts, a faint lightshow drifted over passers-by. Ahead, on the sunken dance floor, put-on smiles fronted those who stepped neatly to overplayed pop hits. Nothing had changed. Compared to the night before, the mood was still sterile.

Will aimed for the bar where he thought Charlotte might be. He couldn't see her, but what he did notice was some guy next to the glass collection area staring directly at him. It was strange. The guy wasn't idly staring. Will could tell he was watching him. He even began to smile beneath the wire spectacles and military cut.

Rounding a pillar circled by a rail of discarded drinks, Will was confronted by two burly men. Dressed in cheap black suits, they regarded him with contempt. He knew they were security, even before he spotted the coiled wires protruding from their earpieces.

For some reason, perhaps assistance, Will searched for the guy watching him. He was still there, only now he did more than watch; he raised a chubby mitt and waved a slow, mocking wave of goodbye.

Before Will could fully process this, the security guards gripped him firmly and lifted him into the air. By the time confusion became surprise, Will's body was at an angle, and his feet were off the floor. A sensation of forward motion and a ringing noise were the last things he experienced before his head hit the nearby pillar, and everything disappeared in a flash of white.

☺

Charlotte waited at the bar near where they'd been sitting. She politely dismissed the barman, who careened over the pumps eager to serve her, and scanned the diner for her girlfriends. Maybe they'd ventured onto the dance floor as well.

Boy, was Will a surprise, both of them removed from the environment in which they were most familiar with the other. She and Michaela mischievously portrayed him as a mythical beast. A brave centaur, fronting the only decent local parties they could find. They tempered their intrigue through a desire not to appear too keen to get to know him. A self-imposed mode of behaviour to keep them aloof. Otherworldly. Did it have the desired effect? Had she landed the coup of the decade by bagging him? She'd go as far as saying the pace of their affair made her nervous. But she was excited to tell Michaela about it.

While Charlotte killed time perusing the top shelf, the barman became agitated, snatched a manky cloth and began scrubbing busily. Intrigued, Charlotte investigated the source of his anxiety and found an older man approaching directly towards them. The lecherous intent on his chubby face implied he was more interested in her than the barman. Hoping she was wrong, she rooted through her purse as a distraction. Where was that bubble gum? Anything would do until Will arrived. She wished he'd hurry up.

'Can I get you a drink?' came the engagement she'd dreaded.

Charlotte ignored his hopeful face, as though she was preoccupied. 'I'm okay,' she hesitated, 'thanks.' She returned to rummaging.

'Anything you want,' he boasted, full of himself.

Flakes of dry saliva filled the creases of his lips, a cocktail of alcohol and stale cigarettes fouling his breath. Charlotte wanted to get away from him. 'I'm fine, thank you.' She nodded politely and gave him a tight-lipped smile.

He leaned on the bar, trapping her. 'You really think he's coming back?'

Charlotte remembered being with Will in the toilet. 'I'm sorry, what?' She wanted to push through this man. Rationale stopped her. She held his gaze, his eyes small and intense behind aviator-style spectacles.

'Anything you want.' His hand dropped from the bar and found her backside.

Charlotte tensed, about to unleash her wrath until his hand delved between her thighs, sending her dumbstruck. Fear and disgust rose through her. She forced her arms onto his podgy chest, pushing him away. In the same motion, she turned sideways and stepped back, the sensation of his damp chubby flesh staining her memory.

'I slipped,' he said, holding up his hands in defence.

Charlotte felt her face flush red hot. She searched for help, but the barman was stunned, frozen to the spot.

'Just a little accident.' The man eyed her with devilish appreciation.

Charlotte's brow tightened. Her nostrils flared. 'Fuck. Off,' she seethed, eager for Will's arrival.

'Suit yourself, duck.' He considered her thoroughly. 'Don't

come crying to me about lover boy.'

The man swaggered away while the barman hastily abandoned his post like the weasel she'd taken him for. Those nearby continued to cavort as though nothing had happened. Obviously, they hadn't seen. She remained at the bar for a minute or two, until her emotions seemed to have settled.

Growing impatient waiting for Will, Charlotte made a half-hearted trip through the crowd in search of him or her girls. Fearing the worst, she imagined Will bragging to his friends about his conquest. Preferring to be alone and dying to get away, Charlotte dashed for the exit before she had to contend with either group.

In the entrance hall, the very same guy stood next to the front doors chatting with security guards. She couldn't believe her misfortune but, at the same time, realised he must be someone important at the club.

Charlotte diverted to collect her coat, worried that he'd come over and say something. She waited for the cloakroom attendant, focussing on the number of her raffle ticket. The whole time, she could hear him laughing with the heavies, all of them boasting about how macho they were and some guy who was up to no good.

Her nerves in tatters, she couldn't help but glance backwards and caught him watching her. If Charlotte failed to conceal her emotions, the girl with the pierced lip and heavy makeup didn't let on when she returned the coat.

Storming, almost sprinting, from Glitter, Charlotte swung on her coat in a manner that shielded her from his view. She hoped the heavy belt buckle would catch the sick nonce in his face.

Among rowdy groups and abandoned fast food trays, scattered over the wide pavement, she was beyond caring where to go. Caught between welling tears and an ill-advised rage that wanted to send her back to the club to shout and complain, she had a good mind to tell the posse of rugby boys outside the kebab house.

Disorderly drunks, stepping onto the road, hindered her hailing of a taxi. Charlotte turned full circle, searching for an escape from the obstreperous fools, helplessness sapping her energy. She shut out the effort the walk would take and set off for home, growling to release her fury.

Crossing the end of an alleyway, a blue light flashed across a crumbling brick wall. An ambulance was parked in the shadows with a group of people watching paramedics attending to a figure. White jeans were visible. They were at the rear of Glitter, and Will had been wearing white jeans.

Charlotte's distress and a desire for a warm bed told her not to get involved. What caused her to hesitantly turn into the alleyway was a bizarre form of hope, a strange desire that wanted it to be Will. She didn't want him hurt; she wanted a reason for being stood up.

Edging along, another flashing blue light became apparent, a police car parked behind the ambulance. Two officers were talking to two doormen. One copper indicated the security camera above the fire exit, but the doormen maintained innocent expressions.

Charlotte's approach distracted one onlooker, but they were too preoccupied to give her more than a moment's thought. Seeing the outstretched leg, Charlotte wished, above anything else, that the jeans were not white like Will's.

Finding a way through, his bloody face ran through her. She regretted wishing him harm. Only moments ago, the same boyish face smiled fondly at her, his kind eyes and well-formed features so pleasing to her gaze.

Dropping to his side, a paramedic held her off with polite

authority. They demanded that someone help, then reassured Charlotte it would be okay, that they needed space to work. A husky-voiced drunk woman helped Charlotte to her feet, asking after her wellbeing and calling her 'my darling'. Charlotte couldn't handle sympathy and turned away, pretending the woman's words hadn't registered.

Will was carried inside the ambulance on a stretcher. The nearest paramedic wrapped a blanket around Charlotte, asking if she wanted to accompany them to hospital, asking if she knew the young man and whether he'd drunk much, asking how much she'd drunk too. Charlotte couldn't answer all the questions at once. It was all happening too fast.

The rear compartment, filled with equipment and compact stores, was claustrophobic enough without Will's unconscious body strapped to a stretcher. Charlotte sank into the seat indicated and watched the paramedic cover Will's mouth with an oxygen mask.

Weaving through late-night traffic, sirens wailed. The paramedic attended to Will while Charlotte, streaked in mascara, rationalised the events she'd witnessed. The comment from the nonce at the bar, his laughter with the doormen. They were talking about someone they'd thrown out. It must have been Will but, until she'd seen him outside, she'd been entirely unaware, and her mind clouded with hate. Charlotte's thoughts of Will were replaced by the emotional scars of being groped. The man thinking he could do as he pleased. Groped, the word seemed insufficient. How about … indecent assault? And the man, he was no longer a nonce. Petty insults didn't do him justice. He was an adult governed by the same rules as everyone else. To let him get to her would be to let him win. Charlotte exhaled slowly. From a dark place, she found hope, not only for herself but for Will. With the two of them being assaulted, there must be enough evidence against the man. Enough for the authorities to take matters further.

Charlotte imagined the man being led from Glitter in handcuffs, her friends and all the other guests jeering as the police escorted him to jail. With the sight of victory, Charlotte's morale lifted, but a bump brought her back to reality. Then another bump. The ambulance was crossing a speed hump. She saw through the tinted window the ambulance bays outside the town's infirmary. A grand stone building housing a modern A&E department.

Charlotte followed the stretcher from the ambulance. The paramedics wheeled Will through the ambulance park, and a doctor with a team of nurses arrived to greet them. The paramedics provided a briefing of Will's condition as the stretcher passed into the bright white hospital.

Advising her Will would be taken for a CT scan, a nurse guided Charlotte from his side, taking her to a circular waiting room, with corridors extending at various angles behind the central admission desk.

Charlotte found a seat and waited beneath the blanket, watching patients come and go, wondering how severe the reasons for their visits were. After a short time, another nurse arrived and escorted Charlotte to a treatment room with a wooden chair and an empty bed along the far wall. She hadn't considered herself a patient but now started to doubt her assumption. Pleasantly the nurse told Charlotte to take a seat before fetching a cup of water from the sink by the door.

Handing the water over, Charlotte studied the nurse's heart-shaped face, maybe fifteen years older than hers, with firm skin and few signs of ageing. A narrow chin sat below wide cheekbones and blue eyes that were alert yet unassuming.

'Can you tell us the young man's name?' The nurse asked in a tone that matched her concerned expression.

'Will,' she said.

'Did Will have much to drink?' The nurse sounded relaxed about it.

'Some,' Charlotte replied, 'he must have. But not too much,' she added, seeing Will in the toilet and not remembering any noticeable side effects.

'Okay,' said the nurse reassuringly, 'Do you remember how much?'

'I didn't really see him drink at all.'

'That's okay.'

'I know he was partying last night as well,' Charlotte added, wanting to help as much as she could, 'but I don't know how drunk he was.'

'That's fine.' The nurse rose to her feet. 'The doctors are completing some tests. They won't be too long.' The nurse went to the door, 'You can stay here for now, okay?'

Charlotte imagined Will in one of those circular scanners, comparing the advanced examination with the time the doctor told her she needed her tonsils removed, aged seven. Her mother stayed with her the whole time because her dad was away at work. Charlotte remembered being with her dad, too, another time. Several hours on his lap with a crooked finger, her dad in trouble for encouraging young Charlotte to mend her broken bike chain. It was strange how it was a happy memory despite the pain of a fractured finger, a time when her parents were together.

Charlotte's hangover crept over her. She wanted to sleep through it but knew she couldn't. Feeling overdressed and conscious people would judge her, she ventured to the row of vending machines and selected a watery coffee for ten pence.

Back in the treatment room, sipping on a second coffee, after waiting for what seemed like an age, a South Asian doctor arrived and introduced himself with an outstretched hand. Charlotte remained seated and took hold of his grip, noticing his cold hand.

Wasting no time, the doctor switched on a lightbox beside the cabinet. From the papers, he displayed Will's tomograms. Having Will's medical condition being disclosed to her made Charlotte uneasy. Realising how little she knew him, she folded her arms, feeling like a fraud.

'The CT indicates there is no damage to Will's brain near to the impact point.' The doctor pointed at a section and drew a circle with his finger. 'Neither traumatic subarachnoid haemorrhaging nor acute subdural haematoma. Your young man didn't even sustain a fracture. This is good.' He smiled tightly. 'We have also assessed his other major organs and also found no damage there.'

'Is he awake?' Charlotte asked.

'No, not yet,' said the doctor as a matter of fact.

'Do you know when?' asked Charlotte.

'That is beyond all of us.'

It was a silly question, but his tone and the weight of his words affected her gravely. What were the implications? There were too many.

The doctor filled a paper cup and handed it over. 'Have some water.' He smiled. 'Much better than coffee.'

Charlotte let the doctor swap the drinks and asked, 'What does all that mean?' watching him presumptuously pour her coffee into the sink.

The doctor remained impassive. 'As we cannot wake him, technically, Will is in a coma.'

'A coma?' Charlotte asked, shocked at hearing such a severe condition.

'He is breathing on his own. His vital signs are good. We suspect he's sleeping off a lively weekend.' The doctor smiled briefly. 'We should have a better indication in the morning.'

Charlotte nodded, absent-mindedly taking a sip of water. This was catastrophic. Charlotte imagined Will's loved ones elsewhere, Will alone in the hospital bed. What should she do?

'It will be okay,' the doctor said kindly.

Charlotte needed to speak to the girls. They would help. Not now, while the party still raged. The morning would be best.

'Shall we go to see him?' the doctor asked.

Charlotte nodded hurriedly, gathering her coat from the chair.

Pacing along the white-tiled corridor, the doctor detailed Will's treatment: 'The worst of Will's cuts required only butterfly tape, not stitches, and to the break of skin beneath his hairline, we applied medical glue. He was lucky not to dislocate his shoulder.' He glanced back at Charlotte. 'His injuries suggest he lost his motor reflexes and landed on it.'

'I see,' confirmed Charlotte grimly, apprehensive of the scene to which she was being led.

'The bruising to his ribs is far worse than that you will see on his neck. We're administering saline fluid intravenously. This will keep him nourished and hydrated until he wakes and is well enough to eat.'

They arrived at a ward. 'Will he be okay to leave then?' asked Charlotte, nervously surveying the rows of beds, some in view, their patients asleep. Others were concealed behind privacy curtains.

'We will need to perform further tests.'

The whole ordeal made Charlotte acutely sensitive. When the doctor opened the privacy curtain, the scrape of rings along the metal bar caused her to flinch.

Will lay there, eyes shut, dried blood and red marks beyond the white sheet pulled square to his chest. A saline drip was inserted in his left arm, the slow-beeping heart rate monitor attached to the pulse in his opposite thumb.

'All yours,' the doctor said before retreating.

Thanks, thought Charlotte. She repositioned the Formica chair between Will's unconscious form and the privacy curtain.

Machines beeped impassively in the tight space. A sense of claustrophobia engulfed Charlotte's fragile psyche. The heat and the chemical odour made her dizzy. She needed air and stumbled to the window. Opening it as much as the hinges would allow, the narrow gap pulled in a cool breeze. Charlotte rested at the windowsill until she felt refreshed.

Back in the unforgiving seat, Charlotte reflected on her mother, remembering her bedside vigil when young Charlotte's tonsils were removed. She'd remained at Charlotte's side for three days, bar the forty-five minutes Charlotte was under anaesthetic; unable to sit and wait for the operation to be completed, she'd dashed home for a wash and change of clothes. This time Charlotte was the responsible party, the person expected to aid recovery. But the circumstances and duration were less certain than those surrounding her own time as an inpatient.

Nurses, undertaking scheduled checks on Will, woke Charlotte with professional courtesy. Her brief, uncomfortable sleep offered no benefits, and she found herself too groggy to follow the explanations for tests being undertaken every hour.

During the next set of tests, which seemed much longer than an hour later, Will's response to a pinch indicated a GCS score of nine. The nurse advised he was in only a moderate coma. Again, hearing the word coma, Charlotte tensed. Her limited understanding drew conclusions that she fought hard to dismiss.

Upon later assessment, this time carried out by the doctor, Will began swearing. The doctor sternly condemned the unrepeatable words and, in response, Will garbled an incoherent sentence. Watching Will's mouth move unnaturally with wide, unfocused eyes horrified Charlotte.

'He's improving,' said the doctor to Charlotte's surprise. 'By my calculation, that little outburst puts him one point away from a minor coma,' the doctor continued. 'When Will opens his eyes of his own accord, this will be a key signal he is on the road to recovery. If he speaks coherently, even better. If, after both of these, he knows what you are saying and can obey your every command, it won't be long before he is discharged.'

At least the doctor remained upbeat. Charlotte took it as a promising sign.

'Don't look so worried,' he said before he left. 'It will do him good to see a happy face.'

By mid-morning, Will still hadn't awoken, and the issues Charlotte might have to contend with before leaving remained daunting and unavoidable. If the worst were to happen, she didn't know who she'd call upon, let alone who she needed to notify.

Thinking about making those calls, Charlotte realised she should phone the girls. Under normal circumstances, she'd have returned home or phoned by now. It wasn't fair for Michaela's travels to start burdened by unnecessary concern, never mind having to help resolve this mess first. Charlotte pushed back the chair. The metal legs shuddered harshly against the linoleum floor, causing an anxious glance in Will's direction. He remained inert. Disappointed there was no change to his condition, Charlotte slipped away.

At the payphone on the corridor wall, Charlotte didn't want to get into details. Despite Sophie's coos and playful cajoling, Charlotte refused to offer a satisfactory response. Yes, she was with a guy but, no, it wasn't how Sophie imagined. Could she speak to Michaela, anyway? No, she was over at Pete's. Charlotte knew the sour tone with which Sophie ended their conversation formed part of a broader game that would allow her to probe further upon their next meeting.

Retaking the plastic seat beside the bed, Will's eyelids flickered. Hope stirred Charlotte to step into the ward and signal to a couple of nurses.

The nurses came briskly to Will's bedside. In a whisper, Charlotte updated them as to what she'd seen. They cast a critical eye over Will. One tidied his bedding. When he didn't react further, they reassured Charlotte and left with well-practised smiles.

Feeling naive, Charlotte took her seat, listening to the machines beep and the hospital ward's hidden events. Occasionally Will's bruised cheek would twitch involuntarily above the thin line of cuts.

Charlotte was tired of the tiny space with every detail excruciatingly studied: the machine's relentless electronic lines, all the wires, every bland and monotone piece of fabric, dreadful injuries, polystyrene ceiling tiles, ghastly light, a mucky pile of clothes on a wire trolley, robust flooring fit for no home. It was oppressive.

Then, a flash of intrigue, the memory of leather, a corner bulging from within the folds of Will's outfit. A blessing if only for its newness. His wallet. Charlotte retrieved it and rooted through the contents: coins in a zipped pocket; a bank card; leisure centre and snooker club membership; three ten-pound notes, one new, two ragged; a driving licence; a half-used book of first-class stamps; a folded piece of paper. She removed the paper and found it to be a flyer for Saturday's Dominator party. She toyed with keeping it, a souvenir of their time together, but decided otherwise. So far, there was nothing to celebrate, and it wasn't a relationship.

Replacing Will's wallet, the question of how long to stay returned to weigh on her. Charlotte thought she ought to be there when he awoke, but no one could say when that would be.

Although his vital signs were improving, he remained in a coma. She'd try Michaela again soon.

Considering that he might never wake, Charlotte saw the wide-reaching implications and the devastating effect upon his friends and family. It tired her out thinking about it. She needed proper sleep in a bed, not on a chair. Then she felt guilty for prioritising her minor needs above Will's more severe predicament.

Unfamiliar with him beyond breezy party chitchat, she considered him a wise-looking boy, who, during their brief acquaintance, provided her with more than enough entertainment. He was fun to be around. Did he promote parties full time? Or was he a missing colleague whose employer left answer machine messages reminding him he should be at work by now? Were there people searching for him? A distraught mother at an empty breakfast table wishing him home. An anxious father making phone calls to friends. What if he missed an exam? Surely, they'd let him re-sit. What if he had a girlfriend!

Charlotte gazed over the bed to Will's battered face. Expecting to find him sleeping, she was startled to see his eyes open, blinking. The flutter of nerves almost got her rising from her seat; she wanted to find the nurses but feared a shout or sudden movement might hinder his recovery. She waited quietly to give him time. She imagined him catching her with his wallet and thinking she was a thief. With hindsight, having seen his face twitching, she should have realised he might wake soon.

Will surveyed the white curtained space before fixing on her, blinking heavily without showing any recognition. After an unnatural length of time in this position, and as though he couldn't control his facial muscles, he smiled vaguely.

Although his smile was slightly unsettling, her concerns were lifting to marvellous, weightless relief. Calmly, she asked, 'Are you okay?'

Will faced the ceiling. His eyes rolled back as though trying to remember. Eventually, he wheezed, 'Partied out,' and, as his head rotated towards her, he croaked, 'big time.'

05 / *Rehab*

There was a girl at Will's side, who he didn't recognise. She was attractive too. Brown eyes above a narrow nose and bow-shaped lips. How could he not recognise her?

At first, all he remembered was being in Glitter with the boys. Then he had a flashback to a warehouse, the pulsing lights beneath a crowded dance floor. Or was that Glitter? It felt like a long night. No wonder his head hurt.

The girl said, 'You're in hospital.'

When he moved his jaw to speak, his right cheek ached. He could feel a lump beneath the skin. He attempted to sit up to get a better view of the girl, but a sting in his ribs caused him to grimace and settle back.

'Take your time.'

A patchwork of recent memories snapped together, reorganising themselves into a familiar arrangement above those immersed deep within his consciousness. His name, his childhood, his home town all hurtled towards the epic warehouse party that descended into hedonism and a heady retreat from the police. Then, after the party at Stuart's, the trip to Glitter. Everything up to the point a girl left the toilet.

This girl.

Charlotte.

Sitting in a hospital ward, calmly observing his return to consciousness.

'Do you want some water?' she asked.

Will nodded, and she rose from the chair to slip behind the

privacy curtain. Her disappearance took him back to the toilet. Their bare skin colliding together seemed like only a moment ago, the times before that fun and light. They didn't know each other well, but they were comfortable together. She was here with him now. Did his parents know what happened? He decided he couldn't have been here long. He hoped he hadn't.

Charlotte returned brimming with optimism. She passed him a cup of water. 'The nurse said lunch won't be long.'

Will took a sip, watching her settle. The bedside vigil had stolen her sheen but her stylish outfit still held together a beautiful young woman he considered profoundly caring.

'Is it Monday?'

'Yes.'

'What happened?'

Charlotte leaned forward. 'We got together.'

He saw them embracing in the toilet. 'I remember that bit.'

She leaned back, partly relieved, partly irritated.

'Was there trouble?' Will asked, 'What happened to Stuart and Adam? Why am I here?'

Two nurses arrived pushing a trolley loaded with trays, a basket of rolls in sealed cellophane bags and two large urns. Without delay, one moved to help prop Will against his pillow. He grimaced, and she asked after his wellbeing in a matronly manner. Will described the pain, and the other nurse retreated.

'We'll get you something for that.'

With Will upright, she tidied his sheets and wheeled the table up from the foot of his bed. From the urns, she spooned a dollop of macaroni cheese and a dollop of rice pudding onto a segregated plastic tray and served it with a bread roll. The other nurse returned with water and a paper cup containing two tablets. She placed them on the table then wheeled the trolley from Will's bay. Along the ward, the elderly and the infirm awaited their lunch with tired expressions.

The lead nurse marked the clipboard at the end of his bed. 'Dihydrocodeine can make you constipated, so there's something to help with that too.' She replaced his notes and followed after her colleague.

Will reached for the tablets and the water and swallowed them in one go. 'I'll pick the restaurant next time,' he quipped.

Charlotte stifled a laugh. Will reached for the cutlery, remembering sitting next to her in Glitter, her smile coming easier than the one he'd just seen. Then they were on the dance floor together, enjoying the music. He felt his appetite return and stabbed some pasta with the fork. 'I haven't eaten since Saturday.'

'I'm getting on for twenty-four hours.'

Will could tell she was tired. 'You want some?' He indicated the food.

'I'll pass. Thanks.'

'It's better than it looks.'

Charlotte wrinkled her nose in dismissal.

'You don't have to stay.'

'Don't be silly.' Charlotte searched the ward like she wanted to summon a waiter. 'It is stuffy in here, though. Maybe I'll go find something.' She fixed him a beautifully serious expression. 'Do you want anything?'

'I'm all right, thanks.'

Charlotte departed. Will finished his lunch, leaving the chewy bread roll because it made his jaw sting. He pushed the table away and settled back. Reflecting on the weekend, he found nothing of concern. He saw Glitter's crowd around him but no interaction. No incident that could have sparked trouble. Compared to the warehouse, Glitter was a relic. Sanctioned entertainment, as banal as the music. A temple of cheap booze for those content with whatever they're served. Trouble was more likely in a place like that. But he couldn't remember any, just being alone, expecting to meet Charlotte.

A man at a bar watching him appeared and disappeared from his mind in an instant.

Will rested his eyes and, through the darkness, pictured the man actively watching him. Will remembered him wave. Again, the trail stopped. Will felt uneasy, like the memory threatened him.

The ward was monotonous and impassive, the lights and softly beeping machines as relentless as the chemical aroma. Charlotte returned, a sprite of health and wellbeing streaking through the room. The folds in her top rippled like petals. She carried a fashion magazine, which, after sitting down, she plonked by his feet. The action was careless, but the way she looked at him afterwards, she was as serious as when she left him.

'Everything okay?' he asked.

'Do you know what I think happened?'

'What?'

'I think the people who run Glitter beat you up for being with me.'

It surprised Will.

'A guy approached me. After I left you.'

'How do you mean?'

Charlotte hesitated. 'He came over to me at the bar.'

'Did he say something?'

'He did more than that.' Charlotte paused, choosing her words. 'He suggested he knew what happened between us. He wasn't too happy about it.'

The image of the man watching him returned, the man waving goodbye. 'What did he look like?'

'A miserable old man …? Big, glasses … kind of sweaty.'

When she said *old*, Will knew he was on to something. 'On my way to find you, I remember this older guy watching me. Properly watching. Like he was waiting for something to happen. I think he waved.'

Charlotte nodded slowly. Will could tell she was back in Glitter.

'Was he big plump or big tall?'

'Plump, not tall, with a flat top haircut.' Her nostrils flared. 'He felt me up,' she said, as though she loathed the words.

That surprised Will even more. 'You all right?'

'You should have seen me last night, all the booze and emotion. I wanted to destroy the place.'

'What did you do?'

'After telling him to do one, you mean? Leave. That's when I came across you.'

'I don't remember.'

'No, you were unconscious.'

'You found me?'

'No, by the time I'd arrived, the ambulance was already there.'

'So other people saw what happened?'

'I guess so.' She shrugged. 'I wasn't there.'

Will didn't know how to handle the revelation. He couldn't remember exactly what happened, so he was separated from events. Beyond his injuries, there was a void his emotions didn't know how to fill. 'How are you about it all?'

Charlotte shrugged. 'The police were there, talking to some doormen. But I don't think they'll come to find you.'

'It's all drunkenness to them. Fights happen all the time on nights out.'

'What happened wasn't a fight.'

'They don't know that.'

Will said, 'You're not the only one who wants to destroy the place.'

☺

Once the doctors completed their tests and were satisfied Will could be discharged, Charlotte went to find a taxi. Alone, getting dressed behind the privacy curtain, Will examined the bruising to his chest. An almost perfect straight line ran down his sternum, separating good from bad. On one side, yellow swirled amongst blues and purple. He ran his fingers across his ribs, feeling his tender flesh. He found his clothes next to the bed and imagined the doctors and nurses witnessing his limp naked body, a minor intrusion compared to the major beating.

Another memory developed of being dragged along a staff corridor before being thrown face-first through fire doors. Deal with it, he told himself and unfurled his jeans to get dressed. The confined space and restricted movement in his right hip made it problematic. Sitting with his leg straight, he delicately worked the jeans over his foot and then slid his other leg in. Standing, he left the waistband loose to avoid pressure on his hip.

Will carefully guided his hand into his T-shirt's sleeve. Keeping his arm in a comfortable position, he pulled the tee over his head and worked his left arm through the opposite sleeve. The motion pulled against his right armpit, causing a sharp pain in his shoulder.

Standing there dressed, Will was far from comfortable. He kicked his socks under the bed in disregard and stood into his scuffed shoes.

From behind the drawn curtain, an abrupt, 'All right?' announced Charlotte's return. He picked up his suit jacket.

Will found her waiting with a wheelchair. 'I thought it might help,' she said.

With Charlotte pushing him through the hospital to the waiting taxi, Will was glad to be discharged. Charlotte remained quiet, and

Will suspected she was contending with her own turmoil.

Arriving on a landing, Charlotte summoned the lift.

'You're awesome,' said Will, 'doing all this.'

Charlotte shook herself from her thoughts. 'Not a problem,' she said, sounding tired.

The lift opened empty. Will's reflection stared back at him. He studied his injuries as Charlotte wheeled him inside. Along his jawbone, thin gouges and clotted lumps extended like rugged terrain, violently dark compared to his pale skin. He tilted his head and found another row of scratches covered by congealed blood. Charlotte preferred to watch the descending numbers on the digital display, her beautiful profile waiting solemnly in stark contrast.

Leaning against the front wing, the taxi driver politely greeted them before opening the rear door for Will. He didn't make any smarmy comments, but his attention lingered on Charlotte while she returned the wheelchair to reception.

'Beauty and the beast, eh?' said Will, and the driver agreed with a chuckle.

Ambling back, Charlotte seemed in a malaise and took three attempts to shut the taxi's door. The driver jumped at the chance to tell her how he'd meant to get it fixed, but she remained mute as they set off.

Will didn't see Ravisbourne as a violent town. Surrounding the grander civic centre, a maze of estates provided shelter to the growing masses who wished to work in London but live affordable lives. A commuter town, built on no great industry, with mostly uninspiring architecture. The only things going for Ravisbourne were cheap rent and being close to the orbital raves that caused euphoria and condemnation in equal measure. Even there, despite the scene's questionable legality, he'd never experienced violence of the sort encountered in Glitter.

Chugging north to his parents' house, Will was glad to have grown up amongst the narrow lanes, where older properties were located in more rural surrounds. Will tried to think of a time he'd witnessed violence. The occasions were remote, limited to drunken fights between strangers in a bar or playground scuffles in school. Neither involved him directly.

Charlotte said, 'What about the police?'

'What about them?'

'We could tell them what happened to us.'

Will didn't see the old bill as his saviours. After Saturday, they were his adversaries. 'I don't see any point. They'll take a statement, and that'll be that. Ultimately it's our word against those in Glitter.'

Charlotte appeared defeated. She viewed passers-by as though they would resolve her dilemma. 'I don't know,' she said finally.

Will didn't think he could face being scrutinised about what happened. 'You really want to tell them what happened, after what we did? We couldn't leave that out, and it make sense.'

'It doesn't have to make sense. What they did is enough.'

Will tried to see it from Charlotte's perspective. At the time this man laid his hands on her, he was unconscious. What could he tell the police? He said, 'If you want to speak to the cops, I'll go to the station with you, to support what you told me. Did anyone else see him do it?'

'There was the barman, but …' Charlotte turned to face the window. Eventually, she said, 'Maybe you're right. Maybe there's nothing we can do.'

They were nearing Will's parents' house, late afternoon, and Will was content to leave the conversation there. He saw enough of a struggle dealing with his own situation. As the taxi arrived, Will found the familiar detached property, hidden beyond drooping willows, comforting. Parked outside the double garage, the Capri, his father's mid-life crisis, gleamed, but the Merc was gone.

'Can I stay here?' Charlotte asked, admiring the property's double frontage. Will was unsure of an answer until Charlotte clarified, 'I mean here, in the taxi.'

'Sure thing.'

They embraced.

'I don't think now is the best time to be introduced to your parents.'

'Probably not.'

Will hobbled to the front door, imagining Charlotte's concerned gaze, waiting for him to make it safely inside. Two pairs of slippers were in the wood-blocked hallway. Calling in greeting, his voice cracked, and he got no response.

After catching one last glimpse of Charlotte as the taxi pulled away, Will slammed the heavy door and paused. With no sound or movement within the house, he became confident he was alone. If his parents were out back, their slippers would be too. There was only one car on the driveway. They'd probably gone out for an evening meal.

Famished despite the hospital food, Will flicked off his shoes and hurried to the kitchen. Seeking further confirmation of his parents' absence, he peeked in the airy front lounge and found it empty.

While bread toasted, Will raided the fridge for butter, jam and chocolate spread and sank a pint of milk. Unscrewing the lids, his shoulder hurt, so he switched hands to get the job done. He buttered the toast, generously topping each slice, and ate them on the spot, kicking any crumbs that fell to the floor under the fridge.

He wiped his sticky palms down his jeans, found a pen, and scribbled a hasty note on the pad propped behind:

Come to visit! Had a bit of a run in.
Fine but sore. Explain tomorrow.
Goodnight!

Will

Clearing away, Will hoped he made it upstairs to bed before his parents got home. He whipped some extra pastries from the fridge and made his retreat.

☺

The following morning, feeling completely drained and remembering his wounds, the trip to Glitter was like an unwanted dream from which he couldn't awake. Lying in his old bedroom, redecorated since he moved out three years ago, he could have been in a hotel room. The small kettle and teacups, complete with sachets of tea, coffee, milk and sugar on a tray next to the bed, were intended for visitors.

The empty packet of pastries lay on top of them. Will regretted not saving one because his stomach ached from hunger. It made him want to move but the awkward conversation required upon seeing his parents prevented him from doing so.

With the bedroom door as he'd left it, he presumed they'd no further insight beyond the note. Will lay there for another hour and a half, hoping sleep would carry him to a more peaceful realm, but the discomfort and the memories of what happened kept him awake.

Eventually, he flung aside the covers and climbed out. Stiff, he stretched until his joints loosened and he was comfortable walking. Peering along the landing, the bathroom opposite was free, and he tiptoed naked across the red carpet, locking the door behind him.

The cold tiles beneath his feet made him shiver. He hopped onto the floor mat and, after setting the bath to fill, examined his face in the mirror.

'Afternoon,' his mother called from downstairs. 'You okay, Shakespeare?'

'Yes, thanks,' Will replied, trying to sound in good spirits.

'You want me to make you breakfast?'

'Yes, please.'

'I'll give it twenty minutes; I know how you are in there.'

'I won't be long.'

'It's fine, lovely.'

Will soaked for half an hour before he began to wash. The nurses had cleaned his cuts, but he wanted to get rid of the dried blood. His task ended when he realised the residue was actually thin scabs.

Getting dressed in his bedroom, the clean pair of pants and socks left behind in a drawer helped make him feel more human. As did the old T-shirt and tracksuit bottoms that covered the majority of his injuries.

Will styled his hair, delicately pushing his fringe across to hide the lump straddling his hairline. Overall, he didn't look too bad. Only a graze along his jaw. That was all. He was fine.

Before heading downstairs, the enticing smell of bacon drifting through the house, he dumped his ruined clothes into a carrier bag. He'd bin the lot once he returned to his flat.

Arriving in the kitchen, his mother looked up from the frying pan. 'Oh dear,' she complained, 'look at you.' She approached with an unwavering frown.

'I'm fine.'

She brushed her natural blonde hair behind her ears and took hold of his shoulders. 'What happened, darling?'

'I had a run in with some lads.' Will hoped she wouldn't grip him any tighter.

'Will, you need to be careful.'

'They were drunk.'

'Where were you?'

'On the way home from work.' Will averted his gaze. His parents still believed he worked in a town centre bar.

'I've told you before. If it's late, get a taxi home.'

'Mum, I know what I'm doing.' At the island countertop, he climbed onto a stool.

'Not everyone else does at three in the morning.'

'I got unlucky.' Through the large window, he admired the back garden, which was in full bloom.

'What did you do?'

'Nothing, they were after trouble.'

'This is what I mean. I don't know what your father's going to say.' She returned to the hob and removed the bacon from the pan.

'It wasn't my fault.'

'Does work know?'

'I told them. I've taken the week off.'

'I'll dish this up,' she sighed. 'That'll help. Do you want anything else?'

'No, I'm fine. Thanks.'

☺

Thursday afternoon, Will remained sprawled at his parents' house, enjoying the bright, airy lounge with its tall bay windows. The room had character, well decorated with coloured soft furnishings, button-backed settees and a wool rug. A wood-burning stove sat beneath a sleek mantlepiece. Stylish ornaments and family photos were positioned on several side tables.

Each day he'd been heading downstairs about midday, after a couple of hours TV in bed. He liked it when the afternoon sun reached the windows, and he could enjoy the warmth on his healing body.

Being back here, it felt like he'd never left. Since moving out, he visited every few weeks to say hello and stay for dinner, an unspoken arrangement that kept his mum happy. He only ever stayed for any length of time at Christmas.

His parents' gaff was far more salubrious than his own flat. It gave him a sense of stability and order he didn't get at home. Too busy planning ahead, his life was undertaken at a sprint. Searching for new equipment and locations, speculatively dropping in on estate agents, designing promotional material, dealing with the printers, visiting record stores or Rob at the studio to keep up-to-date. His flat was more a shelter, where he could take stock and plan for the next party. He wanted and needed a roof for nothing else. Refined luxuries would take care of themselves once he was fully established.

His mother didn't mind him there, commandeering the room, TV remote in hand. She'd pop in to see if he wanted anything between chores or trips to meet friends. His father, however, appeared frustrated at no longer being the only man about the house, after selling his pharmacy to a national chain and taking early retirement. Especially as he'd used some of that cash to help Will with a deposit.

This morning, his father poked his head into the lounge, his wavy brown hair shining blonde in the sunlight. 'Still moping?' he asked before disappearing without waiting for a reply.

Will just wanted to be left alone, get some peace before facing reality. The cooking, the bills, hanging his washing out to dry. All the chores that got in the way. It was like his father thought he might get too comfy and move back in. Afraid he'd become an embarrassment when friends from the golf club visited. His waster son, mid-twenties and not yet with his act together. They'd never make him club president with that sort of baggage.

When his father discovered Will's injuries, the first thing he wanted to know was what Will did wrong. Will didn't often see his father angry, but, on this occasion, his narrow cheekbones flushed red. When Will told him the story about the drunken yobs, who rushed him on his way home from work, his father couldn't contain his frustrations. He huffed to himself before asking, was he okay? Will couldn't decide if his dad was cross with him for getting done in or whether he wanted to set off in his Capri to run the scumbags over.

Yesterday, with Will hogging the settee, getting bored of daytime TV, his father would pop in to chat every now and then. Each time, the conversation would turn into a gentle interrogation, each one designed to find any contradictions in Will's story. 'There were five of them, yes?' his father asked after discussing life at the restaurant. 'Were they in the bar beforehand?' he added casually.

Will regretted lying about the cause of his injuries but still saw that explanation as the easier option. Will answered his father's questions, adding further patches of detail to make the story more believable. Eventually, his father accepted Will's version of events and told Will he'd be okay.

Will knew he was healing well. Each morning his joints felt less sore. Remaining crashed out all day was an indulgent comfort. Despite the lack of desire, he knew he should increase his activity levels. But the closest he'd got to exercise was the hallway, venturing to call Adam to catch up on gossip. Adam sounded happy to hear from him, then shocked to hear what happened. Rob, then Stuart, called shortly afterwards. Will checked his folks were out of range before giving them the details, becoming incredulous as he told them how he'd been jumped for taking Charlotte into the toilet. It was ridiculous.

Occasionally, when Will relaxed, he'd remember the man smirking and become agitated. The idea that someone else consciously decided to cause him harm irritated immensely. If Charlotte hadn't been at the hospital when he awoke, the waving man would've remained a mystery, a vague memory that, by now, he'd probably have forgotten. Instead, Charlotte's troubles presented an uncomfortable truth. Charlotte had no reason to lie or any idea what Will had seen. What else could it be? The man's actions confirmed it. Dwelling on events, Will returned to the club, passing through the outskirts and seeing the man's smirk in all its vitriolic glory. Panic-stricken, Will pre-empted the attack and jolted awake, experiencing a lingering sense of unease.

He decided the only remedy was to get going, get his mind off it. Considering the journey to his flat, he wondered if he could persuade Stuart for a lift. A healthy slice of normality might help him get closure.

Something bumped in the hallway, something solid knocking wood. Will's dad stuck his head around the door and pouted, 'How's my sleepy boy doing?'

Amused by his father's puckered lips, Will said, 'Fine,' wanting to tell his sarcasm to do one.

Will swivelled around to sit upright against the thick cushions, intending to phone a taxi. His father stepped into the room as though Will's movement was an invitation for a chat. Without a second thought, Will asked, 'You fancy taking the Capri for a run?'

06 / *Decks and F.X.*

Will couldn't get over how ratty Daz looked, with his small round head and pointy nose. The resemblance fascinated him. Beyond that, nothing remotely close to interesting could be said. Will thought the short ponytail and round, red sunglasses must be his attempt at projecting character. Certainly, none came across on the few occasions Will had met him.

Daz leaned against the doorframe, with Adam pandering to his sense of humour. The cheery bravado that greeted Will, and maintained after his arrival at Stuart's, disappeared the instant Daz joined proceedings. His abrupt negativity was hard to avoid. Will wanted to turn the TV up, but Adam held the remote.

Rob's cigarette smoke swirled in front of footballers and lace-clad models, who adorned pull-outs tacked to the opposite wall. In the alcove next to the three-bar fire, Adam squatted excitedly on the cushioned armchair, a sock hanging off one foot like a four-year-old. 'We all thought he was getting laid, man. For the first time.'

Will wondered how many more times Adam would make that joke.

'Laid out more like.' Daz didn't share Adam's enthusiasm. 'I thought you boys were lovie dovies, into getting off more than getting on.'

Daz talked through that pointy nose as well, thought Will.

Adam chirped, 'We are, man. Rozzers stole our sound system.'

'You had it out with them?' asked Daz as though they should have.

Stuart entered from the greasy kitchen, stealing everyone's attention. 'Not in our state,' he said, busy stuffing the cash he'd made at the warehouse into a brown envelope. Distracted, he caught his foot on the worn-thin rug and cursed to himself.

Daz said to Will, 'You gonna let them get away with it?'

Will's attention wandered from Stuart's temper to Daz. 'Who?' he asked, unsure if Daz meant the cops or the guys in the club.

'Whoever's getting in your way, pal. Ain't that the rule?' Daz took the envelope from Stuart. 'Sound, my man.'

Will decided Daz was full of gas, talking himself up in front of them. He reached for one of Rob's smokes, causing pain in his ribs. He grimaced. 'You got a light?'

Slouched next to him, Rob passed Will matches while Daz worked the brown envelope into his long black jacket. His business done, Daz left for the front door. Stuart followed him out.

☺

In the cramped porch, Stuart was about to close the front door when Daz stopped on the path outside. Stuart waited while Daz looked along the modest semis across the road. There was no one around.

'What's up?' Stuart asked.

Daz reached into his jacket and pulled out a packet of cigarettes. He put one between his lips and raised a light, making Stuart wait some more. After blowing smoke in the air and pocketing the lighter, Daz faced him.

'Good night Saturday.' It was a statement, not a question.

'Yeah.' Stuart was indifferent. 'Another crazy one.' He could barely remember their split from the warehouse.

'Thick stack of bills you jus' gi' me.'

'It's what you wanted innit?' Stuart folded his arms, unsure where Daz was going with this.

Daz blew smoke. 'How much you make?'

'Enough.'

'Enough?' Daz laughed, playing along. 'I bet you ain't passed me no more than that G?'

'I supposed to?' asked Stuart, keeping it light, grinning to let Daz know.

'Whatever, in one night, that's good going.'

Stuart could tell Daz wanted to know more, but he didn't feel compelled to share. 'Same for you.'

Daz held the cigarette between his thumb and index finger about to take a drag but paused, working something over in his mind. Done, he pointed the smoke at Stuart. 'Ballsy, breaking in there.' He finally took the drag. 'You have them pills on you going in?'

'We knew it was clear,' said Stuart, avoiding the question. 'We got lucky hearing about it.'

Daz took another drag. 'I heard you don't do the football thing no more?'

Stuart was done with those days. 'I don't need those riots no more.'

'I hear that.' Daz scanned the road, his ponytail poking into view.

Stuart thought Daz must get it cut weekly. It was always the same length, ever since he'd known him. Going back to his crazy days at the football. Daz never made games but would show for away days when the firm got the train to London. Daz wouldn't say a word, right in the middle of it, while the lads were all rowdy. If anyone gave Daz lip, one of the top boys would slap them down straight away.

'What about you?' asked Stuart. 'You have grief in Glitter the other night?'

Daz looked along the road, frowning. 'Nothing I can't handle.'

'Matey, you want a new buzz, gimme a call. I'll show you the way.'

'I might just.' Daz strained the last few drags of his cigarette and flicked the butt at a drain. The remaining embers exploded then fell like a miniature firework. Daz shoved his hands into his pockets. 'Keep me in the loop.' He scanned the road. 'It's better business than them riots.'

☺

At last, Will watched Adam point the remote at the TV and increase the volume.

Adam said, 'Why do I kiss Daz's ass, man? Proper Jekyll.'

Stuart returned, and a look of panic flashed over Adam's face, fearful that Daz might be with Stuart.

Will chuckled at Adam's reaction. 'Your shared love of shell suits.'

'Yeah.' Adam dismissed Will with a sarcastic thumbs up, taking umbrage in his typical style.

'Right ray of light, ain't he?' Stuart headed for his seat.

'I know,' said Will, 'who does he think he is? Talking about taking on the cops.'

Stuart grunted in response, getting settled and retrieving his beer.

'Charlotte wanted to go to them the other day.'

Rob said, 'She's a good girl, that one.'

'The owners gave her a hard time too.'

'They gave you more than a hard time.'

'Tell me about it. But it's just drunk drama, isn't it? Cops won't be able to do anything.' Will reached forward to stub out his cigarette, regretting smoking it. He'd been playing with an idea ever since his father dropped him at his flat, his father unintentionally sowing a seed when he meant to do the opposite.

The two of them were in the front of the Capri, Will about to get out when his father stopped him and, with fatherly wisdom, warned him not to do anything silly. 'Like what?' asked Will, unsure of his father's meaning. He explained, he knew Will and his friends were close, but if they were to see the roughs, they weren't to seek retribution. There was no point starting a running battle with a bunch of thugs they didn't care for. Will knew all that and, apart from the fact that the thugs were an invention of his imagination, had no intention to. But while Will was alone in his flat, forcing himself to tidy up, he began plotting schemes of revenge. Those involving violence he put down to irritation and dismissed, knowing it wasn't in his nature. But then he struck upon an idea that held him like a vice. It was so perfect he couldn't wait to put it to the boys.

'Check Daz dancing,' blurted Adam, rising to balance unsteadily on the cushioned seat. He gyrated his hips and pumped his arms. 'Dancing in his red sunglasses. Yeah, I got the groove, baby. Party time.'

To Adam, Stuart said, 'We ought to get you on a podium, matey, all to yourself, our next gig.'

Will saw their next gig being organised with reduced resources and uncomfortable mobility. 'Or not,' he said.

'You'd scare punters away.' Rob threw a cushion at Adam, who caught it.

'Easy.' Adam settled down, tucking the cushion beneath him.

'I was thinking,' said Will, trying to play it cool, 'we find a new sound system.'

'Tell me about it,' agreed Rob.

'You been looking?' Stuart asked Rob.

'You're the man for that.'

'I been keeping an ear out.'

Will said, 'I heard a man in Glitter's got one,' and watched Stuart's face light up like he couldn't believe he hadn't thought of it himself.

Realisation flashed across Rob's face as he saw Will's intention. Unsure whether to take the suggestion seriously, he couldn't help but grin.

'No way,' exclaimed Adam, clutching his head.

Will knew they were hooked. 'Fancy getting me some compo?'

☺

In a brick-walled basement, cloaked in a warm glow, Daz Wiley watched Cal loading a wad of banknotes into a money counter. Cal was drunk, and his concentration waned.

'You need me to do it?' asked Daz, getting impatient in the humid environment, caused by two dozen cannabis plants growing under hot lamps.

'I got it, chops fuck.' Cal sprang upright and took a swig of lager.

Daz waited while Cal returned to the notes, squaring them with clumsy hands. Not happy until they were all neat. Daz suspected Cal was easily on his eighth can. The beer almost making the nasty bastard docile. Daz wondered how many more he'd drunk since his last visit. It would probably be easier to count the number of hours he hadn't held a beer.

Satisfied with his work, Cal hit a button. The notes rattled through the machine, sending vibrations across the floor. 'Two ten,' said Cal, reading from the digital screen, the alcohol making him sound chipper.

Writing it on a scrap of paper, it was the number Daz wanted to hear. 'Stu's playing it straight.'

'Never mind him,' rasped Cal, his scarred face peppered with sweat. 'What about the club fucks?' Cal rolled the stack of notes and wrapped an elastic band around them before dropping them into a carrier bag.

Daz snatched some more from the pile on the floor. He knew Cal would start growling if he told him Wayne had delayed payment again. He said, 'We'll do his now,' and again waited for Cal to get the next set of bills into the machine. If the daft berk hurried up, he'd be helpful.

Cal stopped to take a swig of beer. A damp patch of alcohol stained the front of his scraggy T-shirt. 'I mean, what happened, happened.'

'Nothing,' said Daz, 'He showed, I told him he pays upfront, I left.'

'Bollocks,' barked Cal, swaying clumsily. 'Those door fuckers didn't show?'

'Just me and him,' replied Daz patiently. Then, 'You wanna run the fucking machine?'

'What's it look like I'm fucking doing?' Cal dead-eyed him and prodded the button.

Daz thought Cal would've gone berserk if he was with him on Sunday night, when Wayne, the successful club owner, gave Daz his speech dictating the terms of their agreement. Daz imagined Cal sending Wayne's lead doorman through the nearest wall, then turning to Wayne to flip his arrogant smirk into absolute terror. That would've got Wayne bending over to pay him on time, not, as he did this morning at their next meet, delay further. Wayne's constant bragging about his take from the club stopped Daz from smashing him there and then. Why let impulse ruin good business? Something would have to happen soon, though. Daz suspected Wayne's success caused him to harbour more devious motivations. That was the problem with people who spoke too much. They gave too much away.

Cal squinted at the money counter's display. 'Two eighty-five.'

Daz noted the figure. Then Cal tidied the bills to his satisfaction, dropped them back into the tray and hit the button. They rattled through again.

'Two eighty-five.'

'Berk,' muttered Daz under his breath.

Cal rolled the notes and dropped them into the carrier bag. 'Club boss know you covered his piece?'

'Don't be stupid.' Daz lifted another stack, disguising his lie.

Cal, frowning through scar tissue, snatched the notes off Daz. 'What you going to do about it?' he asked menacingly.

'I'm working on it,' replied Daz, amused by Cal's aggression.

Cal slurped some lager before adding the notes and tidying them. Daz thought it was a blessing in disguise growing up next door to this guy. Best mates since neither of them could remember. Cal looking for a fight at any opportunity, his older brothers' reputations as heads of the local firm the only back-up he needed. Once they got pinched for armed robbery, Cal was grown, with a reputation of his own. The two of them made the most of it, robbing any nobodies who came near the estate. Failing that, they'd nick cars and take them to Cal's uncle. Whenever cops would show at his door, Daz's mother would swear blind they'd been home the whole time. It drove her crazy.

No locals dared be a hero and make an issue of their antics. Cal's temperament was enough to keep them in line. Everyone knew of his unhinged temper. If Cal had downed a few too many and was threatening to cause real damage, Daz could step in, calm him anytime he wanted. The relationship made Daz untouchable. Some locals would even offer Daz gifts to save their car from increased risk of repossession. But Daz rarely accepted to keep his position strong.

One night, Cal got sloppy. Heading home from the pub, it started raining, so he nicked a motor to avoid getting wet. Passing plod caught him swerving across the street and moved in only to experience the full measure of Cal's defiance. Once they caught him, they added two counts of aggravated assault on an officer to the charge sheet of car theft, dangerous driving and driving while under the influence. The daft berk got sent down for five long ones. The judge was no doubt swayed by an even longer list of suspected crimes passed to him behind closed doors. Cal served the whole stretch plus another three for lack of good behaviour. Assaulting inmates mainly. Once, he relieved his temper on a guard, and they extended his stay with his elder brothers by a year for that one incident. With Cal away, Daz got to work shifting whizz and brown across country. By the time Cal was released, cocaine had come along. That mainly went into London for the City boys. The crew behind him was secure and, the way Daz worked it, dozens of hooligans backed him up, even though most of them didn't know it. Now Ecstasy had come along, the kids going nuts for it, he'd keep a sharp eye on Stuart. No way was Daz going back to the poverty of his childhood. After everything was taken from him all at once. His earliest memory, his insurance broker father attaching a hose to their car's exhaust and seeing himself off. He'd conned Daz's mother into believing in his success when in fact, he owed huge debts to loan sharks. Their mortgage unmaintainable after he topped himself, their massive house was repossessed, and they were moved into council accommodation. Daz remembered when he started doing errands for Cal's brothers and they put notes in his pocket, it was like people were giving him money for free. That was all it took for him to become hooked on the paper stuff.

'Three oh-five,' rasped Cal, impressed with the figure.

Daz wrote it down. 'Man thinks he's untouchable inside that club.' He wondered how he could really use Cal against Wayne

Cal stuffed the rolled bills into the carrier bag. 'That one thinks he's special.'

Daz reached for another set of notes. 'I would too, thousand people between my business and the law.'

'Let's have it then,' barked Cal impatiently.

'I said I'm working on it,' Daz gave it some edge for Cal's benefit.

'What you waiting for?' Cal snatched the next set of notes.

Daz laughed, 'Take a chill pill, fella.'

Cal leaned forward. 'Or what?' he threatened, amusement hidden somewhere behind those dark, catatonic eyes of his.

'We'd be at war all the time you were in charge.'

Cal straightened. Perplexed, he located his beer. 'I thought I were in charge, in charge.' He swigged from the can.

Daz let Cal's stuttering ride, pulled a cigarette. 'Opportunity, fella.' He pointed the pack in Cal's direction. 'I see one. I'll let you stretch your legs.'

Impressed, Cal tilted his can at Daz. 'Who's a clever fucker?'

☺

Four o'clock Friday morning, the Transit, with its number plates altered using electrical tape, was parked beneath a streetlight, a short distance from Glitter. The pubs opposite were lifeless. No light shone through Glitter's glass doors. The neon sign was off.

In the back of the van, a torch, wedged between two boxes, provided light for the four of them. Over their clothes, they wore white overalls splattered with paint from countless jobs and grime off the floor.

Adam giggled. 'This is it, man.'

'Pay attention, yeah? No messing.' Will pulled on a pair of latex gloves.

'I won't.'

'Yeah, right,' said Rob.

'We've got the tools. We know what we want.' Will buried his fist into his palm. 'We get in, wheel them out. Five minutes tops.'

'Easy,' agreed Stuart, departing for the driver's seat.

Will distributed painters' masks for them to cover their faces. The engine rumbled, the chassis shuddered, and the van manoeuvred onto the road. Will took hold of a metal rail for support.

Adam stumbled sideways, clinging onto the metal sidewall to stop himself from falling. 'I'm wasted.'

'When aren't you?' Rob carefully lifted the white hood over his tight afro and readjusted the face mask to hold it in place.

The van chugged around the one-way system to the service alley at the rear of Glitter. Will tried to remember the road layout, guessing when they'd arrived by the roll of the suspension.

The motor cut out, and the van coasted for another few metres before it came to a halt. Will's heart thumped. 'Five minutes, we're done.' He raised the crowbar and hovered by the door, waiting for the all-clear.

Stuart banged the partitioning wall, and a surge of adrenaline pumped through Will. He jumped out. Rob and Adam landed behind him. Stuart swung from the cabin, adjusting his face mask and moved to the van's rear compartment. Will and Rob raised crowbars and planted the ends between Glitter's fire doors, pushing until the lock cracked. Stuart stepped up holding both sack trollies. Inside Glitter, a bar of vertical light split the darkness and stretched wide to reveal the corridor. The four ghostly figures pressed forward to join the shadows within the club.

Under faint security lights, they scattered across the main room, the outline of barriers marked by a deeper black. Adam diverted towards the toilets.

'Where you going?' hissed Will.

'Be back now.' Adam ran off, holding his hood up.

Will wasn't going to stop and argue. 'Liability,' he muttered, continuing to the DJ booth with Rob while Stuart got to work at the nearest speaker.

Rob unplugged and disconnected the gear. Will took a turntable off the shelf. In the distance, an alarm bell began ringing. Rob hurriedly tossed aside a wire and, carefully lifted the second turntable onto the one Will held.

Will decided to get going. Rob said, 'Woah, wait up.' He rushed to place the monitor speakers on the amplifier and gathered all the wires they would need.

They caught up with Stuart in the corridor, Stuart pushing the heavy speaker through. 'Not a fan of that alarm,' he said.

When the three of them returned from loading the van, Adam was stuffing liquor bottles into a box at a bar. 'Some quality whisky back here.'

'Knock me up a pina colada,' quipped Rob and got a laugh.

It was the bar where the guy waved at Will and on realising, and remembering the man smirking, a heat of rage rose inside him. Will tried to focus on his task, approaching the nearest speaker, ratchet ready. This would get his revenge.

Will worked the tool at breakneck speed, loosening the four bolts securing the speaker to the floor. What he hadn't foreseen was the lack of a trolley to wheel it away. Stuart and Rob were using them to wheel out the other speakers, leaving Will no choice but to wait his turn.

The distant alarm continued while Adam stocked up and the bottles clinked. There were three other exits besides the one they entered through. They could split in seconds if forced to. Stuart would have to report the van stolen in the morning.

Will wished he could watch the owner's reaction when he realised the speakers were missing. The empty spaces in each corner, marked by patches of dirt, would be Will's anonymous calling card. He could see Stuart letting rip if the attack happened to him, flinging chairs across the room and causing carnage. Then Will saw himself ransacking through, smashing windows and anything else that got in his way. Will eyed a nearby fire extinguisher. It would be so easy to launch it across the room. He saw it ping off the ceiling and nosedive into the floor with an almighty clang before it rolled to a stop, hissing CO_2.

Stuart and Rob returned, hurrying to Will's side. Stuart used a shoulder to help Will tilt the speaker back. Rob jabbed the trolley underneath and the three of them wheeled it away as fast as they could. After lifting it up a step, Will deviated towards the bar. He tucked a bottle under his arm. 'We need to split.'

Adam took note of the urgency in Will's voice and gathered his stash.

Exiting the club, the alleyway was clear at both ends. Will went to the driver's door, leaned in, and placed the bottle in the passenger footwell.

Adam waited behind Stuart and Rob, who were hoisting the final speaker into the rear hold. Will grabbed a corner and helped them push it in, then took the box from Adam. It went in next to the speakers. Adam slipped past to get to the passenger seat.

Stuart slammed the side door, and Rob climbed in behind Adam. Will went to the CCTV camera above Glitter's rear door and raised both middle fingers. From behind the white painters' mask, he said, 'How you like that?'

☺

Lunchtime Friday, riding in his Sierra Cosworth, Daz was alert to all the narrow turnings leading off whichever road they were on. His seat jabbed him in the back with every blip of throttle. The twin exhausts popped and growled to Joe's right boot, all twenty-five stone of him here to give Wayne something to think about. Joe was as capable of flipping quarter-ton tractor tyres as he was dotards who thought they could call the shots.

Even with the bulk to his right, Daz didn't like heading into the town centre on a weekday morning, when so few people were about. All the quiet streets made him feel vulnerable. He preferred it in crowds. Even when he was a rookie and deliveries were small, he'd arrange them for rush hour or when the football was on. Get lost in the crowd if needed. It was easy.

If anything kicked off, it was better to have Joe than not, the man at his happiest in a ruck or behind the wheel of a rapid motor. Daz owned two Cosworths, one black, one white, both race-tuned. There were enough of them on the road these days but none as swift as his, all the work done underneath so they wouldn't draw attention. Sitting in it was as good as being in a crowd. Its speed his insurance policy, necessary after all the years riding miserable trains to miserable destinations, supplying dust to keep people miserable.

Approaching Glitter, Daz was right to feel uneasy. There was a cop car up ahead. The view through the windscreen didn't make sense because he realised it was parked right outside Glitter. Joe saw it too, reaching for the gear stick to drop it down.

Daz felt the man's forearm bash against him. The engine revved high, and he was momentarily flung forward as the Cosworth slowed. Joe eased to the kerb beyond a flatbed lorry delivering kegs to one of the bars.

The engine burbled while they idled. Daz could think of no good reason why a police car should be parked outside Glitter the morning he was due to collect seventy thousand pounds. He could feel himself getting angry. No possible scenario made sense, no matter how sly he thought Wayne could be.

'He can't be doin' the dirty,' said Joe.

Not unless the amount of dirt he stuffed up his nose had finally turned his brain to mush. Daz focussed on Glitter's front doors and waited for the conniving fool to show himself.

The engine was off, and Daz was idly turning his mobile phone when the two uniformed officers finally emerged. Wayne followed them out.

Standing next to the squad car, the filth and Wayne shook hands, the three of them all smiles. The older cop gave Wayne a thumbs up.

'You believe it?' said Daz.

Joe looked over to Daz like he was pickled too.

Daz pointed a finger, the signal enough for Joe to start the engine. Daz didn't know where to go, but he knew he was through with quiet places.

The dark saloon cruised unnoticed past Wayne and the officers: the officers climbing into their car and Wayne, the upstanding citizen, waving goodbye from the roadside.

07 / *V. I. P.*

Friday lunchtime, Will was still in bed. By the time they'd retreated to Stuart's lock-up and unloaded the sound system, it was almost five a.m. Stuart refused to give Will a ride home and, unless he wanted to spend the night on the sofa, left him no choice but to arrange a taxi. Will arrived at his flat soon after six, shattered like he'd spent the whole night dancing.

The ache to his body no longer covered him like a blanket he couldn't remove. Three days convalescing at his parents' house allowed enough time for the swelling to reduce. The regular sparks of pain accompanying the slightest movement were occasional now. A sting in his side only when he was clumsy. But despite his physical recovery, each flash of discomfort caused an unwanted reminder of that night.

He knew pinching Glitter's system was criminal; nothing would change that. But it wasn't like he regularly went around robbing old dears of their life-savings or beat people up for fun. Getting the sound system resolved an immediate problem. If he hadn't been beaten up, he'd have ground it out, paid for a new sound system and soldiered on like before. But the chance to settle a score was irresistible. He could live with the man's insurance premiums rising. They treated the robbery no different to the warehouse party, as another site to access, and the undertaking became a buzz in itself.

It was a far cry from Will's previous job serving pricey pinot grigios, malbecs and brandies to Ravisbourne's executive set. After leaving school at sixteen, Will had been at the restaurant seven years. As a barman, he learnt to organise the bars and the cellar. Promoted to manager, he was put in charge of staff and cash. Before long, the owners left him to run the joint, and he came to see it as the brunt of the work for no share of profits. Despite the responsibility and the pay, every shift came to make Will feel like he was being taken advantage of, especially when the owners would spend all evening at a table drinking. His life led at someone else's behest, the thrill of advancement gone, days off became a release.

He and Adam caught bands like Beastie Boys and New Order or missioned to Rockley Sands weekenders. For years they'd been visiting London for nights at Three 'A's, The Raid and Camden Palace, where they first heard some of the early house tracks being played by Colin Faver. Then there was Shake and Fingerpop and the warehouse scene around King's Cross, where rare groove ruled supreme. They could bring their own beer and party all night to the best mix of underground sounds.

It was a lifestyle formed at school when the two of them shared homemade cassettes. Guided by Adam's older brother who took them on a journey from northern soul to new wave, punk to electro-funk, soul to disco, introducing them to countless artists along the way. They were into hip hop months before anyone in school, regularly taking trips to Tottenham market to buy the latest New York mixtapes. Chasing the latest sounds was a buzz all of its own. An impulse that guided him years later as house music came through the warehouses. Then E made it to the dance floors, the scene got labelled as acid house, and everything went stratospheric. There were a few months of uninhibited euphoria before the police caught on and started raiding the parties. It was like their way of life was threatened. All they wanted was a sound system playing decent music. Established venues were no alternative. They closed early and wouldn't let you through the door without your shiniest shoes and your sharpest suit; alien worlds, where pop music ruled supreme and everyone sucked in their cheeks to show how cool they were.

Will was getting tired of it all. The buzz of E became mundane and would never recreate the same level of sensation and wonder he experienced during the early warehouse parties. He needed something else to chase and arranging a successful party or cracking a warehouse filled the void. The four of them had been talking about it since they met.

The cancellation of the Red Lion gigs didn't deter Will, but work commitments kept hindering weekend manoeuvres, especially when required to find a new venue. There was no way around it except quitting his job. Why give fifty hours a week to someone else when you can take it all for yourself. Will spent some of his savings on a set of speakers, sourced through a mate of Stuart's, and swung into action. He found an unsuspecting local chaplain, who let them use the church hall for a night. The proscenium arch provided a stunning backdrop for the sound system and the wide-eyed crowds, who arrived in numbers and partied until dawn. But it was never going to be anything more than a one-night affair after the chaplain got word of the scene's nocturnal antics. Inspired by the church hall setting, Will held their fourth party beneath an abandoned railway arch. It lacked an electrical supply, but Stuart was able to power the sound system from a nearby lamppost. Despite the rudimentary frills, the crowd arrived in numbers. That night Will got chatting to an estate agent who bragged about all the vacant plots he knew of. Will was hooked and had no problem talking the man into a backhander for this information. Through the estate agent, the following three parties were held monthly in various disused office blocks. Then the agent got rumbled and fired. Will regretted not getting a spare set of keys cut. It was seat-of-your-pants stuff, but he loved it. The following month he managed to secure the basement of a multistorey car park, but the amount of litter left behind prevented a sequel, even after Will offered to arrange street sweepers. It was a steep learning curve.

They worked well as a team: Adam, carefree enough to say yes to anything, was good with people, especially outside pubs and clubs handing out flyers; Stuart the handyman, too enraged by his own struggles to be a leader, did as he was told so long as pills were involved; finally, Rob, quietly driven by his passion and talent for music, would bring his vinyl and take centre stage.

The phone rang. Will lay there in bed, listening to it trill before he mustered the energy to answer. 'Yeah?'

'Where you been, man?' Adam's voice sounded distant, with noises in the background.

'Asleep.'

'Aww.'

'Where you at?'

'You know that squat in the sticks?'

'The old manor house?'

'That's it. The Dance Inc. lads are busy turning it into wonderland.'

'You running with them now?'

'I was over Stuart's when they called. They wanted our sound system, you know?'

'They paying?' It bothered Will that they only ever called Stuart. The gear might have been in his lock-up, but Will was the one who bought it.

'It's a freebie, but we need to test it, so it's all good, bro. You coming?'

Will rolled onto his back. No way could he handle two buses with a mile walk at the end. 'I'm shattered.'

'Aww, man.'

'Last night drained me.'

'I told Dance Inc. what happened, how we got the kit. You're a legend.'

'Get Stuart to pick me up then.'

'I'll try, but you know how he is.'

Will laughed. 'Let me know then.'

'Okay, man.'

Will replaced the receiver and rolled back. If he could do the warehouse party again, he'd have used an outlet to sell tickets in advance. That way, he wouldn't have had to keep so much cash on site. He could have also used advance sales to buy more speakers. A stack on all four points would've been perfect. It'd been an ambitious gig. With the size of it, Will should have guessed the cops might show. The main lesson he'd learnt, he decided, was that he'd been complacent. He'd presumed the luck organising their previous parties would continue despite the step up in size and ambition. For large-scale events, he might have to hire security. But for the warehouse party, there hadn't been time to organise it, and the opportunity was too good to miss.

Part of him couldn't believe last night. Forcing Glitter's rear door. The buzz was unreal. Getting away with the system made it even greater. It still affected him now. A new man brewed inside him. As though his anger at the beating gave him courage. Enough to suggest the break-in and give him confidence to raise his middle fingers to the camera outside. How'd you like that? With the rumours no doubt spreading, Will was putting some weight behind his reputation. The local scene's main man. Maybe they could get ten thousand people at their next gig. Will added the amount he made from the warehouse party to his savings and calculated it would last three months—a lot less if he'd needed to buy a new sound system. Before the warehouse, they'd been arranging a party every month. They wouldn't be able to do large-scale events regularly unless he could find somebody with enough space who'd grant permission to use it. Will wanted several rooms so they could play different types of music. Maybe have a VIP room for the regulars. That would be cool. But so far as Will could see, to make that happen would mean taking the scene into more traditional venues, and he knew how thorny an issue that was. Unless things settled, it would be a while before he could get their gigs into a nightclub. In the meantime, there were plenty of other options, and the ideas were constantly flowing. The opportunity to arrange another large gig within three months would come along. There was no way he was going to remain a nobody.

☺

Riding the train from her student house, Charlotte wondered what Will's flat would be like. Would it be a penthouse or a converted terrace? Living on the border between the old town and the sprawling new estates made it tricky to judge. Maybe it was smart. His parents were worth a bob or two.

After leaving Will's parents' the week before, the taxi ride ended with predictable hoots of excitement upon entering her student digs. Her housemates filled the lounge, the seating arrangement lost to a sea of duvets and takeaway pizza boxes. Sophie held pole position for this particular triumph and led a buoyant round of applause. Dead on her feet but doing her best to play along, Charlotte curtseyed before subtly trying to steer the conversation elsewhere. They were on to her though, haranguing her with a bombardment of salacious accusations and suppositions. She covered her ears and snuggled next to Michaela. They were watching Dirty Dancing for the second time that day.

There was no appropriate moment to explain to Michaela what actually happened with Will the night before, and, as the day drew to a close, Charlotte's desire to explain diminished. Due to her hangover, Michaela was now leaving the following morning. Her retreat to her bedroom to pack put an end to Charlotte's forming of an opening line and Michaela's imagined response.

As the week progressed, Charlotte became the house's only resident. Besieged by dread that her coil had failed, she cracked and took a home pregnancy test. Relieved she wasn't, and kicking herself for a lack of faith, she got into a routine. Before washing and dressing, she'd take her time over a breakfast of fruit and cereals, a luxury denied by term-time dramas, hangovers, and mad dashes to lectures. The rest of her mornings were spent reading through fashion magazines and parts of the Sunday paper that interested her. After lunch, another leisurely affair usually involving eggs, she'd visit the local library for a heavier reading session. They held a decent selection on renaissance art, which she intended to use as background for her dissertation on Caravaggio's influence on Baroque. Although her final year was months away, she wanted her knowledge to be deep and full, so that, when the time came, her prose flowed naturally onto the page. After the library closed, she'd return home to cook whatever took her fancy in the shop en route. In the evening, she'd watch a video she'd hired from Ritz. It was a self-indulgent week that, Charlotte imagined, was how her life might be, minus the socialising, should she choose to pursue a career in fashion journalism.

The only infringement on her placid designs was the occasional recollection of events in Glitter. She wanted justice for what happened but didn't know how to go about it. After a productive week, this morning she decided to skip the library and visit Will to see how he was doing. Charlotte wondered what Michaela's take would be if she were about. With regards to that man in Glitter, obviously she would have been supportive. With Will, perhaps a moment of jealousy would have flashed across her face before she enthusiastically encouraged Charlotte to go for it.

She and Michaela met during Freshers, living in London and away from home for the first time. Charlotte remembered those first few days, wandering around with a pocket map, in awe of the giant capital and its epic contradictions: the privileged grandiose of Westminster and the City, where exquisite Georgian palaces bragged of Empire; yet, nearby, unashamed poverty loitered amongst the landfill of post-war housing estates. This appeared to be the case in all the inner boroughs, where she rented her own piece of two millennia of history: a tiny bedsit behind the facade of a Regency terrace. In secondary school, Charlotte imagined London as one homogenous entity with a unique culture shared enthusiastically by its population. In reality, she found, amidst the pace and the chaos, a city of individuals whose common but varied goal was self-fulfilment.

Nowhere was this more evident than the common rooms of London Institute's art department. During the first week, mingling around a sorry buffet at a departmental meet-and-greet, Charlotte could tell there were many bold personalities eager to make their mark on the world. Michaela immediately caught Charlotte's attention. Mischief sparkled behind her hazel eyes as she swanned about in her easy-going bohemian getup: sandals, flowing summer dress and sharply cut denim jacket. Charlotte thought her own choice of pinstripe suit with cut-off trousers and high-top Converse juxtaposed Michaela's look excellently. The two of them soon found a bar to get acquainted over a glass of red.

Charlotte might never have met Will had Michaela not introduced her to house music, taking her to a private party in leafy Hampstead. The music sounded so fresh, different in so many ways to the music she was raised on—although the DJ did throw in some Bowie towards the end of his set. Charlotte had never heard house played on radio or at the usual student party nights. She had also never heard about Ecstasy, which was also prevalent at the party. In fact, it seemed to Charlotte, E formed the main thrust of proceedings. The music came a lowly second. Michaela participated, but Charlotte, unaware of what she was getting into, declined, preferring instead to enjoy the music with several large glasses of wine.

By the second year, all the talk on campus was of acid house, and the parties to go to were found in East London. She and Michaela would spend their weekends in disused warehouses on the outskirts of Hackney and Bow. Casual dress was necessary to prevent your best clothes from being ruined. Soon it became *the* style to wear—one guy on her course planned a fashion collection based around dungarees and bright, baggy T-shirts. Together they would dance all night amongst the decay before Charlotte drove them back to their new digs in Ravisbourne. Michaela's incessant chatter would help to keep Charlotte awake for the journey. Both were convinced what they were experiencing was the future. Studying art history, Charlotte liked the idea of being part of a movement, imagining, in hundreds of years, people viewing this time as the genesis of house music. It was a measure of their enthusiasm that, at eight on a Sunday morning, the two-hour drive was never a chore.

One weekday evening, a spindly lad, full of bonhomie, approached Charlotte and her four housemates. They were leaving their local pub after some vino. He handed Charlotte a flyer for an "All-night House Party" promising a live DJ and smoke machine. Best of all, the party the following Saturday was local. She and Michaela were thrilled at the opportunity and attended, eager to see what it would be like.

Arriving at the Red Lion shortly after midnight, a lively house beat thumped from somewhere nearby. They followed the perimeter to a wooden door left invitingly ajar. Inside, a courtyard, lit by a solitary security light, brimmed with colourfully dressed people all smoking and chatting. At the entrance, an attractive blonde guy wanted to take three pounds off each of them. They complied, thanking Will, and approached the dry ice billowing into the courtyard from the function room.

Inside, the room's layout, filled with a thick cloud of smoke, was unknowable. Through the haze, they could discern a few people dancing with gusto. At the far end, where yellow light glowed from a couple of spots, was the silhouette of a DJ behind decks, his hunched shoulders rocking to the beats. Charlotte and Michaela were impressed and got into the swing of things. Before long, the air was thick with the heat and sweat of many dancers crammed into the modestly sized room.

A sizeable guy worked his way through the dancing bodies offering pills for sale at twenty pounds a pop. Michaela was glad of the offer, but as usual, Charlotte passed. Michaela never made an issue of Charlotte's non-participation. She was the one person Charlotte believed she could truly be herself with. They both did.

That was the first and only party in that particular pub that Charlotte and Michaela visited, although house music nights in Ravisbourne became a regular fixture on their social calendar. As regular as the spindly guy, who they'd often see outside local pubs and clubs with his trademark shell suit and wedge haircut. A church hall hosted one party, the next beneath a railway arch and then a series in disused office blocks. It was their own piece of East London. Over the series of parties, they became familiar with Will and his happy-go-lucky buddy Adam.

The train arrived at a stop, and a couple took seats opposite.

Dressed for an extravagant formal event, the woman was very dashing and carried herself well. About sixty, she could have passed for fifty in the elegant purple dress and lightweight, cream overcoat. Her husband followed behind in his heavy suit. Neither ugly nor handsome, he was easily sixty. The natural disposition of his roundish face was one of preoccupation, like he constantly churned through a solution to a problem. As they travelled together, his wife acquired a temporary version of this. Perched forward, she cast a hawkish eye over the activity within the carriage while her husband examined embossed, legal documents. They remained this way until the train arrived at the next stop. The husband sloped off, and after a moment, his wife realised and hastily followed, skipping ever so daintily to join his trudge along the platform.

They were clearly successful. The round-faced man who dined well on business lunches in expensive restaurants, and his slender wife who enjoyed wholesome salads to maintain her figure. To some degree, there was an air of convenience about their partnership. But when Charlotte studied their wedding rings, she found both bands thin and made of gold with a bronze hue. In every aspect, the rings were identical, and the style suggested they were forged during the war when supplies were scarce. Charlotte imagined the two of them getting together when he was a bumbling student, and the only thing he could offer his beautiful classmate were mannerisms she found fetching. Through the tumult of modern life, with all its distractions and temptation, they'd remained together, supporting each other to become the affluent couple they appeared today.

Charlotte wondered how devoted they really were. Whether they did everything together or whether today was a rare occasion that gave her that impression. The husband had slunk off without his wife after all. Charlotte's own parents were quite solitary. Her mother practically raised her alone while her father travelled the world working for a motor racing team, home for a long weekend every two weeks, eight months a year. She hadn't thought distance was an issue for her parents until they separated. It confirmed to Charlotte you never really knew what made a relationship work from the outside. Maybe she'd have to get used to this journey.

What happened in Glitter made her feel close to Will. The traumatic events bonding them in ways she hadn't expected. He hadn't called since Tuesday, but given the circumstances, she'd forgive him. She hoped her thoughts of him would soon detach themselves from the awful incident in Glitter. She'd much rather have only Will's pretty features on her mind, without them mixed in with horrid memories of that man and the way he touched her.

Thinking of it, she remembered the brute probing between her legs, and it gave her the creeps. The hair on her neck stood on end, and she shuddered. There was faint hope that her fledgling relationship with Will might repair the emotional damage done at the club.

☺

By mid-afternoon Will was slumped on the cracked leather couch in his living room. He was getting hungry but not enough to tear himself from his seat. It would've been nice to have his mother cook for him for the time being.

On TV, the newsreader presented to camera, beginning a new item: 'Some newspapers are calling acid house music a sinister and evil cult that lures young people into drug-taking.'

Will flicked channels with the remote. He didn't need to be lectured by the press. One minute the tabloids were offering free smiley-face T-shirts to readers, the next, they were running headlines like "Raving Mad" and "Evils of Ecstasy". "We Call It Acieeed" was banned by radio because the powers-that-be thought it was about LSD. Now they were comparing the scene to a cult.

He didn't want to answer the knock at the door, but after the second round of bashing, followed by his name being called, he was pleased Charlotte had come to visit. He diverted to the mirror for a brief inspection. The cuts had thinned to narrow tracks, and the bruising was lighter. It would have to do.

Waiting outside, she posed, hands on hips, showing off leggings and an oversized sweater rolled to her elbows. 'Am I chasing you now?' she said, sounding displeased.

That was a ticking off he could get used to. 'Good to see you too,' he smiled, stepping aside to let her in. Will wanted to laugh, remembering the first time he saw her. Straight away, he'd realised how stunning she was but he always treated her the same as any other guest. Maybe that's why things had taken a while to get going.

Collapsing on the couch, he retrieved the remote and lowered the volume. Charlotte assessed the surroundings, the walls covered in dozens of smiley-faced flyers, the mirror at one end, the leather armchair and couch, the TV in the far corner, VHS tapes littering a hard-wearing carpet. There wasn't much else apart from dirty plates on the coffee table. Satisfied with her evaluation, she settled on the arm of the chair and let her attention wander to thc TV. 'You watch this?'

It was a new Australian soap opera. 'Twice a day.'

'Party animal.'

Will liked her response. Watching her sitting there, he couldn't perceive not being attracted to her like he was right now. He became appalled by how feeble his efforts were previously. What if she'd gotten away? Promoting successful nights seemed irrelevant. He could no longer think why they were important to him.

'Good week?'

'Lonely,' she sighed, 'My girlfriends have all gone home for the summer.'

Distracted by the flip-flop she jiggled between her toes, he asked, 'Why haven't you gone home too?'

'And hear every detail about my parents' divorce? No thanks.'

The flip-flop fell to the floor. Will looked up from the toes he wanted to put in his mouth, and Charlotte greeted him with the same sad expression he'd gazed upon in the taxi.

'Come here.' Will made room, and she plonked herself beside him. 'What do you want to do?' he asked.

'I don't know … Go somewhere?' She shrugged.

'I'd rather stay in, to be honest. I'm shattered today.'

'Poor you.' She ruffled his hair, and a glimmer of amusement passed over her face.

'Watch the bump,' he cautioned, enjoying being in the moment with her.

'Sorry,' she said, sounding only mildly apologetic.

Will couldn't take his eyes from her. He leaned in for a kiss and she caught his face as their mouths joined.

Slowly they got into the moment. She guided him back into the seat to straddle him. Pawing at his chest, they kissed with abandon. He ran his palms under her jumper to her stomach and hips.

Charlotte leaned back and lifted her sweater over her head, revealing her navel and breasts, neatly pressed together by a red lace bra. She raked a hand through her hair and tossed the sweater to the floor.

Will stroked the bumps of her ribs with his fingertips. She ran hers up his chest, squeezing harder this time, and caused Will to grimace.

'Sorry,' she said, remembering his injuries, 'Let's have a look.'

Will lifted his hoody over his head, exposing his bruised ribs on the one side, and settled back.

Charlotte studied the damaged tissue and ran her hand softly over it. 'Poor you,' she said with a sad expression.

'It's not too bad,' said Will.

She lowered her face to kiss him again.

Will wanted to embrace her completely but the sofa was too constricting. He pulled away and said softly, 'Come on.' Will moved to get up and Charlotte obliged, climbing off his lap and following him to his bedroom.

Getting onto the bed, he chucked aside the duvet while Charlotte removed her bra and pushed down her waistband. Will removed his tracksuit bottoms. Charlotte steadied herself on the dresser, pulling her leggings and knickers over her feet. Done, she huffed at the exertion and climbed onto the bed, looking to his engorged shaft.

She held him gently as they began kissing. Then her legs came across him, and in the same motion, she pressing his stiff length inside and lowered herself until their bodies were firmly against each other. They kissed passionately, rocking with the momentum of their mouths. Will could have stayed there forever. The tenderness of her kisses, her smooth, bare flesh and the stroke of her breasts against his chest took him to a place beyond the reach of time. They rolled onto their sides, relaxing into it. Will held the back of her knee, thrusting gently before she submitted further, turning onto her back and taking him on top of her. She raised her knees and used her calves and feet to hold him deep inside before she was entirely his. Her legs dropped to the mattress, and they both let go of themselves, whispering with pleasure, until they reached delirious ecstasy.

☺

Next to Will, Charlotte slept. Unburdened from her parents' divorce for now, her face was at ease. The phone rang, and Will rushed to the receiver so as not to disturb her.

He carried the phone into the living room, aching from the exertion of sex. 'Yeah?'

'Matey,' Stuart greeted him. 'You trying to blag a lift, I hear?'

'I can't make it now.'

'Why not?'

'Charlotte's here.'

'Good. You two can share a taxi. Easy.'

'Maybe later.'

'You two a thing or what?'

'Maybe.'

'I don't want no maybes. This place is awesome.'

'Is it?'

'Don't make me ring you later.' Stuart threatened comically, 'You hear me?' He hung up.

Thinking Stuart was high already, Will returned to the bedroom with the phone. Clothes were scattered across the floor and Charlotte was awake.

'Aye aye, captain,' she said, eyeing his crotch.

Will made a half-hearted attempt to cover his dignity. 'Fancy takeaway?' he asked, climbing in beside her.

'Not really.'

She shook her hair free of her face and lay on the healthy side of his chest. Where did that leave him, he wondered? He wasn't massively hungry, but he thought it worth mentioning. He definitely didn't have anything fancy to cook for her.

'Do you know what I think?' asked Charlotte.

'What?'

Her tone made him think she was about to broach something serious. When she pushed up off his chest to address him directly, he knew he was right.

'I can't help thinking,' she said. 'If we are compelled to go all the way back to Glitter to identify this guy, confirm to ourselves it's the same man, the police will have to get involved.'

'You're pretty pissed off about it, aren't you?' He respected her desire to stand up for herself.

'Well spotted,' she quipped. 'What happened was not cool.' She settled onto his chest.

Will remembered raiding the sound system. 'I doubt it'll be open.'

Charlotte shuffled onto an elbow. 'What do you mean?' she asked, confused.

Will hesitated, realising his mistake. 'I don't know,' he said, not wanting to tell her what he'd done last night but not able to think of a better excuse.

'You don't know?' she asked, exaggerating her doubt.

Her frown was cute. 'It's not somewhere I normally go,' he said, trying and failing to cover his tracks.

'It's Friday night,' she said, puzzled.

'You know I break into warehouses …?'

'Talk about guilty conscience! You don't have to tell the police that.' Charlotte became irritated. 'Do you even care what happened to you?'

'I don't want to be questioned, is all.'

Charlotte dismissed his concerns. 'You're in the music business, big deal. They're not going to ask for a CV.'

Maybe she had a point.

'Okay, say we go,' Will reasoned, 'what if security recognise us?' He was intrigued whether Glitter would be open, but he didn't want another beating to find out.

'We could dress up.'

'As what?'

Charlotte considered options. 'I've got makeup.' She sounded like the idea magically came to her.

'You've planned this, haven't you?'

She scoffed. 'No.'

Will laughed. 'As if.'

'Listen, you got beaten up. I got molested. A man like that shouldn't be running a nightclub.'

Will couldn't deny her conviction. 'So, what we dressing up as?'

'Friday's rock night. We can easily find some black outfits.'

That sounded like a terrible idea. Will sighed. 'It's a mission. We've got to get ready … Go all the way there … Queue …'

'I've got a car,' she said, 'I don't usually use it around town but I'll go and get it especially for you.' She kissed his chest. 'I'll need to fetch my outfit anyway.'

'Sounds like effort. Can't we stay here? I'm shattered.'

'You're bloody not.'

'I am now,' Will laughed.

'No,' she said, her decision final.

Will couldn't see any way out of it. 'You'd better make me look good.'

Charlotte stretched across and kissed his face. 'Sweetheart, I'll always make you look good.'

After a trip to the bathroom, she returned with a tall stool from the kitchen and made him sit down. She found a pair of black jeans in Will's wardrobe and told him to put them on before spiking his hair with some wax she pinched off the sink. Will was trying to hold still when the phone rang.

'You're popular this evening.'

'It's probably only Stuart. He wants me to go to this thing tonight.'

'What thing?'

'A party we're helping put on.'

Charlotte let go of Will's hair. 'Are you going to answer then?'

'I've already told him I'm not going.'

'Why not?'

'Because you're here.'

'Aww, that's sweet.' Charlotte took hold of Will's hair. 'Hold still then.'

Will looked her up and down. 'When are you going to put some clothes on?'

'When I'm done here.' Charlotte tugged the spike of hair she was shaping. 'Is that all right with you?'

08 / *Rock The Night*

Will rode in Charlotte's specially fetched hot-hatch, his hair spiked, his face painted white. He suspected her motor racing father influenced the car's purchase and asked if she was a daddy's girl. Unimpressed with the question, a defiant shake of her head told him not to go there.

Cruising past Glitter, the Golf's rumbling exhaust drew some attention. Lined behind temporary metal railings, a grungy crowd was clad in stonewash denim and leather jackets. Guitar riffs blasted from inside Glitter's doors.

'I'll park further on,' said Charlotte, in heavy white makeup. 'In case any drunks scratch it.'

'Wise move.' Hearing the music, Will was impressed with their efforts to replace the sound system.

Charlotte found a parking spot a short distance from Glitter. A taxi parked up where they'd prepared for the robbery. Will remembered pulling on the overalls and the thrill of that moment.

From the taxi, a group of veteran rockers disembarked, crossing the road to join the queue. 'All right, rock night!' proclaimed Charlotte, raising her index and little fingers. Her upbeat energy contradicted her worn-out look, achieved using heavy eye-makeup. 'This how we like it?'

With all the wax Charlotte used, Will could feel his newly spiked hair sticking to his scalp. 'Rocking,' he said, mirroring her gesture half-heartedly.

Charlotte ignored his downbeat humour. 'I knew you'd get into the swing of things.'

She left him in the car, looking down at the creased black shirt he hadn't worn in ages.

Getting inside Glitter was no problem. Once they were through the queue, surrounded by older guys chatting knowledgeably about all the latest tours, they breezed past security without a second glance. Approaching the doorway, Will clocked the brass plaque above the front door and read:

Mister Wayne Moran is licensed to sell intoxicating liquor for consumption on the premises. Capacity: 1200

After paying, they descended into the club. Will wanted to boast about last night's break-in but knew he couldn't. Entering the main room, what struck Will was the change in lighting, switched from Sunday's swirling primaries to a fixed arrangement of amber sides. It subdued the atmosphere within the club, highlighting the glinting metal chains and multicoloured Mohicans.

It was like a different venue and, with his spiked hair and face painted white, Will felt safe from identification. But anonymity was irrelevant. The boisterous crowd, larking and fooling, stole the more immediate concerns of watchful security. Will wasn't even on their radar.

Failing to recognise any security staff as perpetrators of his beating, he and Charlotte moved into the diner, where groups in sombre conversation hunched around tables. They settled at the edge, near where they first chatted that night. It seemed like a time from a different world, before the tedious week of pain and recovery.

Below them, behind a wood railing, a mosh pit bubbled with pent-up angst. Heads down, elbows out, some thrashed their long hair around. Will thought he could smell weed.

'Looks nasty,' Charlotte raised her voice over an anthem the crowd were appreciating.

'Too right.' Will felt the need to keep moving, to make the most of their visit. 'Come on.'

They descended the few wooden steps and followed the wall along the far side, near the DJ booth. Will stopped at a speaker and found four shiny new bolts securing it to the floor. The speaker's plastic corner pieces shone brand new, with a snag of clear packaging still attached to one.

'What you doing?' she yelled over the noise.

Will found her peering beside him. 'Nothing.'

Charlotte appeared dubious and indicated the stairs leading to the main entrance. 'After I told him where to go, I saw him chatting to doormen. They were all laughing and joking, showing how tough they were.' Charlotte reflected. 'He must have known what they did because of what he said to me at the bar.'

'That one?' Will pointed to the bar in the corner.

'Yeah.'

The busy service area distributed mass-produced lagers to a patient crowd. A camera observed the till where a barman slopped a plastic pint cup onto the bar top. 'There's cameras.'

'Maybe,' said Charlotte.

'No, there are.' Will's attention wandered to the DJ booth. He wanted to nose inside to see what spec the new decks were.

'What is it now?' asked Charlotte impatiently.

Will returned to her. 'I'm looking. Isn't that what we're meant to be doing?'

'You're distracted by something.'

Will held Charlotte's hand. 'There's a lot going on.' He led her past the hubbub at the bar to a space separated from the dance floor by a barrier. Further on was the corridor containing the disabled toilet. 'This is where they grabbed me.'

They entered the corridor with the disabled toilet, and Will immediately saw it. He brought Charlotte round in front of him, so they were both leaning against the wall.

'What now?'

Fixed to the corridor's ceiling was a rectangular box with a pane of glass at one end. In clear sight behind Charlotte was the circular outline of a camera lens peering through the glass. He touched her arm, hoping to keep her calm. 'Don't look, but there's a camera on us right now. Behind you. I saw one above the bar as well.'

She wanted to look but contained her curiosity with a subtle nod.

'Come on.' Will pushed off the wall to return to the main room.

Charlotte stole a glance at the camera as she took hold of Will's hand. They headed through the set of double doors and back into the gloom. Further on, beyond the pillar where the bouncers grabbed him, Will spotted an empty table littered with discarded drinks. Off to the left, a throng of rockers ambled into the second room next door. Will saw the scene playing out, a plan forming. 'Let's smoke him into the open.'

'How?'

The DJ introduced a song that was met with whoops of approval.

'Here.' Will led Charlotte to the table with discarded drinks. They were in flimsy plastic cups. Will raised one to show Charlotte and squeezed the sides inwards with ease. 'These things bounce.'

Charlotte shuffled a curious gaze between Will and the cup, patiently waiting for further explanation.

'That lot could do with a cool off.' Will nodded at the moshing crowd.

Charlotte still didn't get it.

'They're only plastic,' Will assured her, neatly arranging the cups into a line.

'Run it by me again.' Charlotte surveyed the dance floor.

'Maybe, with a bit of action, we could coax this guy out.' Will indicated a nearby door marked STAFF ONLY. 'Maybe from a staff corridor or something?'

'I don't fancy the chances.'

'What else we going to do?' Will took hold of a cup.

'Wait.' Charlotte restrained his arm.

'They're harmless,' Will reassured her.

'That's not what I'm worried about.' Charlotte checked their surroundings. 'What do we do after?'

'Move into that crowd sharpish.' Will pointed to the throng behind them.

Charlotte watched the dawdling group, thinking it through. 'What if there are cameras on us right now?'

'Can you see any?' Will asked. Charlotte checked the ceiling nearby, and he added, 'Probably why they grabbed me here.'

Charlotte made her decision and began nodding slowly. 'Okay, fine.' She exhaled to compose herself. 'Let's do it.'

Will liked Charlotte's reaction, working through her turmoil, the good girl at her limit. He passed her a cup. 'We've got to be quick, clear the lot.'

Charlotte hesitated. 'I don't know if I can run in these.' She lifted a clunky leather boot. 'I haven't worn them since sixth form.'

'Hey, I'm an invalid. Don't worry about it.'

'What a team.' She broke into a laugh.

'Ready?' Will asked. 'No laughing now.'

'Yes. Thank you.' Charlotte composed herself.

Will indicated her boots. 'Are you sure you're going to be okay in those?'

She looked down briefly before she twigged he was teasing. 'Stop it!'

Will laughed. 'Go!' he commanded.

'Will!' she screeched while he moved onto a second cup, tossing it over the railing, a trail of beer flying above the head-down crowd.

Charlotte chucked her cup, and it bounced off a thickset guy. Then she beat Will to two more cups before he finished the lot.

Tumbling cups and a mix of liquids rained onto the moshing crowd. Their patches under attack, the aggression ratcheted up, and they began pushing and shoving each other wildly.

Will and Charlotte dashed to the parting crowd and squeezed among them to shuffle into the next room. Ignoring the odd grumble, they entered the room to have their senses hit by blaring punk rock and irregular pulses of white light. Flashing from corner spots, they highlighted, in prolonged bursts, tattoos, metal piercings and torn denim. More solitary in their dancing, the revellers in here found their own little space to pump their fists and stamp their feet to the anarchistic soundtrack.

Finding the packed space hostile, it was a struggle to find a way through. Will tried not to rush for fear of starting less avoidable trouble. They returned to the main room beside the stairs to the main entrance. Security guards lined the dance floor, issuing instructions to those who refused to settle.

The DJ pleaded for calm then introduced the next track, Motörhead, "Ace Of Spades". After a couple of bars, Lemmy rattled off his brazen lyrics and, if anything, it enlivened the crowd. That worked, thought Will.

Hustling along a walkway, aiming for the diner, Will and Charlotte's progress was slowed by people rubbernecking the drama. Nearby, a bouncer waded into the melee. With biceps bulging beneath a black shirt, he gripped an overly enthusiastic rocker and shook him into line.

Having travelled almost full circle, Will and Charlotte returned to the diner and, at a railing, watched security guards issue commands to another riled section closer by.

'Guess they didn't appreciate the shower,' yelled Will over the thrashing guitars and fast-paced lyrics.

Charlotte didn't respond. Caught in a dilemma, worry wrinkled her brow. At the bar, a shaven-headed staff member provided an animated debrief to his commander-in-chief. *It was him.*

The man's presence got Will's back up. He saw the man sneering, at the exact moment he waved, a week ago, when Will was grabbed by the bouncers and forcefully removed.

Before he knew it, Will was steaming towards the man who'd become the sole focus of his attention. Behind him, he heard Charlotte call, 'Will?' but his stride or gaze didn't waver.

When a guy at a table swigged from a bottle, Will reacted to the innocent drinker as though he was under attack. Without a second thought, such was his hostility, Will snatched the bottle from the guy's lips and ignored the spluttering protests as beer spilt over his black tour T-shirt.

The man at the bar heard the commotion and spun around to find what must have looked like a rampaging goth bearing down on him.

His appraisal was grim. 'What you want, sunshine?'

It was the only defence he could muster before, surprised, he watched the plastic bottle swing in a wide arc and bonk across his forehead. Beer exploded everywhere. The man spun around, clutching his face.

Will became aware of his surroundings and the club's loud music. Adrenaline drained through his fingers. He dropped the bottle, which bounced lightly across the floor, spilling the dregs. Realising he needed to scarper fast, Will searched for Charlotte, who hurried to his side awash with concern.

'We have to go,' said Will with a calmness that belied his sense of urgency.

'You think?' shouted Charlotte.

The barman who'd witnessed the attack fumbled for the radio, his calls for help audible above the music. The man Will hit dropped to a knee, clutching his forehead.

A split second later, Will and Charlotte were moving. Picking up speed with each step, they dashed past the baffled drinker, soaked in beer, and through the diner. The barman discarded the radio and frantically waved for security.

From the dance floor, two security guards began in hot pursuit, pushing disgruntled rockers aside just as Will smashed through the fire doors. The resurgence of adrenaline blocked the pain along his bruised side. They hurtled up steps towards another set of doors. All Will could feel was his legs and lungs burning.

'What the …!' Charlotte gasped between mouthfuls of air. 'That's done it.'

Will didn't know what compelled him to hit the man. 'Sorry,' he gasped, desperate to keep going.

'Sorry!' shouted Charlotte.

Behind, the two bouncers arrived on the steps.

Will piled into the fire doors at the top and had to slowly push until those outside made space for it to open. Will acknowledged their objections with a brisk, 'Sorry!'

He and Charlotte sprinted onwards. As those in the queue were reclosing the doors, two security guards slammed through, causing even louder protests. Will gritted his teeth and redoubled his efforts, vaguely aware of an audience of partygoers smoking and drinking outside the bars across the road.

Their pace at maximum, Charlotte fumbled for her keys. Will arrived at the Golf and began bouncing on the spot. Security guards at the front doors must have heard the commotion because now there were two more, eager to catch up with the first two, while everyone else watched.

'Quick.' Will barked as Charlotte freed her keys.

The look she shot him had lethal intent. She unlocked the door and dived in. Will wanted to rip the handle off to get inside. Security were halfway between them and the fire escape, their expressions fixed firmly on the Golf as they sprinted along the road.

Charlotte unlocked his door. Will scrambled in, hearing the ignition spark before he was set. 'Lock your door,' he yelled, slamming his switch down, the bouncers nearly upon them.

Charlotte put the Golf in gear and stamped on the accelerator. The spinning wheels gained traction and the car surged forward, rapidly picking up speed. The acceleration pinned Will in his seat as the bouncers reached for the door handles. Another lunged onto the bonnet, staring intensely through the windscreen, 'Hey,' he shouted.

'Watch it,' yelled Will.

Charlotte jerked the steering wheel right to take the Golf abruptly onto the road and threw the meathead off the bonnet. The bouncer running on the driver's side was forced into the road but managed to keep pace with the car. Reaching for the handle, he resorted to thumping at the window and demanding they stopped.

'Lock your door,' shouted Will.

But Charlotte shifted into second gear, and the man beside her stumbled after tripping on a traffic island. By the time Charlotte reached third, several thousand revs too late, he was visible in the rear window, picking himself off the tarmac. The other three gathered around him, watching the Golf speeding away.

Moving through the commercial streets surrounding Glitter, the only sound was Will and Charlotte catching their breath. Stopped at the first set of traffic lights, Will resisted turning to the rear window. He knew they were far enough away. Charlotte focussed on the rear-view mirror, the dashboard lights illuminating her features from below. Her jaw tensed, and he expected the engine to begin shrieking at any moment.

When the traffic lights changed, to Will's surprise, Charlotte took a sharp left, crossing lanes without indicating. Feeling the momentum fling him inwards, Will clung to the strap bolted to the roof.

They screeched onto a street bustling with brightly lit takeaways. Will remembered it was nearly chuck-out time on Friday night and found the hordes of people reassuring. Mindful of enraging Charlotte further, he found it easier to get distracted by the drunk pedestrians, championing their own dramas, while the Golf joined the slow passage of traffic.

Will watched an overweight girl tear into a large pizza while shouting to her friend to wait. Sitting on the grubby kerb outside a takeaway, her pink skirt was short enough to reveal white knickers. He was fascinated by her trashiness: her inebriated state, a loose pink top hanging off a shoulder, the garish makeup with its mix of reds and purples, black club sludge smeared across her white platform shoes.

'What were you thinking?' said Charlotte.

'I didn't think anything,' he said, trying to appease her.

'Too right,' she snapped, impatiently sharing her attention with the stop-start traffic.

Will took his time, trying to explain it. 'I've never been hit before. I flipped when I saw him.' He held out his hand. 'I'm still shaking.'

Charlotte dismissed it with a frown. 'You could go to prison.'

'No way.'

'You could.'

'I think I had a flashback.'

'So what? What if you've killed him?'

'I haven't.'

'How do you know?'

'I saw his face when he hit the floor.'

'Will!' she shouted.

'I'm not being flippant.' Will squirmed uncomfortably. He'd never hit anyone before. He didn't want Charlotte to think this was normal behaviour. When the guy fell, he was definitely conscious. A plastic bottle wouldn't kill you. How else did you say it? Why was Charlotte getting angry with him anyway? He hadn't planned to do it. 'It was your idea to—'

'Don't,' Charlotte snapped. '*That* was not *my* fault.' She glared at him beneath the dark, heavily layered mascara until she could bear him no longer. Will thought she might order him out.

'So much for going to the police,' she said.

'Maybe—' Will stopped himself. He didn't want to get into a row about rough justice.

'What?'

'Nothing.' Will shook his head. 'It doesn't matter.'

Charlotte scanned the road ahead. 'Where are we going?' she asked impatiently.

Will thought he heard emphasis on *we*. Was she referring to their relationship or the destination? Tentatively he said, 'Where do you want to go?'

'I don't know.' Charlotte flicked another irritated glance his way.

'You want real fun?' Will remained ambiguous, wanting to satisfy both options.

Charlotte's attention remained on the road.

Will said, 'Take a right up ahead.'

09 / *After Parties*

Will directed Charlotte away from the chaos of cheap takeaways to join the main road through the northern half of town. The whole time, she didn't take her eyes off the road.

Older townhouses, reappropriated as offices, lined the route until they got to the newly developed estates clad with white plastic facades. Further up the road, a supermarket glowed brightly, its large car park empty except for the small cluster of cars surrounding the entrance. Will presumed they belonged to the staff he could see inside stacking selves, their dutiful night-work distinctly subdued compared his own.

Joining the dual carriageway that looped around north Ravisbourne, wind roar and tyre roll accompanied the engine's purr on the short, fast stint to the next junction. Charlotte turned off and coasted the slip road, the engine's whine dropping to a low hum.

Will told her to take the third exit. Charlotte changed to second gear and maintained speed through the sweeping curve. Will wondered if she'd heard him as they fired past the first exit. She changed up. With the third exit nearing, Will said, 'The turning's tighter than it looks.'

'I know,' Charlotte's tone rang with authority. She was in total control and wanted him to know it. Circling the far side, she dropped a gear and took the corner with the skill of someone familiar with the road layout.

Travelling up Ravisbourne Hill, the hatchback weaved between hedgerows on the single-track road, the glowing town below them to the left. Will became entranced by the headlight beams sweeping over the tarmac. The journey reminded him of a previous trip to Manchester, to the Hacienda, when the four of them hitched lifts to an after party twenty-five miles away at a warehouse in Blackburn. After a sketchy drive through the countryside, they arrived at the party, which didn't even have a name. Everyone was mad up for it, having an absolute blast until mid-morning. But their comedowns were hit hard when they learnt how isolated they were and the trains didn't run on a Sunday. Mercifully offered rides back to Manchester, they spent another night at the Hacienda before catching a train to London Monday morning. None of them made work until Tuesday.

Twisting through the cambered corners, venturing further from the lights of suburbia, the sky darkened, and the stars became visible. Wispy clouds floated over nearby woodlands, like bunting leading them to the parade. Will hadn't been to their destination since school, when those with cars drove everyone out there to get loaded on a Friday night. There were plenty of jokes that the house was haunted. Apparently, the council converted it into a mental asylum for a while. He didn't know if the story was true. Maybe Charlotte knew more about it.

At speed, they ascended a rise in the track. Passing the apex, it felt like they'd momentarily left the road. Will's stomach tumbled. Charlotte's jaw remained tense as the suspension bounced back down.

Sooner than Will expected, a wide stretch of tarmac appeared abruptly on the right. 'Here,' he blurted. It would have been almost eight years since his last visit.

Charlotte hit the brakes and indicated, but there was absolutely no one around to see the signal. 'Here?'

'Yeah. Sorry,' he said, watching the orange indicator light flash over the two stone gateposts that were exactly as Will remembered them. Their defunct iron hinges the only remnants of a large set of gates that once hung there.

Past the gateposts, the driveway became a narrow, inclined path, where thin branches brushed the bodywork. Cresting the brow, beneath countless stars, a white, pillared manor house rolled into view. Illuminated with coloured lights from within, the opulent property appeared much grander than Will remembered.

A pumping bass line became audible. 'Nice,' he said quietly.

Charlotte didn't respond.

The path forked right towards a gravel semicircle at the front of the house. Along the closest side, vans were parked in the shadows. Charlotte continued left past the unkempt front lawn, scattered with groups sitting in huddles. The moving lights inside the house caused their shadows to shift and stretch across the grass. Faint patches of coloured light danced over Charlotte's face.

The path dipped away. The lights and noise faded behind them. Passing through a gap in a hedgerow, they found a gravelled enclosure full of cars haphazardly positioned. There was clearly more desire to party than parallel park.

Once they found a parking space at the far end, they zigzagged between the cars and retraced their journey to the main building. Will heard the heavy chug of a diesel generator behind the house. All the lights and the sound system would be drawing kilowatts of power.

The wide front doors were protected by perforated steel panels and concealed a grand marble hallway flooded with people. A curved staircase led up on either side. In the dim light, the atmosphere was vibrant. The patter of many conversations merged to form a gentle murmur above the relentless house music playing elsewhere. Will could hear one, maybe two, other sets of beats fighting for attention.

Weaving through the groups stood together chatting, Will became conscious of his black jeans and shirt, terribly outdated style-wise, and a reminder of his days as a barman. Charlotte didn't appear bothered by her out-of-place attire.

Aiming to the right, towards an open doorway and an orange glow, they found themselves in a square room with a temporary bar in one corner and a stuffed grizzly bear in another. Reared on its hind legs, claws outstretched, the bear was the only one that looked like it needed a drink. People were crashed against the walls. A small group laughed rowdily at the bar. They were too busy chatting away to notice Will, forcing him to the far corner to order two Red Stripes, served onto the bar top beside forgotten drinks.

Clutching cans, they continued through to a glass-roofed room, hot and humid, like a tropical incubator, with a high ceiling full of plants and exotic greenery. A tall, thin tree sprouted through the wooden-boarded floor. The bittersweet smell of soil and leaves mixed with cigarette smoke and tangy body odour. People crashed on wicker chairs and coloured beanbags.

The door in front led to a bigger room, this time half-full with people dancing. Will sought out the DJ, working away in the corner, and recognised Mike, one of the Dance Inc. promoters, stood behind him.

Mike, like the rest of the Dance Inc. crew, attended a rival school. Will got to know their faces from Sunday league football matches and events like roller discos during the school holidays, way back before house music even existed. They were never close. When Will found out they were promoting too, it seemed like an extra layer of competition had become wedged between them. Conversations were always brief and seemed forced, underpinned by necessity rather than any sense of affinity. Perhaps there was begrudging respect at best. Will thought they were try-hards with their showy Dance Inc. logo. At least they were willing to pay upfront for his sound system. Maybe he'd up the price to get them in line.

'Will!' came a call.

Spinning round to the corner, Will found a quadrangle of low sofas full of people and identified Adam's contorting face among them. Wasted, Adam strained at the neck and yelled, 'What you wearing, man?' He struggled to contain his amusement.

Tell everyone, why don't you, thought Will, realising the group were friends of the Dance Inc. crew.

'Mister Promo,' said Charlotte like she was confirming it to herself. She looked to Will, awaiting his response.

'What you waiting for?' called Adam, 'Get over here.'

Will foresaw an awkward inquisition aimed at his expense. Caught in a quandary, he hooked a thumb backwards and winked. 'Be with you in a bit, buddy.'

Adam became chagrin. 'Rob and Stu are upstairs,' he said, trying to save face. 'Rob's playing.'

'Okay, mate.' Will turned on his heels.

Behind, he heard laughter as Adam complained drily, 'That girl's definitely changed him.'

The door opposite led onto a long, dimly lit corridor, lined with people sitting along each wall. The marble hallway was at the nearest end, where Will could also hear a different set of beats. They ventured right, where a shimmering blue light flickered intriguingly against the walls and ceiling at the far end.

Waist-height, running along either side, the edges of square cupboard doors were sealed and painted over. Perhaps they were empty storage cupboards. Will saw them filled with TVs playing psychedelic visuals. That's what he'd have done if it was his gig.

When they arrived among the lively voices, echoing from the far end, they found themselves in a glass conservatory with a ten-metre swimming pool as its centrepiece. The water's rippling surface was covered with dozens of balloons and a layer of sparkling confetti. Unlike the exterior glass, caked in moss and lichen, the pool, with its white tiles submerged under clear water, was scrubbed clean before the party.

On the far side, people mucked about, either soaking wet or stripping off. One of them hurled themselves through the air to dive-bomb the water. Charlotte stepped back, anticipating the splash.

'Fancy a dip?' asked Will as the bomber slapped the confetti-covered surface, sending a column of water into the air.

Charlotte watched another person launch into the pool. 'Not tonight.'

Droplets landed nearby.

Deadly serious, Charlotte said, 'Don't ever do anything like that again. I mean it. Can you imagine if we got caught?'

'We didn't. Chill out.'

'Chill out?' she raged. 'Why don't you?' She shoved him with both hands.

Before Will could do anything about it, he was stumbling over the edge of the pool, and his can of beer was flying from his hand. Instinctively Will reached out and caught Charlotte's wrist. She screamed, trying to break free, and threw her can at him, but it was too late. She was coming in with him.

Will rapidly submerged. His soused jeans and shirt wrapped to his body. Charlotte's wide-eyed expression of surprise was the last thing he saw before he went under, and she landed on top of him. Her arms and legs flailing, she nearly kicked him in the crotch. Trying to steady herself, she leaned on his head. Will could hear muffled shouts through the water and swam sideways to get air.

He broke free of Charlotte's grip, the water dragging against his clothes. 'Prick,' he heard when his head emerged. A splash of water hit him in the face.

She swam for the side. 'I'm going to drown in these boots,' she gasped.

Charlotte pulled herself onto the edge, the sodden black shirt clinging to her slender body. She heaved a leg from the water and untied the first of her shoes. Blotches of white and black makeup were smeared across her cheeks beneath matted lines of hair.

His clothes made doggy-paddling a struggle. 'At least I've cleaned my makeup off,' Will gasped.

'Thanks.' Charlotte pulled off the boot and launched it at him.

Will caught a mouthful of water dodging the shot. The boot splashed next to him and sunk before he could catch it. 'What you doing?' Will gasped, 'You might need that.'

Charlotte removed her next boot and aimed at him. 'Fetch.'

'Don't,' yelled Will, 'I've got enough injuries as it is.'

'Poor you.' Charlotte changed her aim and threw the boot in the pool. 'They could have been made a whole lot worse if we were caught.'

Will swam to her, steadying himself against the edge. 'Maybe that guy will think twice before he goes grabbing women again.'

'You don't take the law into your own hands, Will.'

'I didn't mean to.'

'You hit him with a bottle.'

'A plastic one,' Will grinned, remembering the hollow bop.

'It's not funny,' Charlotte snapped, 'You knocked him out.'

'I don't think I did,' said Will, 'And besides, he got off lightly compared to what happened to me.'

'You try anything like that again,' insisted Charlotte, 'you wait and see what I do.'

☺

Inside Glitter, the club empty after closing time, Wayne Moran exited the staff corridor with his head bandaged. Off-duty door staff were across the room, spread about the diner, swigging beer in high spirits. Wayne was sure he heard someone mention his name. They were probably mocking him, joking about how easily he hit the floor when the kid put a bottle across his forehead. Behind his back, Wayne knew he'd never live it down.

After the attack, Wayne clambered to his feet and rejected the assistance of bar staff in a bid to show he was okay. Once he came to his senses, leaning against the bar with a blue paper towel held to his forehead, two of the guys escorted him into the staff room, where he washed the cut. Blood wouldn't stop dripping into the metal sink. The bottle was only plastic, but the rigid base ripped his skin. Wayne didn't like the door staff fussing over him. Their manly hands touching his face made him feel uncomfortable. Then a barmaid came to have a look. That was okay. She gently held his jaw, inspecting the cut and suggested it might need stitches. Wayne wasn't sure, but when it was still bleeding with the pressure off after half an hour, he ordered a staff member to ring a cab, and he took a solitary trip to A&E. Being relatively early in the night, there was no great mob of drunks delaying his admission. Just in case, he removed the temporary bandage and made the cut bleed again. Entering A&E with blood streaming from his forehead, the receptionist took one look and immediately called a nurse. A large, middle-aged woman arrived, devoid of sympathy, and escorted him to a corridor with rows of beds, an array of bandaged limbs and the addle-headed on display. While the nurse undertook some painful prodding, he wondered if she could be cheered up by a shag. She washed the cut with iodine and administered two thin pieces of tape to keep the wound closed. Then she wrapped his forehead in a bandage. A second cab set him on his way two hours later.

He wanted to go home and sleep, but that would've felt like defeat. Eager to get at the security footage, he cabbed it back to the club, where door staff were surprised to see him. In his office, in front of the small CCTV monitor, he found concentration gruelling. He decided it could wait until the morning, switched off the screen and plodded over to lock the door before dropping into his chair. Feet on the desk, he kipped for an hour but awoke amidst a sensation of being under attack. Not only from the kid with the bottle, but from this morning, too. When he arrived at the club to find the speakers missing. Not what he was expecting on his way to fetch the money he owed Daz, all seventy K of it. Twice the cost of one week's sniff since Daz decided he wanted cash before product from now on. It would appear Wayne's personal financial arrangements had conspired to lower his credit score with the bossy little reprobate.

A year ago, when Lewis came to him with the deal, the two of them were only dabbling in the white stuff, and Wayne was dead against involving his club in anything substantial. But the more they spoke about it, the more it made sense. All the pissed punters, any one of them could be bringing it in. And besides, the sizeable packages wouldn't be there long because buyers were already arranged. Lewis reckoned he could get it in weight if Wayne would use the club as a front. Keep the packages moving, keep the cash rolling, and they'd get a decent rate. That's what Lewis promised. What Wayne hadn't banked on was dealing with Daz, who paraded in and out like he owned the joint. Sunday night, the greasy little streak thought he could make a scene, giving lip to door staff. What made Daz think everything should go his way? It pained Wayne to bow down to anyone, let alone a delinquent like Daz, with his misguided sense of status. As far as Wayne was concerned, Daz was nothing but a peddler. A middleman. Those he moved between held the power because they were the ones with the cash and the resources.

Crossing the empty dance floor to the off-duty door staff, Wayne remembered his stolen speakers. The stress of it all made him sweat, and he scratched his chest. It always itched when he was angsty like this. His spectacles slipped down his nose and, caught up in his vexations, he almost poked himself in the eye, prodding them back into place. He wanted to destroy whoever stole from him last night. Was the one who put the bottle across his head in the same gang? Did Daz have a part in it? Paranoia crept over him. Wayne blamed tiredness after the day he'd had: entering the club prepared for Daz's visit, finding the missing equipment, the fear the club's safe had been looted, then relief when he saw the door to his office undisturbed, the CCTV footage of four masked men breaking and entering, the cheeky sod who flooded his toilets while the other three proceeded to steal his sound rig, the cops arriving twenty minutes too late, sniffing around with a torch without even exiting the vehicle. Wayne made the decision to open tonight, whatever the cost. After calling the cops, they returned later that morning to receive the CCTV tapes. All while Wayne juggled arrangements for new equipment and made an insurance claim. Using his own copies of the CCTV, he'd make it his job to find those responsible. Why spend all that cash on cameras otherwise? He hadn't heard from Daz, so he presumed the feral child had forgotten their meeting. After the day's nuisances, Wayne was glad to get a session underway.

Wayne stepped among the tables, where a barman had propped a broom after sweeping the night's debris, leaving a pile of plastic cups and cigarette butts for the cleaners to remove. With Wayne's arrival, laughter dwindled, and the door staff appeared to seek out the damage to his forehead.

Dan, his head of security, swivelled around to get a good look like the rest of them. 'You all right, boss?'

'Tell me that little shit is in pain.' Wayne was so annoyed he couldn't help sticking out his chin, show them he was tough too.

A reply came. 'Got away he did, with some girl in a motor.' It was Mags in the corner. Wayne struggled to distinguish the voice amongst all the heavyset guys in matching black jackets.

Another one piped up, 'We got the registration plate.' That was Craig, over by the dance floor.

That sounded positive. Wayne suspected it was Craig he'd heard mentioning his name when he left his office. 'They'll keep.'

'Want a line boss?' asked Dan.

Wayne said, 'I knew I was paying you for something.'

☺

Resigned to his unfashionable outfit, Will restyled his hair in one of the conservatory's mucky glass panels. Charlotte watched him closely, having quickly tied hers into bunches.

'You look fine,' she huffed and pulled him away from the improvised mirror.

They squelched from the poolside with Charlotte carrying her heavy boots after making Will go fish for them. Moving through the downstairs dance floor, Will checked to see if Adam was still in the corner and saw him in conversation with one of the girls. Holding her hand, he looked like he was trying to propose. Charlotte's attention was on the music as she made an effort to dance her way through.

Getting drinks, Will considered the requirements for hiring a mobile bar of his own: the quantity and cost of booze, profit margin, plus another van to lug it to site. Would Adam be capable of running it? He thought not and decided it was too much effort. They were making a decent wedge. Maybe he could charge someone else for the privilege. It might be worth making enquiries about a licence. Then again, to get around the licensing laws, the parties were considered private, so what was the point?

Navigating the marble staircase, they guarded their drinks like they were completing an obstacle course, dodging a gauntlet of people with no concept of, or ability to, move politely out of the way. Near the top, a guy with yellow sunglasses and a giant Mohican sang, 'E, get your E. Happy with all the people.'

Charlotte shared a smile with Will, amused by the performance.

The guy continued, 'Happy, happy pills here, beautiful.'

Will held Charlotte's damp waist. 'We're sorted, buddy,' he said pleasantly. 'Have a good time, yeah.'

Ahead, smoke wafted from an open double doorway, enticing them across the landing towards the music. They were long forgotten by the guy with the Mohican who resumed dancing.

The vast, darkened room was a heady dance floor. Nothing except the dancers and the music existed. It was the source of the bassline they'd heard from the car, the party's brooding soul. Will indicated the far side, where he could see the DJ setup and the top of Stuart's bald head next to a speaker.

Considering the wall of gyrating limbs and smiling faces, Charlotte said, 'Probably best to put these on,' and stepped into her boots.

Once she was fixed, Will entered the revelry, but making headway was impossible with everyone caught in their own delirium, too wasted to notice the plight of another. Will retreated and found an easier path along the far wall, which dripped with beads of condensation. Feeling the music and the vibe inside the room, Will wanted to get going. Glimpsing Charlotte, she already swayed to the rhythms in that familiar way of hers.

Making it to the other side was like exiting a jungle. In the small space between themselves and the far wall, Stuart and Rob were behind a table piled high with sound equipment.

'Oi oi, matey. Look at you,' beamed Stuart.

Busy cuing the next track, Rob only glanced up briefly. Will wasn't sure Rob recognised him. He shook Stuart's hand, introducing Charlotte, who nodded coolly. Stuart offered a perfunctory greeting in return, his main concern on Will's outfit. 'Switching your style, is it?'

Will feared mockery. 'Something like that,' he said, wanting to move on.

'Black is in,' chuckled Stuart. 'Here, speaking of dark, you found the basement yet?'

'No.'

'Not for the faint-hearted,' he warned with a knowing wink. 'Hey,' Stuart nudged Will with an elbow and encouraged him to look down. In his palm, Stuart held a little red pill and offered it discreetly. 'Get that down your neck, matey.'

Will shook his head, hoping Charlotte hadn't seen. After their night so far, he didn't want fresh controversy. 'We're gonna chill tonight.' He'd never seen her on it.

Stuart looked over to Charlotte, who leaned against the wall watching the crowd. 'You ain't going soft on us, are you?'

'No.' Will smiled to reassure.

'She's all right she is.' Stuart nodded as if it wasn't clear who he meant.

'Thanks.'

'Just remember your priorities.' Stuart laughed, popping the pill in his mouth. 'Down the hatch.'

Will wanted to get back to Charlotte. The distressed wall she leaned against could have passed as a backdrop to a magazine photoshoot, with her the model.

'Matey,' Stuart stopped Will, 'we're at the end of a rainbow here, drowning in gold.'

In his euphoria, Stuart was getting poetic. 'I know,' said Will with an amused grin.

'The other night was decent. I want more of that.'

'I'll have our next party locked in no time.'

'Top man. No distractions.' Stuart nodded at Charlotte then nudged Will with an elbow and winked. 'I'm gonna find water before wonderland takes hold.'

Will watched Stuart go. He held out a fist for Rob who, working the controls, seemed to realise who it was and smiled warmly. 'Yes, bro.' He waited for an appropriate moment to bump it in return.

'In a bit.' Will left him to it.

Over at the wall, Charlotte nodded her head to the beat. 'You look like a model.' Will said, admiring her pose.

Charlotte appreciated the compliment. 'A rock one?' She came away from the wall.

'Exactly.'

They held each other's hands.

'You finished gossiping?'

'I'm all yours.'

Her eyebrows raised. 'Lucky me.'

There was affection there. Will felt like things were about to loosen up. 'Fancy a dance?'

Charlotte looked over the crowd. 'Why not?'

☺

Five in the morning., Lewis Steele stepped from Glitter sniffing cool fresh air, amazed how a bit of coke could help put aside your general dislike for people.

The club's front door latched shut with a click, and Lewis rattled it out of habit. What a night. Wayne getting bottled by some kid, the blood, the shocked whispers of bar staff and the boys making light over the radios while Wayne took a trip to hospital. Then the blow-out once the club shut. All the lads getting on it, things getting loose. The bar getting raided, Wayne complaining but too blitzed to stop anyone. No one knew what was going on after that.

Lewis had kept it steady and bowed out at a reasonable time. He'd get home, put the dogs out, kip until lunch, then get ready for the afternoon's footy before travelling to the Midlands to drop off a bar early evening. If his missus complained about his late arrival home, he'd blame it on the trouble at the club.

Lewis lifted the collar of his thick black jacket. He could have called a cab from inside instead of chancing it on the street, but he wanted to get going. The opportunity to slip away presented itself, so he took it, not wanting to deal with nagging from hangers-on.

Approaching the taxi rank outside the kebab houses, he was bemoaning his team's prospects, playing away, when the white saloon rolled up beside him. Lewis recognised the front arches and the bonnet's bulging vent from the corner of his eye. The throaty exhaust was unmistakable. He heard an electric window unwind. Keep going, he said to himself.

'Guess who wants a lift?' came the gruff statement.

Lewis recognised Cal's voice and barely squinted sideways, plodding along at his own pace. 'I'm good,' he said, but metal chinked against glass and Lewis was brought to a halt by the gun barrel resting on the lowered rear window. The saloon rolled to a stop.

'Ain't we still friends?' Cal peered out from within the Cosworth, an ugly smirk across his face.

'Bit early, isn't it?' replied Lewis, trying to sound chummy.

'Shut it,' barked Cal. He kicked open the rear door, and a

tattered trainer returned inside. 'In,' he barked.

Lewis knew he couldn't do anything else, expecting Joe behind the wheel to lend his considerable weight to whatever Cal wanted. He climbed inside, hearing the engine over-rev before the saloon rumbled off.

'Keep it steady,' ordered Cal, hovering menacingly behind his scrawny younger brother, Leigh, not Joe, at the helm.

The kid was a known joyrider, with dozens of points on a licence he didn't yet own. Lewis was alert to the gun in Cal's grip. If they got pulled now, Lewis didn't know what he'd do. He said, 'Nice and easy, pal,' and could hear the tension in his voice.

They were moving west towards Ravisbourne's industrial sector, along the old road out of town. They passed telegraph poles plastered with weathered flyers advertising a travelling circus. Empty parking spaces for carpet warehouses and independent electrical wholesalers, closed at this time of day, were littered with waste. Lewis tried to determine the reason for the pickup. He hadn't done anything wrong as far as he was aware. His last dealings with Daz were to introduce him to Wayne to line up the deal. He expected a decent cut but ended up getting cut out. He hadn't made a fuss about it.

Lewis could feel his heart hammering inside his chest, its rate and his senses elevated by the coke. If Cal could hear it, he'd probably got a kick out of it. Lewis shuffled in his seat and received a brief, cold stare.

The independent stores and commercial offices ended at the Westpoint roundabout, where the road network expanded to accommodate the vans and HGVs of heavy industry. They circled past several exits leading towards industrial compounds. Taking the fourth exit, they passed unmarked warehouses, bays of them on both sides of a long stretch. The road eventually stopped at a T-junction. Behind a wire fence, the town's waste disposal facility lay dormant, brimming with junk beneath a huge, metal awning.

They took a right, rolling alongside rugged wasteland and a vast expanse of ruined foundations, to reach industrial facilities with white smoke rising from tall, brick chimneys. Past these, they approached another concrete wasteland. Beyond a wire fence that warned away intruders, Daz waited by a black saloon similar to the one Lewis rode in.

They bumped over a collapsed section of fence and weaved through piles of rubble spiked with rusted iron rods. Weeds, sprouting from the cracks, replaced the building that once stood on the site.

Slowing to a stop a short way off, Lewis watched Joe join Daz in front of the headlights. Joe so big, he could play front row rugby league and not break sweat.

At Cal's indication, Lewis hauled himself out, with Cal and his gun following behind.

Lewis couldn't shake his growing tension, feeling it in his legs as he approached the centre-ground.

Watching him with a callous stare, no red shades on at this hour, Daz said, 'Relax.'

Lewis eased up and nodded slightly. As though Daz had spoken to Cal directly, Cal put the gun inside his jacket.

'I think ol' Lew's sore from last time,' said Cal.

'Last time's nothing, believe me.'

Lewis could do without the two of them speaking about him like he wasn't there. He said, 'I'm good.' trying to sound relaxed.

'Good.' Daz pulled a smoke and hooked it in his mouth, 'Unless you wanna go spend your days in prayer, it's about all you got.'

Lewis waited while Daz lit the cigarette, taking his time before getting to the point of all this. Lewis hoped for workers in the nearby buildings. Anyone within earshot of gunfire would help his chances.

Daz shook the burning match and dropped it. 'You may think we cut you for Wayne. I can see why you would. Truth is, Lew, you never stopped working for us. You jus' didn't know it.'

Daz offered Lewis the pack of cigarettes, and Lewis gratefully stepped forward to accept.

'Good,' said Daz, 'Now, how'd you fancy rocking the old man's boat some? Be our man on the inside?'

The glimpse of Daz's intentions led Lewis to a place fraught with trouble. 'I get a choice?'

'You get a light.' Daz tossed Lewis the box of matches.

The box arched through the air, and Lewis caught it. He struck a match and lit the smoke, willing his heart rate to recover.

Taking a welcome drag, Lewis said, 'You hear the cops were over Glitter yesterday?'

'Hear?' said Daz, his tinny voice rising with outrage. 'I was fucking there.'

10 / *Chill Out*

Saturday afternoon, Will woke on a cushioned wicker seat. The bright sun shone through the glass roof onto blade-like leaves, way up there, basking gloriously. Will tilted his head so their shadow would shield him from the immovable daylight. Charlotte slept on his chest, her cheek squished against his black shirt, creased even more after his outing in the pool.

A lanky guy bounced through on the balls of his feet, his eyes wide. When he spotted them, consternation passed over him. Barely pausing for thought, he licked his lips and picked up his pace as though the encounter never happened. It was too much to hope that he and Charlotte were the only ones there. Will knew there would be others, the extravagant manor house now a den for the deeply hedonistic. Charlotte showed no aversion to those on a chemical high last night, but Will was concerned about those still up during the cold light of day, deprived of sleep and nourishment since who knew when. She preferred to keep her vice to alcohol, and must harbour some sort of judgement, even if she chose not to share it.

After their dip in the pool, the hot dance floor dried them off in no time. Captivated by each other's charms, they danced without a care. When Rob's set finished, he came over to join them. It was the first time Will had noticed anyone else in hours. Rob kept it cool as always, not giving much away, replying to Charlotte with short measured responses and minimal gestures, always respectful. Charlotte was pleased to meet him then headed to the bar to hunt for food. While Will talked with Rob, one of the hardcore came over to compliment him on his set. The guy was high and full of enthusiasm, waxing lyrical about the tracks Rob played. When Charlotte came back with three packets of crisps and three beers, Rob used her return to shake the guy off.

After Rob left them, Will and Charlotte took a break at the windowsill and chatted until sunlight shone between the newspapers covering the glass. Charlotte told him all about her life, where she grew up, what she used to do as a kid. A similar story to Will's, a normal happy childhood, but in a different part of town. Will liked it when she spoke about her degree in art history and tried to relate it to acid house. Drunkenly, she explained how the scene was part of the progression of musical expression within society, but became tongue-tied after all the booze. Then Charlotte told him about Caravaggio, her favourite painter, comparing him to music and how he painted in a naturalist style that was a progression on the classical. Will couldn't visualise what she meant, especially when she called Caravaggio the world's first director of photography. It sounded like something to do with lighting. He steered the conversation back to music, asking how Caravaggio related to acid house. Her point was, acid house was like disco, only newer, like Caravaggio was to Michelangelo. Will nodded, thinking northern soul was a better comparison than disco but happily agreed. Her passion for her subject was endearing.

This morning, flat out against his chest, he didn't think she could be more at peace.

When she stirred, groggy from sleep, she sat up and pressed her hands against her face. 'I don't want to know what I look like.' She looked to Will, appalled with her hangover.

'It'll be okay.' He laughed.

'I've got to go home,' she said, as though thinking about it was an ordeal. With a self-pitying laugh, she lowered herself back onto his chest. 'This is all your fault.'

He checked to see if that guy was still around and found the plants and the sunlight, making him squint. Without anything planned for the day ahead, he was content to stay there and dozed until Charlotte got up without warning.

'I've got to go.' She removed her bunches, ruffled her scraggy hair and tied a loose ponytail. 'Right.' She began flipping cushions, searching for any possessions that may have fallen loose. Satisfied there weren't any, she rubbed her bleariness away and stood.

Home time looked for real this time. Will swivelled upright and lifted the cushion behind him to check he hadn't lost any belongings either.

'Are you coming?'

Will wondered if he'd get invited to hers, to chill for the night. 'Could do,' he said, remaining indifferent. He wanted to stay at the party if he didn't't. There was the equipment to think about.

'What does that mean?' she asked impatiently.

'I might need to sort the equipment,' he said. Then, trying not to sound too keen, 'What you doing today?'

'Not sitting around here waiting for you.'

Will laced his trainers. 'Good plan.'

'I'm going to the loo. I'll meet you outside.'

'Okay, I'll go and check for the others.'

'Fine,' she said as though she wasn't interested in what he did.

Alone, Will moved into the room with the bar and the grizzly ear. The bar was gone, but the bear remained on guard, a figure rled by its feet as though for protection. Will tried to identify e lone sleeper. 'You alright, buddy?' He prodded him with a e.

Half asleep, the crashed-out reveller muttered something oherent before wrapping himself tighter around the grizzly bear's leg.

'Fair do's.' Will didn't know him anyway.

In the hallway, the grand space was eerily quiet compared to the night before. The bleak marble was left strewn with beer cans and plastic bottles. Some people slept against the staircase, stragglers who were either too mashed or lost elsewhere when the rides back started. He could hear voices from below, but first, Will climbed the staircase to check on the equipment. Crossing the landing, he could see nothing but bare wooden floorboards in the empty room, once home to a couple of hundred dancers. Stuart's legs poked into view from the far corner. He slept under the table that housed their gear. Will knew his former-football-hooligan pal chose to pass out there to protect the equipment from thievery. Will was tempted to sneak it all out himself to give Stuart a scare, but it was too much effort to carry it all on his own.

Will left Stuart to kip. He could be intolerable if woken unexpectedly. Will retraced his steps and pushed through the heavy main doors across the hallway. Charlotte waited beneath the awning, leaning against a stucco pillar with its cracked paint peeling away.

'Grim.'

She was referring to her trip to the toilet. Through her dissatisfied expression, Will saw the cramped, unmaintained cubicle with its grimy corner sink, broken tap and no mirror.

On the patch of overgrown grass behind Charlotte, a solitary jacket had been forgotten. Miles below them, one corner of Ravisbourne was visible through the afternoon haze, sprawling into the distance beyond a copse of trees. Charlotte hooked finger in one of Will's belt loops and pulled him close. Wisps of her hair swayed in the breeze.

'Can I call you later?' Will searched for a kiss and got one.

She tugged the tails of his untucked shirt. 'If you must.'

☺

From Charlotte's luscious goodbye kiss, Will headed downstairs towards the nattering voices, curious about the depravity after a night and a day of hedonistic impulses. If Rob and Adam were still up, they'd be no help packing up the equipment.

A steep, wooden staircase turned tightly at right angles. Will decided it would have once been used by staff. Without a handrail, he supported his footing by steadying himself on the damp, uneven walls. The bottom steps flickered with an intriguing orange glow.

The basement had a dusty concrete floor and a small gathering was crashed on cardboard mats around a fire in the corner. Adam was flaked against a wall, oblivious to the conversation. A sturdy desk housed a single turntable and monitor speaker, left as a gesture. "Pacific State" played quietly in the background. Dust marks indicated where the main stacks were once positioned. The room covered the property's entire floorplan and was lit by fairy lights, spiralling around every pillar supporting the low concrete ceiling.

'You got a permit for that fire?' asked Will, grinning when everyone whipped around shot with surprise, their conversation interrupted.

'William,' cheered Rob, propped on an elbow.

'Good afternoon, chaps.'

'It is.' Rob lolled happily. 'We're about to go to another party.'

'Where?'

'Across town.'

'What about the equipment?'

Rob took a moment to consider his reply. 'I don't know, man. I'm just the DJ.'

'How you getting there?'

Rob was patient with Will's questions. 'Jamie said he'd book taxis for us once he was set up. Have you seen them?'

'The taxis? No.'

'That's a shame, man. Have you seen Stuart? Maybe he can drive.'

'Maybe.'

'Sweet, man, you up for it then?'

'What else we doing today?'

Rob beamed broadly. 'Legend.' Then, remembering something, 'Hey, I've found a new venue we can use.'

'Oh, yeah?'

'You know that gym, Power Train it's called. On High Street.'

'Yeah.'

'It's closing forever. Sean told me earlier. Site's got no takers at the moment. And he reckons the landlord could be keen.'

'I could have a chat with him.'

'Think about how perfect it is. It's got all those different levels where the exercise machines used to be, the stretching area, the bike area. The changing rooms could be used. And it's got toilets, man. Nice ones. But it would totally have underground vibes, I'm telling you.'

Will was buoyed by the news of a venue near the town centre. Precisely what he needed. He'd make it his job to chase it up during the week. 'I'll get on the case,' he said.

He could be on his way to creating their first regular night. A permanent home to advertise in local listings. Maybe he'd apply for that alcohol licence after all. They would need to think of a name for the night as well. Then again, Power Train might actually work for their purposes. If all the signs were left behind, it could save them a bunch of cash on rebranding.

Leaving the basement crew to gather themselves, Will returned upstairs with an elevated sense of purpose and found Stuart sitting against the far wall, his legs spread in front of him. A bottle in hand, he took a swig and held the water in his mouth, staring vacantly at the floor between his legs.

'You up for a party?' Will's footsteps clipped through the room.

It took Stuart a moment to react. He rubbed his bald head. 'Chill out, matey.'

'Too soon?' At the table, Will unhooked the leads, connecting the mixer to the two turntables. Playing the martyr, he said, 'It's okay, I got this, don't you worry.'

'What did I say?' grumbled Stuart.

Will coiled the leads. 'Chill out?'

'Well done, matey.'

Will secured the lids to the turntables' and stacked them one atop the other.

'Where the others?'

'Basement. Very messy.' Will stuffed the coiled wires under one of the lids.

'Twats.'

Will placed the mixer onto the amp.

Groaning, Stuart staggered to his feet. 'Why do you have to be so keen?' He eyed Will suspiciously. 'What's with the black clothes?'

'No reason.' Will lifted the amp and mixer and held them for Stuart. 'You can have the lighter load.'

'Cheers.'

Carrying the equipment down the marble staircase, Stuart said, 'I'd love to have seen the owner's face when they arrived at Glitter yesterday.'

'It didn't stop them opening last night.'

'How'd you know that?'

'Me and Charlotte went down there.'

'Why?'

'Charlotte wanted to see if we were talking about the same guy.'

'Were you?'

'Yeah.'

Stuart frowned as they bumped through the front doors. Will was sure he'd have to tell him more.

Stepping off the concrete slabs beneath the pillared awning, stones crunched under their feet. They squeezed between the property and the first van under the shade of tall eucalyptus trees. On this side, the mansion's windows were painted black with tape crossed over them in case they shattered. One van was gone. Stuart's yellow Transit was parked beyond the vacated space.

Stuart placed the amp and mixer on the ground and unlocked and opened the side door. He studied Will as though re-evaluating his friend. 'So, what are you going to do now?'

Will could tell Stuart was wary, the former football hooligan anticipating trouble. 'Not much. Charlotte wanted to report him, but I kind of ruined that one.' Will placed the turntables inside the van.

'What do you mean?' Stuart retrieved his equipment from the floor. Then considered, 'Is that why you're wearing black?'

'As a disguise. Her idea.'

Stuart placed his equipment next to Will's. 'You tell her about this stuff, how we took it?'

'No.'

'What happened then?'

Will hesitated. 'I put a bottle over his head.'

'Matey,' Stuart rubbed his head. 'My comedown's bad enough as it is.'

'It was only plastic.'

'Well, that's all right then.' Stuart laughed uneasily.

☺

Saturday evening, Charlotte snuggled on the two-seater in front of the TV. With only a few hours uncomfortable sleep in that greenhouse room, some semblance of normality was a little way off. Boy did her legs ache from dancing in those heavy boots. Not even a long soak in the bath helped them recover. Traipsing from the bathroom in her PJs and dressing gown, the lounge was as far as she could manage, and her plans to get dressed and have a productive day were placed on hold. She hadn't moved since.

On the television, the argument the fictitious couple were having rose in volume. They'd been breaking up for the entire episode. Charlotte wasn't sure yet how she and Will would turn out. Straight after the incident, she was furious, but talking it through, and seeing Will's hand shaking, calmed her to a degree. She felt for him again.

She knew he'd been badly beaten up. She'd never been in that type of situation but could understand his reaction. Less than a week ago she wanted to hurt the man herself. How different was violence in reality?

Will's actions didn't bring her justice, and she knew going to the police was now out of the question. They wouldn't have a chance once they were recognised. But after the emotional experience of Will's actions, it was as though she'd moved on. The trauma of the indecent assault became more distant and easier to ignore.

She checked her fingernails. They were still covered in black paint. The TV programme with the arguing couple was finishing. With the remote control lost in her cocoon, she began picking at her nail polish, waiting for the next show.

The party was wild. With white tees and MA1 flying jackets the order of the day, she and Will must have stood out like sore thumbs. But she hadn't been at all self-conscious. The party was full of warm vibes. All those different rooms with everyone so relaxed. It reminded her of her Hampstead Heath days. She noticed Will declining Ecstasy and suspected it was only due to her presence. He must know she didn't participate.

Will was naturally enthusiastic about the music, like he thought acid house was about to become ubiquitous. The money he made gave him enough of a reason to believe so. She tended to mock that level of confidence in a man, but Will kept it cool, even if he could be too idealistic at times. But then again, wasn't she an idealist? How often did she hope for a better world? House music was full of hope. That was the reason she liked it so much. The scene had become the antithesis of Thatcher's Britain. A counterculture a million miles from what the PM must have imagined when she espoused the virtues of entrepreneurialism. Acid house embodied all the bits forgotten or ignored by her government. A vibrant youth culture at home amongst urban decay. Music at its heart. No discrimination over race or sexuality. Charlotte was proud of her generation and how they denounced bigotry. With attitudes changing, shameful policies, like supporting apartheid in South Africa, would be consigned to the history books forever. Maybe, she reflected, anyone with progressive views was an idealist one way or another?

A knock at the front door interrupted her train of thought. She threw the duvet aside, resenting the interruption. Opening the door, feeling fresh air pass over her, she stiffened. Not because of the coolness to the breeze but because the creep from the club stood in front of her. She couldn't believe her eyes. He seemed surprised too. In fact, he looked amazed, like he'd just lucked out. Charlotte was absolutely, inconceivably, aghast.

'You,' he exclaimed and the big one in the dark bomber jacket, who she'd barely given a second thought to, marched her backwards into the house.

Charlotte heard the door click shut and the creep's heavy

footsteps follow them inside.

'Where is he?' he asked, but Charlotte was so overwhelmed she couldn't muster a reply.

Still trying to comprehend the situation, the empty lounge emphasised her isolation. Finally, Charlotte yelled, 'What the hell are you doing?'

Her rancour failed to penetrate his thick skull. He surveyed the cosy room and nodded with mock appreciation. 'Nice,' he said. Then he ordered the big one to, 'Check the house.'

The muscle in his black jacket and dark jeans disappeared up the staircase leading directly from one corner of the room.

Charlotte's mind became hyperactive, like she could feel the physical activity within her brain. The electrical impulses of her synapses flashed off and on, rapidly computing the scenario.

'Where is he?' the creep asked.

Charlotte found the courage to hold his stare. 'Who the hell are you talking about?'

'One of many, eh?' he sneered. 'Sit.' He indicated the two-seater.

Charlotte remained standing.

'Brave.' He adjusted his bandage. 'Brave and stupid.' He bared his teeth. 'You're wasting your time playing dumb with me. Or maybe you're all confused. I'll find out, though.'

How had she got to this situation? Two minutes ago, everything was well. She was warm and snug, tucked under her duvet. She couldn't believe this guy—the nonce! —had the gall to barge his way into her home.

Charlotte couldn't think of anything else, her mind was gridlocked. A few heavy clumps registered somewhere. Then the thickset guy reappeared. His deep-set eyes, beneath bushy brows, were full of guilt, as though the personal effects he'd seen upstairs formed an image of a person with whom he empathised. In a flash, the expression was gone.

'Don't look like he lives here.'

Piqued by the news, the creep said, 'All alone, eh?'

Charlotte assumed the question rhetorical and stayed silent, holding her ground with both men watching her. It was the best she could do.

'Where's he live?'

'I don't know.'

'Bullshit.'

'I don't!' She hated Will. She was lying for him. 'We only met the other day,' she conceded, trying to convey sincerity, trying to throw him a curve ball.

'Don't want to rush into anything too soon?' he mocked. 'Okay, ring him.'

Charlotte stared with incredulity at the man who had the audacity to intrude on her world and relay orders.

Her distress must have been plain to see because his comforting tone was rich with sarcasm. 'Aww, you want, you can come back to mine, be nice and safe while you think it over.'

As if it was his cue, the big bloke, the muscle, stepped forward.

'Okay,' Charlotte raised her palms to halt him. She snatched the receiver from the windowsill and stabbed each button slowly and deliberately. When he arrived next to her, she became jittery. His foul smell was a visceral reminder of their time together in Glitter.

Listening to the dial tone, Charlotte was at a loss over what to say.

The creep snatched the receiver and Charlotte was relieved to have him step back from her. Judging by the length of time he stood listening, Charlotte guessed Will wasn't home. Was that a relief? She didn't know any more.

He lowered the phone. 'Oh dear, what are we going to do now?'

Charlotte loathed his affectations. All she could do was stare at his smarmy face, wishing to everything holy he'd leave her alone.

Then he said to the big one, 'You wanna knock her out for me?'

Horrified, Charlotte stepped backwards, banging her heel on the skirting board. Her back was literally against the wall. 'Don't,' she pleaded.

His face lit up at her response. He leered closer. 'Well, how else am I going to get you in the car?'

11 / *Acid House*

Being marched from her house was a transcendental experience. As though someone spiked her drink at the party, and she was tripping out. Still wearing pyjamas and dressing gown, the big one held her by the back of her head, keeping her low like he wanted.

Forced to keep her eyes on the ground, Charlotte didn't see any more than the car's footplate. It flashed by as the big one guided her onto the rear seat. 'Poke your head up, I'm likely to knock it off,' sounded his all-too-believable warning. It was enough to keep her compliant.

Flattened against the seat's musky cream leather, the squeaky brakes and soft suspension caused her nausea. She presumed they were fighting their way through traffic. The radio presenter's convivial prattle was no better than Wayne and Dan's dreary exchange. She couldn't believe they'd volunteered their names.

After travelling for maybe twenty minutes, the engine note told her they'd hit a dual carriageway. Rapid vibrations passed through the seat to her body. Her urge to vomit quelled. It wasn't long before they slowed and, after a few more twists and turns, finally came to a permanent halt.

God, they could be in her parents' neighbourhood. Charlotte imagined her dad visiting and both her parents in the front room, watching her climb out in a dressing gown with two strange men. Maybe her dad would come running to save her. The experience bringing the three of them back together as a family.

She was marched across the driveway, over a porch's black and white tiles and into the unknown house. The strip of carpet on the parquet floor led to stairs, where the burgundy weave continued upwards and along the landing to a dimly lit room. The big one shoved her inside and locked the door.

Through wooden blinds, shafts of sunlight fell across an unusual arrangement of nineteen-fifties furniture, giving the impression the room was more a store than a space to live. A jumble of antiquated objects cluttered the shelves of a glass-fronted cabinet positioned against the far wall. A smaller cabinet housed a tiny, built-in television screen, like the one Charlotte remembered at her grandparents' house. The same lacquered wood formed the slender-legged dining table, complete with plate settings laid neatly. Three wingback armchairs were positioned around a circular coffee table that matched the larger dining version.

Charlotte slouched across the carpet's swirling browns and took a seat on a wingback. It was surreal, like an out-of-body experience. As though her entire life condensed into this bizarre moment. She could feel herself sitting within the room, but she didn't seem present, as if her mind denied her senses.

She imagined someone spiked her drink at the squat party. The perverse scenario was unsettling. She couldn't be hallucinating, the details were too real: the room was fitted with old-style round plug sockets, and she could see marks where the armchair's weave had been rubbed thin by countless elbows. It couldn't be true.

Charlotte was desperately alone, aware of her breathing and her sense of touch. A strange sensation of emptiness gathered in her belly. If someone told her this would happen, she imagined she'd be terrified. Instead, she was calm, detached from the situation, her mind trying to tell her: this is the single most terrifying situation you have ever been in. But she didn't believe it.

Voices and laughter reverberated from the landing, then a click as the lock turned. She shied away, but Wayne's attention only briefly passed over her. He strode straight to the glass-fronted cabinet and rooted through the artefacts. Dan, the muscle, remained at the door while Wayne retrieved an old-style Bakelite telephone. 'Forgot about this, didn't we.'

As he carried it to the dining table, its degrading cable became taut and toppled a candlestick. Unconcerned, he withdrew a dining chair to sit. Charlotte wondered if she'd have made a call if she'd noticed the phone. Perhaps it was best to do nothing and let events unfold.

Wayne hooked an arm over the back of the chair, surveying the space himself. 'How'd you like it?' he asked proudly.

She already despised the furniture the conceited oaf prized. What was there to boast about apart from, unfortunately for her, the subordinate who guarded the door? All she could do was shrug, as though she'd been trumped by his wit.

'My parents' stuff,' he informed her, 'before they popped it. I didn't have the heart to throw it away.' His smile bared neatly aligned teeth that Charlotte decided were dentures.

She couldn't tell if the guy was taking the mick or trying to get along. Both approaches were equally unwelcome. She remained impassive. He appeared calm and confident and, under the circumstances, to be that relaxed suggested a profound intellectual deficit. Or an arrogance beyond anything she'd encountered before.

'So,' he said, drumming his fingers on the table. 'let's try again.'

Charlotte needed him to be more explicit and waited, stony-faced, until he said, 'Well, come here then.'

Approaching the dinner table, Charlotte didn't take her eyes off him. It felt like she was walking on a choppy sea. He handed her the phone and she dialled, turning the wheel for each number, then waiting for it to rotate back every time. Please pick up, she thought as the line rang and rang. She imagined Will still at the mansion, clearing out the equipment. Or perhaps at a carry-on. Could she have called somebody else and screamed for help? Would that have worked?

The line rang off. Charlotte lowered the earpiece, helpless. What do you want me to do now? she thought, watching him revel in her displeasure.

'Quite the conversationalist, aren't you?'

He pushed back the chair and stood, seeming taller than before. She watched him take the phone and unplug it at the wall.

'Looks like you'll be here a while longer.'

'You can't keep me here forever …' Charlotte tailed off, envisioning dire outcomes.

Wayne glared at her like he found the comment deeply patronising. 'Hey,' he said, as though just realising, 'I never thought, this kid better actually like you.' He chuckled. 'Then what would I do with you?'

He set the chair under the table, caught a leg, and rattled the silverware, causing her to jump.

'You want to go wee-wee?' he asked, feigning sympathy.

Charlotte shook her head. It was best to say nothing. Maybe then they would leave.

☺

Will and the diehards from the party were at a country pub on the outskirts of town. The bar, with its rustic decor, had become a weekend hangout for those in the scene. Ever since it became a meeting place for one of the orbital raves. Unofficially, of course. The temporary doormen that night, complete with staff terriers, knew nothing except to take twenty quid off those who wanted a ride on the coaches parked outside. Pete, the landlord, who was now on first name terms with everyone, remained equally tight-lipped but appeared glad to swap his yokel clientele for a more vibrant set. Will floated the idea of a night there once, but Pete didn't have a late licence or want to draw attention to the pub. As a compromise, not wanting to miss out on a good thing, he'd taken to playing acid house whenever a crowd showed.

This evening, the pub was crammed with kids from town, listening to the latest sounds. Most were at last night's party. Including Dance Inc., who, Will decided, he ought to make more of an effort with. For now, though, he was glad to enjoy a pint.

It had taken ages to get the sound systems packed up and everyone out of the manor house. When he and Stuart returned inside for another trip, they were confronted by the exodus from the basement. None of them were with it enough to concern themselves with the equipment and, taking positions on each stairway, hurled empty drink containers at each other. Particular amusement was had when someone found a half-full one, and beer exploded everywhere. Finally, with Stuart's irritable disposition hastening order to proceedings, everyone got in line. Those more capable helped carry out the heavy speakers. The rest sat about the front lawn making plans for fresh cigarettes. Stuart's persistent warnings made sure the equipment was handled sensibly. With a load of wasted guys riding in the back, Stuart joined them to supervise the journey.

That left the responsibility of driving to Will. Rob tried to help, giving directions, but he was more of a burden. When they arrived at the party's alleged address, no one answered the door. Will suggested the party was a figment of Rob's imagination. Rob, coming under pressure from those who'd taken refuge from the uncomfortable rear hold on the kerbside, insisted they drove to a nearby phone box to try calling. Stuart acted as a marshal, and everyone piled back in the van complaining about the ride.

At the phone box, Rob and Adam tried to operate the phone, undertaking the one-man job together. With the group of partygoers hanging around the phone box, it reminded Will of trips to the orbital raves, when whole convoys of cars and vans would converge on motorway service stations until the location was revealed to whoever commanded the phone box. Then they'd shuttle off again, tracks blaring from stereos, people hanging out of windows, horns blowing. If the cops arrived, they'd blockade the cars in to stop them leaving. At a major event a couple of months ago, the promoter fired a powerful green laser into the clouds. With everyone's cars impounded, the whole crowd arrived on foot, like a swarm of fireflies drawn to a giant mate. Tearing across the countryside, there wasn't a fence, hedge or wall that could prevent several thousand revellers descending on the party.

There was no such theatre today. Jamie, the guy who promised the party, didn't answer the phone. While alternatives were debated, Adam cranked up the van's stereo and encouraged an enthusiastic roadside shindig. To any neighbours watching, it must have looked like a scene out of a high-tempo musical. With spirits lifted, the final stop on Will's magical mystery tour was chosen, and the journey to the pub began.

'You're saying they got that massive laser to outdo police?' Stuart hunched over the table, littered with pint glasses.

'Yeah, at the Sunrise gig,' said Will.

Stuart quit trying to roll a cigarette and passed it to Adam, an expert no matter what his state of inebriation.

'Man, that Guy Fawkes night was awesome,' said Adam.

'Who told you about it?' asked Stuart.

'The guy we rent the phone lines off.'

Stuart poked out a lip in appreciation.

'My point is, one laser and before you know it, three thousand people show. That's the level we need to get to.'

Rob muttered agreement, slumped at the head of the table.

'We ain't getting one,' said Stuart 'Ain't room in the van.'

'Remember Back to the Future Three the other week? To get that party going, the organisers told the cops they were filming a music video. People filtered in, wondering where the music is. As soon as there were more than the cops could handle, the promoter slapped on the first track, scooted into the crowd. See you later, mister policeman!'

'How'd you know they said that?' Stuart was in one of his moods.

'I told you, sorting the phone lines for Dominator. The guy who rents them out also promotes.'

Rob sat up. 'A mate nearly got arrested at that gig. He wouldn't unlock the DJ booth to let the cops in.' Satisfied with his contribution, he settled back.

'That's why you guys are heroes.' Will angled his pint glass in Rob's direction and received a misshapen smile.

Stuart turned to Adam, 'You finished that roll up or what?'

Nearly,' said Adam, his tongue poking from the side of his mouth.

☺

The girl upstairs was making Wayne sweat. He was all right while Dan was there, watching the boxing with a takeaway curry. Now he was alone, Wayne was worried if he fell asleep, she'd make trouble screaming the house down. He told himself the booze was making him paranoid. His affairs were in order. There was no need to get insecure.

Opposite him, when the late-night TV show faded to black, Wayne caught an ungainly view of himself, beached on the bulbous sofa. Amidst the entertainment unit's shelves, stacked with Betamax cassettes and CDs, spirit bottles twinkled invitingly. Wayne admired the luxury brands, latest technology, and designer furniture. How could this little girl get to him? The room was his most comfortable of places with its thick-pile carpet that smothered your feet, an ocean of fuzz beneath the matching furniture. The combination of black leather and black veneer wood, offset by gold-trimmed, white wallpaper and lavishly coloured art prints. He was surrounded by his most treasured possessions. Items that filled him with confidence. Their value, a constant reminder of his success. If his diffidence continued, he'd have to swim back to the already raided drinks cabinet for a top-up to oblivion.

Stained plates and crinkled foil trays littered the low table in front of him. The last remaining clumps of food bathed in congealed sauces, as appealing now as they were when fresh. But Wayne was stuffed. He couldn't even manage a beer afterwards. Maybe if he offered the girl food, it would help pacify her. Struggling to sit upright, he collected the leftovers and took the foil trays upstairs. It was an excuse to see how she was doing.

Wayne didn't think he was in bad shape for a fifty-seven-year-old but climbing the stairs, a wave of heat spread throughout his bloated form, and made him sweat. Usually, when a woman was at his house, he'd only want one thing. Chances are he would've picked her up at the club and, by the time they arrived home, he'd be riding high on a couple of hours flirtation. Failing that, there was always the dick-pump stowed in his en suite bathroom. There was no chance of any action tonight. Jeez, did he know how to pick 'em.

Entering the room, he found her waiting impassively. Wearing her chequered bathrobe, she was on the wingback, pushed to the wall so they could cuff her to a pipe.

He placed the foil tray on the arm of the chair but, thinking better of it, dragged the low table to the wingback and laid the selection there. 'You want a spoon?' he asked, but she didn't respond. He went and got her one anyway.

Back downstairs hugging a bottle of bourbon, TV on quietly, Wayne's shirt was still damp from the exertion. Just a couple became half a bottle, trying to remain calm. Staying there gave him a greater sense of control. As though he was on guard. He would see how long he could last.

Who knew the girl would end up chained to a radiator in his house? When he and Dan arrived at the address the getaway car was registered to, he was surprised, but not shocked, to see the girl from the previous week. Dan gave her man a hiding for taking her into the toilet for a quickie. Presented with this girl at her front door, Wayne suspected it was the same guy who put the bottle over his head. The incident happened so quickly it was hard to remember, the coward heavily disguised under all that white makeup as well. Whether that was another man or not, he'd soon find out.

His heart thumped. He'd only grabbed her backside for a joke, to teach her a lesson about how he liked his punters to behave. Wayne exhaled a long heavy breath. He'd go easy on her while he figured a way to end it. If things got testy, he'd shore up his alibi and dump her in the woods outside town. That would be best.

☺

Eight Sunday morning, Will peered into the tall food cupboard of his narrow kitchen. Naked beneath his dressing gown, he held the garment together. He wanted something to munch on until the others woke and they could go for a full English.

Man, partying could take it out of you. After the pub closed, the four of them hit Will's to blast tracks through the night. Will was glad to step up the pace and let off some steam after the tension of Friday. But the booze drained his energy and he was out for the count way before the others. He would have slept longer, but once the sun cleared the flats opposite, it became too bright, and he couldn't get back to sleep.

There were the biscuits, hidden behind the hot chocolate, the cheap brand compared to the swanky stuff he was smashing back to pass the time at his parents' house. Will manoeuvred his arm inside to retrieve the pack and got a draft of air across his exposed belly. He lifted the long packet free, careful not to tip any jars. In his fuzzy state, it was an effort that required total concentration.

Will plodded from the kitchen, gathering his dressing gown together. Lights off, blinds drawn, the living room was lit by the TV, which no one had bothered to turn off. Adam and Stuart slept on the chairs. Adam regularly sofa-surfed, sometimes for days, but it was unusual for Stuart unless he was in a state. Rob must have pulled a sneaky after Will crashed out. Stuart had a job, but they were still both slackers. Neither he nor Adam possessed any foresight. They stumbled from one party to the next, leaving Will to do the organising. He'd call Rob tomorrow and arrange a catch up in the studio, see if they could get a record label involved in the next party.

Perched on his bed, Will fumbled with the sealed pack of biscuits. The phone's abrupt trill tore his concentration from the fiddly task. Thinking it might be Rob, unable to find a taxi and wanting to come back, Will answered, 'Yo.'

There was a notable silence before Charlotte's voice came over the distorted line. 'Will?'

She sounded strange.

'Yes, my lady?' he said fondly.

Then a male voice came on, 'Hi Will,' he said, sounding elated, 'your friend from Glitter here, remember me?'

Will's mind whirred through the situation. He didn't exactly recognise the voice, but who else could it be?

'You there, little man?'

'What?' Will said, thinking it was a joke.

A long, ragged sigh came down the line.

Will roused, 'What is this? You're not funny.'

'Aren't I?' The guy said, 'Me and your lady friend have been thinking. In fact, you've caused us both a bit of grief.' He snorted at what he considered a joke.

Will heard another man chuckle in the background. 'If you hurt her,' Will's voice quavered as he realised the implications.

'Well, why don't you pop to the club sometime. You know …' The guy considered how best to impart his message. He settled on, 'Payback.'

'Payback?' Will frowned.

'Payback, little man. You got it. It ain't her I want to hurt. Understood? The question is, how much do *you* not want to get hurt. Because let me tell you, *this*, this is happening. For real.'

As the line clicked dead, Will's beating, his subsequent hospitalisation, aching in his parent's lounge, that stupid trip to Glitter all flashed through his mind. The repercussions were inescapable, and he released his fury by tearing everything from his bedside cabinet.

He stood amongst the clutter, wishing he could rewind time. He had to find Charlotte. What else could he do? He reassured himself that he had acted on impulse. He hadn't meant to hit anyone. There had to be room for reason. He'd get dressed and take Stuart's van. If she wasn't at her house, then what? Did he really want to go to Glitter? He'd have to call the cops. Moving to get dressed, he trod on the fallen lamp and stumbled.

Cursing loudly, Will kicked the junk across his floor. If the cops wanted him to go to the station, then that's what he'd do. The outfit he'd been wearing was jumbled amongst the debris, like his life in ruins. Will growled through a tense jaw.

'You all right in there, matey?' From outside the room, Stuart sounded worried. He leaned in. 'I was asleep, matey. What's going on?'

☺

Through half-closed blinds, bars of sunlight streamed over Charlotte. Despite being exhausted, the situation, let alone having one arm handcuffed to a metal pipe, made sleep impossible.

Her mind had raced all night, picturing her parents, wherever they were, oblivious to the predicament of their only child. If they knew of her dire situation, they would immediately come in search of her, each travelling a direct path to provide her with a warm embrace. The type of reassurance only a parent could give.

Now Will knew what had happened to her, he would contact them when he remembered her student address and paid a visit. Employing his breaking and entering skills for more constructive purposes.

She'd convinced herself he'd arrive in her bedroom and find her address book in the top drawer of the bedside table. She wouldn't mind the intrusion of privacy. He'd know that as he found details of her parents' property on the inside front cover. Her father's temporary address added more recently below it. Between these, he'd read the houses' phone numbers. At the bottom of the page, he'd find the number of her father's new mobile phone. They were all there, neatly written.

At one point, Charlotte panicked wildly, imagining the heavy found the book when he searched upstairs. There was nothing she could do if that was the case. She put it out of her mind, clinging to her previous fantasy in desperation: Will, with the support of her parents, was now notifying the police of her kidnapping. He would tell them everything, how the club owner had indecently assaulted her, how he was beaten up by security. The police would understand these as mitigating circumstances for the second trip and Will's subsequent assault.

Without further violence, Will would be waiting safely at the police station while officers stormed the club and rounded up staff for questioning. Bar staff or cleaners wouldn't be under suspicion. Their knowledge would only assist police. There was no need for them to feel intimidated. After an event like this, the club would surely change hands. The new owners would appreciate the strength of character and honesty staff showed by keeping them in employment. Paper records of the club's management and security staff could be seized. They would contain personal information, like the address book Will had found. If, after these were checked and leads followed up, information was insufficient, the police would arrange an identity parade for Will to point out the guilty party. Based on the overwhelming evidence that was emerging, resistance would be futile. The fool would have no choice but to disclose her location. Police would be on their way shortly. An investigation as finite as that couldn't take much longer.

'See you later, honey,' Wayne called from outside the room.

He was mad. How could he sound so happy? He was about to walk into a police trap. Maybe that's why they hadn't already broken down the front door. Police were waiting outside to make sure he was present. To catch him red-handed.

Charlotte heard the front door close and waited for signals that the impending police operation was about to begin.

☺

Will retrieved his discarded jeans his head spinning after explaining the situation to Stuart.

Stuart said, 'You can't go down there now. You're a state.'

'I've got to.'

'You could get hurt, matey.'

Will knew that was a possibility but shook his head. 'The coward's blackmailing me.' He fastened his belt. 'What else can I do?'

'Think it through.'

'I have.'

'So, you got enough cash on you?'

He did, but … Will was overcome by the reality of the situation. He became flushed, feeling like he might vomit. He didn't want to spew over his floor and pushed past Stuart to get to a sink.

Staggering through the living room, Will's mouth filled with saliva, which he was forced to swallow. At the sink, he waited to retch but it never came. The kitchen's cooler air seemed to help. He gulped mouthfuls of fresh water from the tap, wiped his face, and found a towel to dry himself.

Stuart hovered in the doorway, unsure how close he should approach. 'Come sit down, matey.'

Will shook his head. He'd won his game but didn't realise it: they'd stolen the sound system and were in the clear. Why had he gone back to Glitter? He should have talked Charlotte round. If she'd known about the raid, she'd have never suggested the trip. She might even have left him. Perhaps that's why he went. To keep her happy.

'What about Daz?' said Stuart, 'He's got contacts in Glitter.'

Will couldn't see his logic. 'I'm not getting him involved.'

'Listen, if this messes things up for him, it could mess things up for me.'

'What?' Will couldn't understand it. 'Stu, mate, Charlotte's been kidnapped, and you're worried about scoring pills.' He pushed past him and through the living room before Stuart got any more ideas.

In his bedroom, Will pulled on his jeans, eager to get out of there. He didn't care how he looked but ran his fingers through his hair to get it in shape, help him feel awake. He grabbed a T-shirt from the wardrobe then threw his tie-dye sweater over that. Pulling the hood up, he found some socks in a drawer and laced his kicks. Stuart better not try to stop him taking the van.

Back in the lounge, Adam was awake, watching the silent TV with bleary-eyes. When he peeked over nervously, Will knew Stuart had told him what was going on. Will found the keys on the windowsill.

Stuart said, 'I'll make some calls if you want?'

He looked wary. Will could tell he didn't really want to get involved. For all his tough-guy bravado, Stuart hadn't even offered to come with him. Will decided to save him the hassle: 'Let me head down there, see what I can first.'

Exiting his flat, Will passed along the short path separating two overgrown patches of grass and bumped through the rotting wooden gate. He'd drive past her house. If there was no one there, then what? How much cash was the guy after? He could call the club first. Then the cops. Be evasive about his own identity but tell them exactly what happened. Give the man something else to think about. What if he was at Charlotte's house right now?

'Where you off?'

Will found Daz standing behind the passenger door of a black saloon, its squat, angular bodywork rigid, like a flexed panther ready to pounce. A massive guy he'd never met before stepped out of the driver's side. There was a dull cruelness to his expression, and he held it with nonchalant ease. Will was rooted to the spot. 'Getting some smokes,' he said.

'Some smokes,' said Daz, as though he was confirming to himself what he'd heard.

'Yeah.' Will shrugged, trying to keep it casual.

Daz said, 'You on your own in there?'

Will shook his head. 'No.'

'Then why don't we step back inside, fella.'

For a split second, Will thought about running. Turning around and getting away as fast as possible. But the guy with the bull neck made him think twice. What could he do against him and that hulking car? Will retrieved the keys and reluctantly retraced his steps towards the wooden gate. 'I've gotta be somewhere.'

'Shut up,' said Daz.

The two unwelcome guests followed Will into the living room. Upon spotting Stuart's glance towards him narrow, Will decided Stuart must have called Daz while he was getting dressed. It didn't seem enough time for them to arrive but why else would they be outside? Will was astounded Stuart had gone behind his back. Adam had shrunk into the sofa but conveyed no sign of guilt.

'All right?' Stuart asked, watching Daz take up the middle of the room. Stuart seemed confused by the massive guy, who blocked the front door and didn't acknowledge him directly.

Daz held their attention, looking over the remnants of last night's antics, the empty beer cans and open cassette tapes. 'I hear you guys got a problem.'

No one answered him.

'Well, get your dancing shoes on,' he said as though he'd lost patience. 'Five of us going for a ride.'

12 / *Their Law*

Stuck between Stuart and Adam in the back of Daz's saloon, Will could almost taste the bitter odour of stale cigarettes, such was the stench. The interior was foul, the plastic trim vandalised with burn marks and rough gouges. The tint on the windows concealed their identity from passers-by, who remained as oblivious to Daz's intentions as he. No matter which direction they travelled, the distance between him and Charlotte was growing in magnitude.

Yesterday, after a week of pain and discomfort, Will thought he was back on track. Today, his plans were in tatters. Things changed literally overnight. Now he was at the mercy of those no one wanted to think about, deviants who made an existence putting pills in your pocket. He was guilty of it himself, failing to consider Stuart a threat.

Stuart had made his allegiance clear. He must have tipped Daz off. Daz knew already. The pleasure he was taking by getting involved was written all over his smug face when he ordered the three of them out of Will's flat. Will thought he was joking until the guy with a torso bigger than a wrecking ball plucked Adam roughly from the sofa. Adam yelped, and the big guy barked, 'Shut it,' inches from Adam's alarmed face. That got Stuart standing to attention. There was nothing else Will could do but follow along.

Will was furious with Stuart for betraying him. He was being pinched on all sides by those with criminal intent. Who knew how much malice lay behind their designs? A simple trade-off for

Charlotte now seemed out of the question.

Up front, Daz prodded the buttons of his chunky mobile phone, carefully checking the number was correct. Adam's face was blighted by stress. Stuart preferred to keep a permanent watch out of the window.

Will couldn't sit still and say nothing. He asked, 'Where we going?'

Daz's attention remained on the keypad. 'Someplace nice.' He put the phone to his ear.

Will was plagued by thoughts of Charlotte. He tried to focus on the here and now and listened carefully to the faint dial tone.

Without introduction, Daz said, 'You gonna make tonight.'

The response was unclear.

Daz let his displeasure be known. 'You had the filth round for breakfast.' Then, to some unknown slight, he seethed with contempt, 'Dammit, Wayne.'

Upon hearing Wayne, Will's attention piqued. It was the name on Glitter's licence.

Daz barked, 'You don't call nothing no more, you hear me? Tomorrow morning, like we do. Understand?'

From the other end came a faint and brief reply.

'Tomorrow, like I said.' Daz hung up.

'That the guy causing all this?' asked Will like it was no big deal.

With a shake of his head, Daz returned to the phone. 'Jus' 'cause you're sat here, fella. Don't mean you got an invite.'

Will imagined Charlotte chained somewhere. He wanted to answer back but thought better of it. He watched Daz slowly and deliberately key another number into the phone. Daz placed it to his ear. Will heard the dial tone ringing.

Irritated his call wasn't answered, Daz lowered the phone with a tight grip. After a moment of deliberation, he placed it by his feet. The journey continued in silence.

Will was stuck in a car, with all that space outside, an estate's roads and paths interspersed with small grass commons. A tower block loomed nearby. All around, pockets of small semis were hidden behind high garden walls, their upstairs windows concealed behind untidily drawn curtains. A high proportion of cars had dented bodywork or needed repair. They were in south Ravisbourne, somewhere Will rarely ventured.

The saloon rumbled around a corner and parked on a short road between sides of houses. Along an alleyway in front was a row of private garages. Daz reached for his phone and climbed out, slamming the door behind him.

The car shook, and the big guy turned on the radio. He dialled through the frequencies and paused on a pop tune Will was unfamiliar with. Unimpressed by the chirpy presenter, the big guy flicked off the radio. Stuart and Adam both preferred the view through their respective windows. Will couldn't even escape if he wanted to. What would the big guy do if he forced the issue and tried to bundle Adam out with him? There's no way he could catch all three of them. But Stuart was an unknown quantity and Adam would resist, especially when the big guy intervened. They were miles from home in the wrong part of town, so Will decided against anything foolhardy.

The four bodies sitting there made it uncomfortably stuffy. Will's discomfort was worsened by his legs straddling the exhaust tunnel. He was glad when the big guy unwound his window to prevent the glass steaming and cool air came rushing in.

Through the clearing fog, Daz rounded the corner looking shifty. Will saw the same expression on Stuart when he was working his way through a dance floor. Daz climbed in without a word, the engine started, and they rumbled away from the kerb. Will needed to know where they were being taken.

Daz said, 'Tomorrow, you boys gonna get something of mine,

bring it to me.'

'What about Charlotte?' asked Will.

'You obsessed with her or what?'

'She's been kidnapped,' Will snapped and instantly regretted it. Quietly, he said, 'By someone you do business with. That's not good for any of us.'

'I do what?' Daz looked to the big guy and waited for a response, but the big guy, concentrating on driving, didn't notice. Daz gave up, faced forward, and laughed to himself. Will didn't know what was funny about the situation. He wanted to shout.

Daz said, 'Man, I need to start running,' like he was excited by the prospect.

Will waited for more, but Daz didn't continue. Will had to see it through. Whatever *it* was. He focussed on that thought, trying to hold it together for Charlotte's sake.

Daz lit a cigarette and took several long pulls. 'I've been hearing a lot about London lately. The music scene you boys pissin' yourselves silly about.' Daz poked his ash into the slipstream above the window. 'I heard one story, some guys, they threw a grenade through a rival promoter's front window. The man, this promoter, spent the night cowering under a table 'fore he got the balls to get up, discover a novelty cigarette lighter.'

Daz took a quick drag before discarding half his cigarette, flicking it out above the tinted glass. 'It worked, though. Man played his last party, and those guys,' Daz closed the window. 'Those guys become the biggest thing since Elvis.'

'Cool,' said Adam sincerely.

Daz laughed, a hearty, high-pitched cackle that was unsettling. It dragged on and caused Adam to look to Will for reassurance.

Will said, 'Earlier, what you said … What do we have to do?'

Daz ignored Will. They left the estate and retraced their route across town, travelling north to the inner ring road. Daz lit another cigarette, then a third. No one spoke.

Arriving outside Will's flat, the big guy switched off the ignition and surveyed the mirrors while Daz shifted round to face the rear seat. 'Home time for two of you,' he said, clearly enjoying the position he held over them.

Will thought Daz looked even more like a rat when he smiled. Up close, he could see in detail the pockmarked complexion and uneven, yellow teeth. Maybe the red sunglasses were meant to distract from his harsh features.

Daz's crooked smile faded, considering them individually. Then, he reached inside his jacket to reveal a matt black pistol with squared edges. Daz admired the weapon. All Will could focus on, feeling his chest tighten, was the barrel's gaping hole.

The gun hovered between them, its threat severe, like an invisible ray was hitting whoever it targeted. Daz aimed at Adam. Adam swallowed, the noise of his throat loud in the quiet interior.

'Mister cool,' Daz said to Adam, 'you're up tonight.'

Will could feel Adam's leg trembling against his.

With menace, Daz swung the gun between Will and Stuart, causing Will to tense whenever it crossed him. Daz let it settle somewhere between them.

'You two get set for morning.'

'What do we have to do?' asked Will, the barrel threatening to punch him at any moment. Then it was rising, and Will saw Daz sneer, momentarily, before he pressed the barrel onto Will's forehead.

'You'll know soon enough.' Daz pushed hard to leave a mark. 'Think of this like buying your freedom. And your girlie, she's the deposit you get back at the end.'

Will waited, motionless, the gun still against his head.

'Out,' barked Daz and returned the gun inside his jacket.

Stuart and Adam both opened their doors.

'Not you.' Daz yanked Adam back inside. 'Idiot!'

Adam slammed his door shut. 'Sorry,' he blurted, desperate for forgiveness.

Stuart held one foot outside, waiting for further instruction. 'You two. Go,' said Daz, his scorn remaining on Adam.

Stuart nodded obediently and climbed out. Will followed, glad to be away from Daz but not much else. The engine roared, and the saloon peeled away, leaving Will and Stuart outside Will's flat.

'How could you?' Will seethed, trying not to shout.

'How could I what?'

'Call Daz!'

Stuart acted surprised and offended. 'Are you serious?'

'What else am I supposed to think when he's parked outside?'

Stuart dismissed Will with an irritated head shake, like he pitied him. 'If I had, I wouldn't be stuck here with you, would I?'

Will growled and paced towards his front door.

Inside, he couldn't stop pacing, trying to figure out what was going on. Who did Daz think he was, ordering them around like that? Then he brought out the gun. That was all Will could think about: Daz had a gun. Will couldn't see anything but the gun pointing at him.

Stuart lay across the couch, feet up like he owned the place, playing with the cord on his hooded sweater.

Will said, 'I have no clue what to do.'

Stuart remained mute, his grim expression contrasted by the smiley-faced flyers covering the walls.

'This is fubar.' Will slumped on the other seat.

'Yep.'

'What would you do?'

'There's nothing we can do,' said Stuart. 'We got to ride it out.'

'Seriously?'

'Matey, you have no idea.'

'About what?'

Stuart frowned, reluctant to reply. Will wondered if he'd stopped to think about Charlotte or Adam. Will didn't want to think about the state Charlotte might be in. Adam would likely be in pieces, whatever Daz had in store for him.

☺

Adam preferred to be left alone in the back of Daz's car. Then he could pretend this wasn't happening. But oh man! Daz was turning again, twisting to lean over the front seat. Nudging the gun forward for him to take. There was something evil about Daz. Adam didn't know what he'd do with the pistol, but fear compelled him to take hold. Daz let go, and Adam felt the gun's weight. He hadn't expected that. Inspecting the detailed etching, he wondered what the levers did. It was nothing like the guns cowboys used in movies, all chrome and shiny. Adam wanted to go home and see his parents. He knew he couldn't say so.

'All you do is release that catch and pull the trigger,' said Daz, pointing where he meant. 'Aim high, 'cause I wouldn't wanna be you, you hit any innocent bystanders.'

'No one ever died because of tracks, man.'

Daz smacked him across his head. It didn't hurt much, but the shock upset him some more. He told himself this would be over soon. Then he hoped he could return to having fun.

'It's gonna be a piece of piss,' said Daz. 'I even got you a way in round back.' Daz indicated the gun. 'Put it away.'

Adam hid the weapon under his sweater. The metal chilled his belly, so he pulled his T-shirt between the two for comfort. Tucking it under his waistband, the heavy barrel squashed his penis. He imagined the tip of it being blown off but quelled his cowardice and folded his arms when he was finished. There was a gun where his dick should be. Oh, man!

'Empty the chamber, then take it to your boys. Get any ideas of your own an' you keep running.'

The blue-bricked building towered above them. Adam could see a layer of clouds but no stars. The noise of Glitter didn't even register. He didn't want to go in. For the first time ever, he didn't want to set foot in a nightclub. People there were having fun. He wanted to have fun too. But from where he was sitting, he didn't think he'd ever experience fun again. He wanted to be with his mates, getting high and listening to the latest tracks. Anywhere but here.

Daz grabbed Adam's collar and shook him. 'You hear me?' Daz barked. Again, he clipped him across the head.

'Yes,' shrieked Adam. He wanted to go home, and he wanted to cry.

'You'd better run forever you don't do as I say.' Daz squeezed Adam tight. 'I'll have my boys go to work on you for days.'

Adam nodded hurriedly. He wanted to run. Once this was over. He was going to run and hide. So no one could see him. Then he was going to stay there. Forever if he must.

'You remember what I said?'

'Yes,' said Adam obediently.

'Tell me.'

Adam realised he was trembling. He didn't want to do it, but he recounted the instructions to keep Daz from hitting him.

☺

Clutching a leather satchel, Joe Mann paced past Glitter's lively queue and got a kick out of those angered by his pushing in. Try it, he thought. Joe liked to boast there wasn't a room he couldn't step into and handle himself should the need arise. His confidence came from stripping all types of trucks and cars at his father's scrapyard from a young age. The size and duty of tyres and the bulky engine blocks he'd regularly lift made him see the human body as incredibly fragile. He never gave anyone a second thought, no matter what they said.

Being taller than most, the door staff spotted him coming and allowed him inside. The lead doorman muttered his arrival into a mouthpiece. Joe continued straight past the pay booth, where a girl with a bushy ponytail took money off a swaying drunk. At the bottom of the stairs, the dampened pop music came into clarity as he pushed open the double doors and found himself amid swarms of people enjoying themselves.

Out of the glare of the lights, Joe skirted the dance floor, dodging the happy crowd. He knew his route and, at the far corner, allowed himself access behind the bar and into a maroon-walled corridor, the music and the lights fading behind him. Around the next corner, Joe pushed through the door to Wayne's office to find Wayne peering at the CCTV monitor. Startled, the dope asked, 'You know how to knock?'

At the desk, Joe unzipped and shook the leather satchel empty, the whole time fixing on Wayne to let him know he wasn't pleased to be there. The contents fell onto the wooden surface between them.

'Where's Daz?' asked Wayne keeping track of the parcels landing in front of him. 'I thought we were doing this tomorrow?'

'Busy.' Joe felt the last package fall from the satchel and zipped it shut.

'The cops would be busting in right now they knew anything.'

Who was worried about cops? Joe clocked Dan, standing to the side with his chin raised. It made Joe smirk. The man thought he was in charge because he got to wear a badge.

'Fine.' Wayne waved a hand in dismissal. 'If that's how he wants it, makes no difference.'

'Except you paying double tomorrow. Like D' told you the other day. Don't forget.'

The club's front doors were still bustling when Joe exited, calm as you like. Up ahead, Daz was alone in the Cosworth. That meant the scrawny flake was on his way, and they'd have to do one soon. He wondered if he'd get a chance for a blast. If the cops showed, that'd get them motoring. The tuning he'd done to both Cosworths: the silenced, large bore exhausts that drove two specially imported turbochargers; the re-bored engines with oversized filters; nitrous oxide systems if he wanted to use them; uprated brake discs; wider alloys; stiffened suspension—all wrapped in a subtle body kit to accommodate the race-spec components but not draw attention. Daz said go all out, and Joe knew he had cash, so it was no problem. He'd turned two already rapid sets of wheels into complete savages. Should the worst happen, Joe was in no doubt they had the horsepower to outrun whatever the powers-that-be threw their way. He climbed behind the wheel, said, 'Wayne don't have a clue what's about to happen.'

☺

Adam arrived at the double doors they'd forced early Friday morning. The dark alleyway empty, a brisk breeze made him shiver. Beneath his sweater, his skin was cold and clammy. He could see the repair work done to the lock, now disabled by the beermat poking through the gap between doors. He wanted this to be a joke, to find Will and the lads laughing at him on the other side. How could he be so gullible, they would say. And he'd laugh. They all would. He thought he might cry at the relief. He didn't want to do this, but he was too scared not to. The way Daz and the big guy dragged him to the river, making like they were going to drown him if he didn't do as he was told. It was fear that compelled him. It compelled him to agree, to take the gun, and now it compelled him to enter Glitter. He readied himself and slid inside. There was no happy welcoming party, no laughs or slaps on the back. Just an empty corridor that led to the doors at the far end. He crept low, alert to the slightest of movements. Man, did he want somebody to arrive unexpectedly. So he could turn right around and get out of there. It wouldn't be his fault. He'd tried, but someone stopped him doing it. Right up until he reached the next set of doors, he hoped someone would interrupt so he could run the other way. But no one did. Tentatively, Adam pushed through the doors.

The sights and sounds of Glitter's heaving main room assaulted his senses. Such was his frenzy in the corridor, the rumpus didn't even register. Now, the familiar sights and sounds appeared like they were from another world. A world he once knew. Before all this. He could feel its presence, but he dared not reach out and touch it. He drifted in a bubble, separated from the partying crowd, an uninvited guest. With everyone oblivious to his forced intentions, he wanted to warn them, to tell them to get out now, before the rush. So they would be less scared.

Adam jumped when a drunk bumped into him. Adam willed him to leave, but the drunk staggered on through the club, as though Adam wasn't there. Adam felt the gun's weight. The journey was surreal, and in a moment of clarity, he realised he was straying further from the exit than necessary. Do it now, quickly, he told himself. He could see his path back to the doors. Please, let no one block the escape. He pulled the gun free, reached up with it.

Pulling the trigger, the recoil nearly snapped his wrist. That got his attention. The weapon's power was terrifying. Enough to break a bone. Adam steadied his grip with both hands and, screeching through gritted teeth, pulled the trigger again and again. To get it done. Up in the roof, sparks flew as one then two lights exploded. The shots blasted over the music and, as though they were one organism, the crowd ducked and screamed in unison. The music stopped, and Adam heard the last few shots in all their booming glory before the gun clicked empty. His ears rang, and his heart pounded. All around, people hunched over. No one noticed him. Instinctively he crouched and pulled up his hood. Stooped low, he scurried towards the double doors sharing the same trepidation as everyone he passed. Darting along the corridor, his mind, his heart and his limbs were all racing, and he nearly dropped the gun trying to stuff it under his top. He slammed through the fire doors. Disappearing into the night without breaking stride.

☺

From the front seats, Daz and Joe watched the crowd stream from Glitter. The distant chaos silent, Daz took pleasure watching the mayhem take its course. People were bumping into each other they were so hysterical, their faces twisted with fear and panic. It was like a comedy. The numbers increased rapidly when the fire exit burst open, and a whole new swathe of people emerged in a stampede. The taxi drivers, hanging around their cars waiting for chuck-out time, didn't know what was going on and stood transfixed, watching the road become swamped. Such was the confusion, no one asked them for a lift.

Daz took a drag on his cigarette and let the smoke drift from his mouth. He knew it was only a matter of time before the opportunity came to him. If these kids had a problem with Waync, use it; theirs could solve his. He knew he could intimidate them. It would be easy. Get Joe involved at first, Cal if he really wanted to make his point. They'd soon fall into line. Lewis had set it all off, his call coming through when Daz was about to leave Cal's for the night. Lewis telling how Wayne was taking the night off to attend other business. At first, Daz thought Wayne was scheming against him until Lewis explained Wayne's reaction after some kid put a bottle over his head. Wayne had visited a house and found a girl he gave grief to at the club. Wayne thinks she must have set her man on to him, so what does he do? He kidnaps her. Anyone else, Daz wouldn't have believed it, but Wayne's ego was untapped. As lord of all Glitter, he thought he could do anything. Even by Wayne's standards, this was something different. The man was a liability to himself. Opportunity or not, Daz needed to do something before things got out of control. Stuart wasn't answering his phone, so they took both Cosworths to stake out Stuart and Will. Who else could it be after what he heard over Stuart's the other night? That's when Daz conjured his plan to shoot up the club, out of boredom, waiting in the Cosworth for hours. It was a smart first step. No way Wayne would believe it was anyone else but the kid. It meant Will was his, and Daz could control the fallout in his favour. Tomorrow, Wayne would pay double the usual, which Will could nick and bring to him. It didn't even matter if he didn't play ball, Wayne would still have to pay, and Daz could give Cal a chance to vent his anger on the littluns. If Daz was lucky, maybe he could keep the feud going long enough to make more from other drops. Or set himself up for the easiest protection money anyone had ever earned. He hadn't figured it all out right now.

Daz flicked his cigarette through the window, deviousness lingering on his face. 'Let's go,' he said, 'before you get a chance to run into any innocent bystanders.'

Joe flipped the headlights on and sparked the ignition. He blipped the accelerator to get the revs up and pop the exhaust, then pulled away from the kerb, taking a turning before reaching the unconstrained bedlam that continued outside Glitter nightclub.

☺

Will and Stuart were sitting in silence when the bump at the front door came. It was the moment Will both wanted and dreaded, having decided to wait for Adam before considering what to do next.

Framed by streetlight, a figure leaned against the frosted glass door. Will imagined Adam in a battered heap and opened up, fearful of his friend's condition.

Adam collapsed inside, panting hard.

'Are you okay? Are you hurt?'

Adam nodded and shook his head simultaneously, trying to speak between breaths.

'Are you hurt?'

Stuart arrived, switching his concern from Adam to the street outside. 'Get in, close the door.'

'I can't.' Will indicated Adam was blocking the way. He scanned the two-storey block of flats opposite to see if anyone was on a balcony.

Adam gasped, 'Man, that was insane.'

'What happened?' Stuart said, 'Adam, matey, you want to move away from the door?'

Adam shuffled against the inside wall.

'Tell us what happened?' said Will, trying not to stress Adam further.

With a pained expression, Adam tossed the gun from under his top. Stuart looked along the street with urgency. 'Close the door.'

'Come in, buddy,' said Will trying to coax Adam away from the door. The gun pointed at his feet like it would blow his toes off any second. Adam scrambled clumsily inside. Will shut the door.

'I shot up Glitter, didn't I?!' Adam rolled onto all fours, still catching his breath.

'You fired that?' said Stuart in disbelief.

Adam climbed to his feet, complaining, 'I wanna go, man.'

'Just chill for five,' said Will, 'Come take a seat.'

'Man, I need space.'

'What about that?' Will pointed at the gun. 'It loaded?'

'Empty.' Adam eyed the door like he was about to make a run for it. 'We got to use it tomorrow. To shake him up.'

Will remembered the moment he hit the guy with the bottle.

'Great,' said Stuart.

'It's all set up. We wait outside the multistorey car park nearest Glitter, half ten, tomorrow morning. The man's got a sky-blue Cadillac you can't miss. An American car.' Adam took a breath. 'We follow him, and when he gets out, we take his bag.'

'We're going to be in broad daylight.' Stuart grimaced.

'Hey man, you won't be firing nothing like I did. We gotta make a show of it, like we mean business. A robbery, nothing else. Don't go mentioning the girl.'

Will and Stuart stood there, looking at the gun.

'We get what he's carrying. Then we take it all to Daz's man, the same one as in the car earlier. He'll be outside the Fox and Hounds. The one at Westside Park.'

'You believe this?' Stuart asked Will.

'If it makes any difference,' said Will. 'It's the same guy we robbed Friday.'

'Yeah, right, I suppose that was practice.'

13 / *Ride On Time*

Monday morning, outside Glitter, remnants of the fleeing crowd littered the road. Paper wristbands and cloakroom tickets, plastic cups and discarded flyers kicked up in the dusty air, fluttering past the marked police car parked outside.

Inside the club, Wayne hosted two police officers who regarded him as a blight on their schedule. His clammy palms were sticking to the desk.

DS Jackson said, 'You're adamant you have no knowledge of the perpetrators? No one you suspect my harbour a grudge against your organisation?'

Wayne pleaded his innocence. 'Of course not, officer,' he said, smiling to show he was relaxed. That was a mistake, he realised, as the other one turned sour.

'Mister Moran,' Sergeant Abingale said sternly, 'what Detective Sergeant Jackson would like you to understand, having gunshots fired inside your nightclub is a severe incident. One we are taking extremely seriously.'

Wayne addressed the one in uniform, his bell-shaped hat tucked neatly under an arm. 'I appreciate that.' He looked to the heavens. 'Lord knows I've got a living to make.'

DS Jackson referenced his notepad. 'You reported a break-in last Friday. By what means did you receive that injury?'

Wayne became conscious of the bandage tied around his forehead. He sighed. 'Like I told the two who came Friday, I slipped at home.'

'It's funny.' DS Jackson raised the notepad as if for

confirmation. 'They don't mention it?'

Putting on a show won't have any effect, thought Wayne. 'I don't remember,' he said flatly. 'It's funny what bumps to the head can do.' Never mind it actually happened afterwards. What did it matter to these two stiffs?

'Sir, if you have any concerns, let me assure you we can provide more than adequate protection.'

Wayne could do without the suit's persistence or protection. 'It was probably some kids. What are they on these days, Ecstasy?'

The one in costume didn't like that. 'If anything, that makes the situation worse, Mister Moran.'

'I realise that,' said Wayne backtracking swiftly. 'The point I was making is that it has nothing to do with me.'

'It has everything to do with you, Mister Moran. We want a review of your security, subject to any future licence renewals. Do not forget we have the power to revoke.'

Now the suit was trying to play bad cop. 'I can assure you,' said Wayne, 'I'll be scrutinising my club's security in minute detail.' He added, 'Starting as soon as you leave.'

Jeez, they didn't half want to chat as Wayne, not so politely, ushered them out of Glitter. There's no point concealing your inquiry as casual conversation, he thought, I ain't telling you squat. He skipped over the fact he didn't actually know squat. Granted, he had a girl chained to a radiator in his house. But that wasn't evidence for this. Even if that boyfriend of hers was behind the shooting. He wasn't getting into all that with these two. If the kid liked to play with guns, Wayne had drastically underestimated him. He wanted an end to the situation. Tonight, after his business with Daz, he'd blindfold the girl and drop her outside town. If she reported him to the police, or lover boy persisted, Wayne would set the twenty security guards, who doubled as his alibi, upon them. Who needed police protection.

Wayne finally got the cops to the front door, unsure of anything said on the way up the stairs. He hoped his nods and yesses were appropriately timed. Ignoring their perturbed faces, Wayne closed and locked the door behind them.

They weren't the only ones to keep an eye on. Last night, he'd been working through the ramifications of Joe's unannounced visit when the screaming started. According to the CCTV monitor, his customers were all going nuts. Over the radio, someone shouted, 'gunshots fired.' Wayne didn't like the sound of that. Then he realised the police would be on their way—while the coke was right there in front of him! That got him moving, furiously stuffing the packages into a carrier bag and racing to meet his head of no-good security to have it removed from the premises. He remembered pounding from his office shoving aside terrified customers who'd strayed into the staff only corridor. He bet one of 'em would write to complain about that, like the whole thing was his fault. Miserable leeches, the lot of them.

Wayne was still raging when he returned to the stairs, having removed seventy grand from the safe and stuffed it into the designer shopping bag he now carried. Double! He might have to set some of his heavies on Daz if he kept up this game. He locked the front doors behind him.

Storming along the street, Wayne aimed his silent fury at the establishments opposite, as though it might burn them to the ground. The cops were gone, but he remained oblivious to the approaching woman—he wasn't going to let some mad kid interfere with the running of his nightclub.

'Mister Moran?'

Mid-stride, Wayne was confused as to who this woman was and how she knew his name.

'My name's Kirsty Pry from the *Gazette*. I would be very grateful if I might schedule time for a brief conversation?'

Wayne appraised her suit dress, unimpressed that she thought she could make requests of him without first making an appointment in writing.

Unfazed by his irritation, she added, 'It's about last night's shooting at the club.'

Wayne screamed, 'Fuck off,' so loud, his voice cracked and squeaked.

The woman stopped in her tracks, and Wayne continued on, feeling his dry throat turn sore.

☺

Will, Stuart and Adam were in the Transit, parked along from the multistorey car park. An anonymous office block cast the narrow, dead-end road in shadow. Most workers were in their offices. Those still outside either hurried or looked important enough to dance to their own drumbeat.

Will had formed a plan and was itching to get going. To him, what Daz wanted didn't make sense. How did Daz know this guy, Wayne, wouldn't lead them to Charlotte? Or what if Wayne and Charlotte were together now, on the way to the car park? How could he not mention her? She'd know it was him! Then what were they supposed to do? Presuming neither of those things happened, Will intended to find out about Charlotte when they robbed Wayne no matter what. Then he'd get to her before anyone else. He'd even brought a pocket map to help navigate. For now, Stuart and Adam were none the wiser. It would be better that way.

Once they rescued Charlotte, they'd take the money to Daz's man as agreed. Will was gambling on Daz being placated by whatever they delivered, as required. When Daz no doubt learnt about Charlotte, Will would swear blind she was with Wayne when they robbed him. It was his word versus Wayne's. What could Daz do?

When Wayne came plodding up the street, it got Will sitting up. As much as Will had considered his plan, nothing could have prepared him for that moment. All of a sudden, the situation was very real. Stuart reacted too. It could've been the bandage around Wayne's forehead or the designer shopping bag that gave Wayne away because Will knew Stuart had never seen him before. Adam folded his arms, made wary by their reactions.

Will fastened his seat belt while Wayne entered the car park's graffitied stairwell. 'Let's get this over with.' He reached forward and took three white painters' masks off the dashboard. He gave two to Adam, who kept hold of Stuart's.

Stuart said, 'No offence, Adam, but you stay put. I'll point the gun. Will, you take the bag. We all get out of there.'

'Fine by me, man.'

Will said, 'I'm having the gun. You can hit him if you want.'

Stuart was miffed. 'Why am I hitting him?'

Will needed to be the one in control, not Stuart. 'Just because,' he said, 'You're bigger.'

The sky-blue Cadillac, with its fins and white roof, arrived at the barriers, and Wayne inserted the ticket into the machine. Stuart turned the ignition. The barrier raised, and Wayne's Cadillac exited the car park. Stuart put the van in gear and manoeuvred onto the road.

They followed Wayne at a reasonable distance, but whenever the Cadillac's brake lights popped, Stuart overreacted, pumping the pedals and causing the van to rock back and forth. Normally, Will would've made an issue of Stuart's driving, but he needed him calm. As soon as they caught up with Wayne, Will would be in control.

After a mile or so, the Cadillac turned onto a back street that ran parallel to the town centre shops. It turned another corner, and when they did too, they caught the Cadillac's rear wings zipping into a delivery yard. Will alerted Stuart, but Stuart was already easing off the accelerator.

Stuart checked the mirrors and brought the van to a halt in the middle of the narrow road. Double yellows were painted on both sides. Opposite the yard, a row of commercial bins were lined at the foot of a tall brick building.

Through the slats in the yard's fence, Will could see Wayne reaching onto the rear seat. There weren't any exits besides the one Wayne drove in through—unless he planned to walk into a store's loading bay. But why would he do that? Will became anxious. He'd have to follow on foot if that happened.

Wayne was out of the car and, to Will's relief, started back towards the street. 'When he gets to the road, pull up in front, and we'll do it then,' said Will.

Wayne emerged from the compound carrying the shopping bag. Will positioned the painters' mask over his face. 'Let's go.'

Adam followed Will's lead, pulling his mask on. Stuart put the Transit in gear to begin after him. The engine revved, but the van didn't shoot off. It trundled forward, hardly picking up any pace. Will anticipated the high whine of acceleration, but it didn't occur. What happened, Stuart changed to second and rolled towards Wayne, who was walking away from them, at a pedestrian speed. 'Get in quick,' said Will, wondering what Stuart was doing.

'Nah,' said Stuart, 'I'm going to run him over.'

'What?!'

'Only gently.'

'Gently?!' Beyond Adam, Stuart brimmed with amusement.

'It's easier than hitting him, ain't it, matey?'

'No, not really!'

'Daz don't care how we do it, so long as we don't mention the girl.'

'Her name's Charlotte.'

'Of course it is, matey.'

'What do you mean, of course it is. It *is*!'

'It'll be a harmless accident, matey. One where he loses his shopping in the confusion.'

Adam watched in fascination, eagerly switching between Stuart and Wayne.

If Stuart accidentally killed him, Charlotte would be stuck. At even more risk. 'Don't kill him,' Will blurted.

'Don't be a tart.' Stuart's beady eyes were fixed on Wayne. 'I need to get some street cred back here.'

'Oh yeah, nice one, buddy!'

It wasn't until they were barely six feet away, when Stuart mounted the kerb and the nearside suspension thumped, that Wayne became aware of them. He looked back, despite the thump, like he wasn't expecting a thing. Like he was about to routinely cross the road. But there was a bright-yellow Transit slowly advancing on him, and he panicked wildly.

With a little skip, Wayne started to run like his trousers were loose. He hugged the swanky bag as though to protect it, flicked a terror-stricken glance backwards, and diverted onto the road.

Stuart lazily rotated the wheel to follow Wayne off the pavement. 'Quick, ain't he?'

'Pull up,' yelled Will.

Wayne was looking backwards more than forwards now, his face frantic, his cheeks flushed red. He trotted back onto the pavement, trying to avoid the swerving van.

'I'll get him when he's on the road,' said Stuart, 'It's safer.'

'It is *not* safer,' yelled Will.

Adam sniggered.

Wayne was running faster than his stout legs could carry him. With another thump up the kerb, Stuart swerved after him. Switching into neutral, he gave the engine a burst of throttle, and the clattering howl made Wayne jump. Immediately, he darted back onto the road without the slightest care for traffic.

'There we go.' Stuart slipped the van back into gear. He followed Wayne onto the road and caught him with the faintest increase in revs.

Will pressed his foot into the floor, trying to brake for Stuart, thinking they were going too fast, that they were about to flatten the man. But Stuart stamped on the brake just in time. Tyres shuddered, the van dipped to a halt, and, with a thud, Wayne disappeared from view.

Will watched with an open mouth.

'Hurry up and get the cash then, matey.'

'Hurry up!' yelled Will. He was about to climb out when Wayne popped up beyond the bonnet. Bubbling with so much anger, Will thought he might explode.

Stuart noticed at the same time. Cursing, he popped the van into first, jabbed the accelerator and immediately stamped the brake. There was a jolt and a thud, and Wayne disappeared from view for a second time. 'Go on then,' shouted Stuart, 'quick.'

Will was so furious he would have run Stuart over himself given the chance. 'Arsehole,' he shouted, jumping out to confront Wayne.

Will found Wayne writhing on the tarmac, the carrier bag fallen loose.

'What the mother …!' Wayne half screamed, half spluttered, trying to roll off his back.

Will surveyed the empty street. If a lorry arrived with a delivery, they were screwed. He pinned Wayne to the ground and gripped his collar. 'Where is she?'

'You're dead,' Wayne spluttered.

Will shifted his knee onto Wayne's throat. 'Where is she?'

Wayne groaned as Will increased the pressure, resisting until he could resist no more. 'My house,' he gasped, his voice weak.

Will kept the pressure on. 'If we knew where that was, we'd have been by now.'

'Dawlish Rise!'

'What number?'

'One seven eight!'

'You best not be lying to me.'

With Will's weight on him, Wayne was almost inaudible. 'I'm not!'

'You'd better not be, you want to see that bag again.'

'I'm not.'

Will stepped off, and collected the loose shopping bag from the roadside. Wayne rolled over gasping for air.

As Will climbed into the van, Stuart said, 'Did you do what I think you did?'

'What?'

There was a thud on metal as Wayne got up, clinging to the bonnet, his eyes bloodshot, the bandage around his forehead skew-whiff. 'Give it,' he ordered through the glass.

'Fuck off, matey,' Stuart stuck the van in gear, blipped the accelerator and stamped the brake. With another thud, Wayne and his rage were gone.

Stuart climbed out, complaining, 'I don't know which of you is stupider.'

Will leaned out the window. 'What's the problem?' He knew Stuart wouldn't want to go against Daz.

Stuart clipped Wayne around the head to subdue him, then lifted him by the armpits. 'You want me to leave him here to tell everyone?'

'Tell everyone what? He ain't going to the cops.'

'No, matey, but maybe he'll tell them to move Charlotte somewhere else. Or maybe he actually lied to you. Or maybe his crew are protecting her? Then what? You gonna talk your way out of that?'

Will hurriedly climbed out.

'You're useless, you are.' Stuart dragged Wayne alongside the van.

'I've never done this before.' Will rolled open the side door. 'At least I had the balls to try something.'

Stuart waited for Will to grab Wayne's feet.

'Don't talk to me about balls, matey. I just run this clown over three times.'

☺

Charlotte pulled at the radiator in the dusty old room. She'd given up on Will some time ago and, after hours—days! —of shaking, she'd finally managed to loosen the radiator's fixings. Such was her single-mindedness; she gave scant consideration to the consequences of being caught.

In vain, she called out, but her voice was sapped of energy. She didn't know if Will was with the police or trying to find her himself. Although she suspected she'd have heard about it, it upset her to think he might have been found by Glitter's thuggish bouncers. She hoped he hadn't been hurt or forced to run away.

She maintained her optimism by reminding herself that the radiator's wall fixings were now loose and took hold of it to pull it away from the wall. She had to wait for the creep to leave this morning to get to this point.

Compared to the night before last, when he was quiet and

mostly left her alone, last night, he'd returned very angry. A racket of crashing and shouting downstairs left her praying he wouldn't come anywhere near her. But her nightmare became real when she heard him climb the stairs and approach. She curled into a ball, refusing to engage while he paced the room, shouting and asking her ridiculous questions about guns and blaming Will for a shooting in Glitter. She found that unbelievable. She hadn't known Will long, but at no point did she ever imagine he could be mixed up in that type of thing. She believed the fool was mad and discounted everything he said. Will didn't even want to visit Glitter when she suggested it!

The thought compelled her back to the task at hand. It was her fault she was in this situation. As a result, it was her responsibility to remove herself from it. She needed to detach the handcuff from the water pipe that fed the radiator. The only way she could do this was by lifting and dropping the radiator until the pipe snapped. It might take some time, and water would start leaking, but it was her only option. She'd gone too far with her plan to change tack.

Charlotte dropped the radiator to make the pipe kink then pressed her weight on top to increase the damage. Lifting the radiator was made cumbersome by the handcuffs. They wouldn't allow her to raise her right wrist more than a foot from the floor. She shuffled backwards and, with a grunt, pulled it at an angle before letting it drop again. She huffed and pressed her weight on top.

Charlotte was caught holding the radiator upright when she heard the fast-approaching vehicle skid to a halt. Moments later, the house's front door slammed shut. The house shuddered.

'Charlotte?'

She heard her name, but the voice was unexpected. Her mind must be playing tricks on her. It couldn't be Will, could it? She wouldn't allow herself such a beautiful glimpse of freedom. It was too much to bear. She let go of the radiator and dropped onto the wingback, resigned to her fate.

Her stomach tightened as footsteps pounded up the stairs. There was nothing she could do but hope for a passing visit. The manner of the arrival made her doubt this. She clung to her hopes while the clobber of feet got louder and more intense. All she could do was wait, feeling her muscles tighten further. Please don't come in, she begged silently. The door to the room swung inwards.

☺

Will frisked Wayne for his keys, then shut him in the van. On the move, they removed their masks. Will checked inside the shopping bag and found what must have been tens of thousands of pounds of rolled banknotes beneath neatly folded shirts. 'Wow!' He stuffed the gun in there and shoved it beneath the seat.

'What is it?' asked Stuart.

'Cash.'

Will retrieved the small map and issued directions. Stuart did well to circumvent the town centre traffic, cutting through side roads and using whichever lanes were free regardless of their direction of travel. They left a cacophony of beeping horns in their wake. Stuart wasn't happy, but with the threat to Charlotte, not even he could ignore his conscience.

They joined the A-road, travelling south-east, passing housing estates and rows of commerce. The road was clear and easy to navigate.

Stuart said, 'You need to know what you're getting into, matey.'

'What?'

'Tread carefully,' his tone was as sincere as his glance over.

'How'd you mean?'

'One trip.' Stuart hesitated. 'Back during football days, me and the boys are on an away day in London. We're on the train, and Daz is with us, among the lads, not saying a word while everyone else is having a laugh, doing their best to intimidate Joe Public. The train company announce a problem with the track and move everyone off a stop early. We're doing the last half-mile on foot, singing and chanting, rowdy as you like, when the opposition firm comes bowling round the corner, bats, blades, you name it … The way we moved Daz out of there,' Stuart checked to see if Will was listening. 'We was told to. Like, protect him, or you're dead, told to.'

They were silent until they reached the exit they needed to take. Will tried to see how he could have done anything differently. But if anything, he'd done exactly what he should have. 'What's done's done. You wanted to warn me, you should have said sooner.'

Adam looked at him nervously. Stuart didn't.

Weaving through the upmarket neighbourhood, Will was relieved to spot the sign for Dawlish Rise. With it informing of a dead end, getting trapped became a concern. Will would deal with that if it happened and saw the van hammering along the pavement to escape.

The street was literally on the edge of town. The houses lined only one side, with fields opposite, stretching to the motorway beyond, a hazy streak of concrete embedded between green fields.

Outside Wayne's house, there was no sign of life. The secluded detached property with a wide frontage and short driveway was hidden by a row of pines. Stuart parked across the driveway.

Will dashed across loose gravel to the front door. He found the correct key and rushed in, calling Charlotte's name. There was no reply, but he heard a thud from the room above. He surged up the stairs on a wave of adrenaline. Hoping she was there, he dared not think what condition she might be in. For Wayne's sake, she'd better be unharmed.

On the landing, Will listened carefully. He'd kick every door in if he needed to. His heart pumped. Will approached a door where a chain dangled from the lock. It was at the front of the house, where he heard the thud. His hopes hung on the turn of a key.

Inside, he found a cluster of old furniture and household junk. He thought he saw a reflection in a glass cabinet. Leaning around the door, he found Charlotte in a chequered dressing gown, sitting upright on a chair, her face tense. Beside her, a radiator lay on the carpet.

Her eyes widened. 'Will!' she cried. She tried to rise to her feet but something stopped her halfway.

Will reeled forward. 'Oh, my god. Look at you.'

She shook a restrained wrist as much as she could. 'We need to break this.'

Her eyes were wide and she was handcuffed to a pipe. 'I'll get some tools,' he said, turning on his heel without hesitation.

'Where from?'

'The van,' he said over his shoulder, passing through the door and back down the stairs at a sprint. He couldn't believe he was here.

'Hurry up,' she shouted after him.

Pacing outside, Will called to Stuart, 'Bolt cutters.'

Stuart, who'd been hovering by the side door, opened up and pulled a heavy-duty canvas bag from inside the bulkhead. With the door open, Wayne complained about his treatment and the pain in his hip. In unison, Will and Stuart told him to shut it.

Stuart found the bolt cutters and waved them at Wayne. 'You're lucky we don't use these on you.'

Will snatched them off Stuart before he did any damage.

Returning inside, Charlotte was back in the seat. She watched as Will placed the pincers around the pipe and squeezed. The paint flaked as the pipe narrowed then sheered with a satisfying ping. Brown water sloshed onto the horribly patterned carpet.

Charlotte shook the cuff free and whimpered with delight. Will took hold of her wrist and carefully manoeuvred the heavyweight tool between her skin and the metal ring. Closing the pincers, the metal snapped apart with a brittle click.

It required great effort to stretch open the ring of metal. Charlotte placed her free hand over Will's and pulled with him. In her desperation, she tried to remove her wrist too soon, and the jagged metal scored her skin.

'Wait,' said Will, changing his approach. He repositioned the bolt cutters and clipped through the opposite side. The ring's two parts dropped to the floor.

Charlotte bounded to her feet. Will could tell her mind was racing. They faced each other, and with the eye contact, she seemed to calm. It didn't feel like they needed to speak. Charlotte's expression of delight was all Will cared for. After a moment, she noticed the mucky water pooling around her slippers.

'Shall we get going?' she asked.

When they exited the house, Stuart slid from the passenger seat and, without thinking, heaved the van's side door open. Wayne looked up with a hot, sweaty face and Charlotte blenched at the sight of him. Will let her know she was protected, but her reaction gave Wayne a minor victory.

Wayne's fixation on her was so intense, he didn't notice Stuart stepping into the hold until Stuart gripped him by the shirt. A moment of surprise flashed over Wayne's face before his indignation returned. 'What you doing? Get off.'

'Shut it,' said Stuart as he pulled Wayne unceremoniously from the van.

After guiding Charlotte onto the front seat, Will watched in the wing mirror as Stuart sent Wayne stumbling onto his driveway. Charlotte was watching too.

'Are we leaving him there?' she asked, 'Why aren't we taking him to the police?'

Will didn't have an answer for her. They were running on impulse. Stuart finished barking instructions at Wayne and slammed the side door.

Will said, 'We'll call them.'

She was suspicious of his answer.

Stuart climbed in and appraised their charge. 'All right?' he asked in greeting.

Charlotte studied him cautiously. 'Hi,' she said before turning to Will.

Will realised she was looking for him to take the lead. 'Can we get out of here?' he asked.

'Right, matey.' Stuart turned the ignition and put the van in gear.

Pulling away, Will watched Wayne's shrinking reflection become clouded in smoke.

14 / *Sinister Strings*

Carrying a white cardboard shopping bag, Daz rode the shopping centre escalator up towards the horseshoe of fast food outlets. It must have been the school holidays because the place was packed with mothers and their energetic brats going wild for colourful tat. He could tolerate the irritation since it provided cover for his meeting with Wayne, arranged for a table in the food hall. *If* Wayne showed. If Daz's plan worked, he wouldn't. Or he'd be late, armed with an excuse that, although Daz knew it to be true, would be dismissed.

Daz placed the tray of wrapped food at an empty table, set down the shopping bag containing old books, and took a seat. His business was as easy as that. Waiting on the call from Joe, he retrieved his phone. He liked people to see him with it, an expensive device that demonstrated his success, and was happy for it to sit next to his food so long as it didn't get covered in grease. He didn't want to miss Joe's call and expected good news. Joe would report that Will had done as he was told and that the money was in his possession. Wayne would be none the wiser, and Daz would be on his way to an extra seventy thousand for doing not much at all. Daz would savour Wayne arriving in person, as out of sorts as he would be out of pocket. Daz would put the old fool in no doubt the situation was unacceptable. What Daz would offer as a solution depended on Wayne's reaction and how much information he shared. Knowing Wayne as he did, Daz thought he'd be fuming, and if he came straight here, would vent his fury about the kid who robbed him at gunpoint. He hoped Wayne could keep it together, not to scare any nearby mums and their irritating little darlings.

Daz had a mouthful of burger when his phone rang. He took a napkin and wiped his fingers clean before answering.

Joe's voice came on the line, said, 'We got a no show.'

Daz felt his grip on the phone tighten as his anticipation turned to annoyance.

☺

The Transit left Dawlish Rise and followed the same route back towards the town centre. Will felt Wayne's keys in his pocket, unwound the window, and launched them into a garden hedge. Charlotte remained alert to the road ahead.

'Are you okay?' asked Will.

'Fine.' Her view barely left the road.

'Did anything happen to you? You know …'

'No. Thank god.' Her attention briefly passed in Will's direction, and he glimpsed irritation in her sideways glance.

'Right.' Will pressed play on the cassette deck and set the volume.

Charlotte pressed stop. 'Where are we going?'

'We've got to get this finished,' said Will.

'I thought you said you'd call the police.'

'I'm going to.'

Why not now?' She pointed. 'There's a phone box there. While there's still evidence of me being at his.'

They were approaching a row of shops. Will hesitated. Then, as though he was tired of hearing it, Stuart said, 'What evidence?'

'I'm sorry?' asked Charlotte.

'I said, what evidence? What is there evidence of?'

'Err, my kidnapping?'

Stuck between Charlotte and Stuart, Adam switched between the two, anticipating confrontation.

'No, there isn't. You're here.'

'Stu, mate,' cautioned Will, urging him to keep calm.

'I pulled a radiator off the wall,' she said as a matter of fact.

Stuart sighed. 'He can explain that however he wants.'

'I'll do it then.'

'Fine, you do that. All I'm saying, there's not much we can say that he can't deny.'

A frown fell across Charlotte's brow, her attention returned to the road.

'We got you out,' said Will, trying to keep things upbeat. 'We'll have you home in no time.' He wanted to believe it, but he realised now they were at a beginning, not an ending. He wanted—no, he *had*—to protect her from repercussions. He had to know there wouldn't be any, to keep her safe until then.

In the town centre, the streets bustled with office workers. It was lunchtime, and the delis boasted queues outside. Some workers ate from paper bags as they walked. They were getting close to the pub arranged for their rendezvous, and Will was glad to see people in the streets.

Westside Park was a diamond of fields west of the town centre. A convenient space for shoppers and workers to congregate at lunch, as they were today, when the weather was nice. The Transit followed the south-western edge, where joggers plodded through a rose garden. They passed the children's play area and recently built tennis courts. The courts were empty, but the play area was heaving with mums and their children, enjoying the holidays.

The Fox and Hounds was at the far end, away from the bustle of commerce. Its reputation suffered despite its recreational location. On match days, it was an early meeting point for those going to the game. The first of a dotted string of pubs that led to the town's football stadium.

The pub stood desolate, abandoned like a supporters' bus during a game. Will saw the row of picnic tables where he was meant to meet the big guy, Joe, and wished he was still there.

'He's gone,' said Stuart flatly.

'He could be inside,' said Will.

'No, we're too late.'

'Park up anyway.'

Stuart pulled into the car park and looked impatiently to Will, who gathered the shopping bag. 'Are you coming?' he asked.

'Not likely,' said Stuart, 'This is all you.'

Will couldn't tolerate Stuart's blame game and got out of there.

The single-storey pub was purpose-built in the seventies and displayed Fox and Hounds in large gold-coloured lettering. A concrete car park surrounded it on three sides, like a gritty, urban moat keeping nature at bay. Plants in window boxes were poorly maintained, littered with cigarette butts and empty fag packets. Next to the door, a blackboard promoted the upcoming football season like it couldn't come soon enough.

Inside was a single, characterless room furnished in a modern style. Behind the bar, lined with brass taps, the barman looked up lazily from his paper when the door rattled. Horse racing entertained the old-timers who sat, each at their own table, behind a newspaper and solitary pint. Football memorabilia and pictures of celebrated players covered the walls. Will knew Stuart was right. Defeated, he headed outside, past the picnic tables where his fated rendezvous should have occurred.

'I told you,' complained Stuart through the driver's window like Will needed to hear it.

Will's irritation burst through. 'What do you want me to do about it?'

'Call him, dickhead.'

Will threw his arms up and returned towards the pub.

This time the barman looked up with more urgency. Will called over, 'You got a phone?' and the barman pointed a finger at the far wall. One was positioned between the toilet doors.

Will dropped in a coin and dialled the number he'd scrawled on the map. After an anxious moment, he heard an engaged tone.

☺

Daz rode alongside Joe, caught in lunchtime traffic. At first, he wasn't sure where to go but told Joe to drive while he figured it. What troubled him was the opportunity. Or his lack of ability to see it. Working through the situation, he decided there wasn't one until he knew what happened. For now, finding Will was the priority. Then, when he did, he'd strike hard and take it from there. He made his decision and told Joe to head for Will's flat. Daz didn't think Will would be stupid enough to return there straight away, but at least he'd be able to send him a message.

With Joe inside Will's flat, Daz impatiently twirled the phone in his palm, waiting and wondering about who he'd hear from first, Will or Wayne. They said there was two sides to every story, but Daz didn't give a damn about either of theirs. It was a case of how he'd react. The pair of them interfering with his business in their own unique way. He'd be better off rid of them both.

Spotting opportunities was all you needed. Daz knew it in school. Forget standing in English and have the class laugh at you, stuttering through, barely able to read. That's why he started bunking off there. He bunked off maths because he could do arithmetic better than all of them and didn't see the point going. What else did you need maths for? Geometry was stupid. Most teachers were lazy, that's why they gave you homework. The only thing school ever offered him was the cane. Daz had been running errands for Cal's brothers for years, and pushed to let him take on more. After that, he stopped going to school completely. Cal had already left. They were both sixteen. All the school board could do was write to their mothers, insisting they went to night school to sit the exams. Talk about clueless. Bailing early was the right decision. Get ahead of the geeks that liked technicalities. Hash was easy to shift on the estate. Once he had that covered, Cal's brothers got him into whizz, sometimes brown. He wasn't always sure what colour he carried out to the counties, but they all added to his totals. By his estimations, he'd be a cash millionaire before he hit forty, a little under five years. Not bad for a dropout with zero qualifications.

When Daz's phone beeped, he registered the familiar number and placed the phone to his ear. 'Yeah?'

'We've had a problem,' Wayne said over the line, 'You'll have to head to the club for your dough. Later tonight.'

'You decide that would be easier?' said Daz. 'Your problems ain't mine.' Through the driver's window, Daz watched Joe exiting Will's flat carrying the TV.

Wayne sounded like he was trying to keep a lid on it. 'I don't know if being robbed is easier.'

'Why you always stalling, fella? Three times now.'

'Stalling! Don't make me laugh. You know I'm good for it.'

'If I saw it, I'd believe it. How you get robbed?'

'It's nothing. Some kid. I took his girl 'cause he got bold.'

Knowing full well, Daz said, 'You had his girl?' Then he spotted the opportunity. 'How'd you manage that, then, Wayne? What happened?'

☺

At the phone in the Fox and Hounds, Will slotted the coin and re-dialled the number scrawled on the map. With the dial tone, he huddled against the wall so as not to be heard. He'd keep it cool, let Daz know he had everything he wanted, that there was no problem.

When Daz answered, Will said, 'I got your money. Here. Now. How do I get it to you?'

Daz said, 'You had your chance. Now I wanna see what happens when Wayne gets hold of you.'

Daz knew already. Will said, 'Let's not mess about.'

'That girl must be something special.'

'What did you think I'd do?'

'I'm waiting to see. The man's offered ten K to find you.'

Will hadn't expected to hear that. 'To get however much is in that bag? It's not worth their while turning me in.'

'You said it, fella. What else they gonna do?'

Will searched for the words that would make everything okay but he couldn't find them.

Daz said, 'You should have done what I told you.'

'And then what would've happened?'

'Who knows now.'

'Look,' said Will, 'if all that matters is money, I'll throw you another ten. You know how much I can make from my parties?'

'That all you got?' said Daz, 'You know what, let's see how this one plays.'

The line went dead.

Will stared at the keypad, considering options. He pressed the receiver's catch then dialled the emergency services. When the operator answered, he said, 'A young woman has been kidnapped.'

'Pardon me, did you say kidnapped?'

'Yes. A young woman has been kidnapped. If you go to one

seven eight Dawlish Rise, you'll find all the evidence you need. This is not a hoax.' Will replaced the receiver and left the pub, nodding at the watching barman who'd nothing better to do.

Will traipsed between the faded wooden benches to the waiting Transit, trying to show a brave face. Stuart watched him expectantly as he rounded the front of the van and climbed in next to Charlotte.

'Well?' asked Stuart.

Charlotte asked, 'What's going on?'

'He was engaged at first,' said Will.

'Did you call the police?'

'Yes.'

'What did he say?' asked Stuart.

'I don't know.'

'You don't know?'

'We've got to wait.'

'What for?'

'Are you in trouble, Will?'

'Can we please go?'

Stuart started the motor. 'Where?'

'I don't think it matters for now.'

Stuart's frustration bubbled over. 'Speak sense, matey.'

Charlotte said, 'Tell me what's going on.'

☺

In the brick-walled basement, the heat from the lamps caused Cal's scarred forehead to sweat heavily. Being in the hot, sickly room was the most annoying thing to happen to him that day. As far as days went, it was a decent one. This afternoon, he came downstairs to find his scrawny younger brother, Leigh, passed out, TV blaring. Amongst all the junk, the discarded food boxes, empty beer cans and overflowing ashtrays, the lightweight, no-hoper had left a two-litre bottle of cider untouched. Never one to let booze go to waste, Cal drank it for breakfast. The sweet cider made his tongue furry so he woke Leigh and sent him to buy some lager to celebrate his win and take the edge off. Bored of the lame TV shows and being alone, he went into the bedroom for a wank before the rest of his booze arrived and made him too pissed to have one later. Life could be boring as anything when your reputation meant the filth would come knocking if you so much as flicked a cigarette onto the street. It was why he never went out these days. Just when needed. But even then, keeping a low profile. No way was he going back inside. Every now and then, Daz talked about giving him a proper day out. A chance to go nuts and let rip on someone or something, but it never happened. Maybe Daz was playing him for a fool, running his mouth to get help. Maybe he'd have to give ol' Dazza a slap to keep him in line if he maintained the chatter with no action coming at the end. He could feel himself getting aggy, but then the lager arrived, so he downed a couple of cans to wash it away and leave him fuzzy for a bit. Leigh wanted a spliff and ventured into the basement to get some of the buds he'd picked the other day. Leigh took an age, so when the fuzz faded enough for him to care, Cal went after him to stop the twerp smoking too much of his profits. Lucky for him, he wasn't. In fact, the dozy oik was being useful for once. Or trying to anyway because he didn't have the strength to carry the male plants up the stairs. He stood there like a mardy ponce, and Cal was about to tell him to chop them if they didn't yield any sweet stuff. But from the grubby boards, the house phone started ringing. He was in a good mood, so he answered, saying, 'Puff factory.'

'Be ready,' said Daz, 'I think I got you your day out.'

'Have people fucked up?' asked Cal, but Daz had already hung up. Cal liked the response and smirked deviously. If Daz was pissed off, today really was a good day.

☺

Will felt the tension in the Transit. Charlotte had her arms folded, her eyes glued to the road in front, while Stuart took them around the town centre for what felt like the umpteenth time that day, cursing the traffic and every situation that didn't go his way: a red light, someone not letting him turn across traffic even though they were in a queue, a ditherer at a roundabout. At first, Charlotte released her displeasure through sighs and little shakes of the head. On the other side of the van, Stuart wasn't aware, increasing his tirade against anything that moved, barking insults and profane criticism until Charlotte let rip. Will could see it coming.

'Shut up,' she yelled as Stuart launched another verbal attack. Adam jumped, startled. She screamed into her lap. 'I can't take this anymore. I've got to go. I want to go. Let me out.'

She lunged across Will to make an escape, and he had to restrain her. 'You can't,' he pleaded, 'You're in pyjamas. We're going to yours now.' It couldn't come soon enough, but at the same time, Will was still worried Daz or Wayne would come looking for her.

Without a hint of sympathy, Stuart barked, 'It's the traffic. If it wasn't for that, we'd be there by now. All right? Keep it together, will you.'

'Get stuffed.'

Stuck between the two of them, Adam shifted uncomfortably.

'We'll be there in five minutes,' urged Will.

Charlotte turned on him. 'I've asked you what's going on, but you won't tell me. I don't know what to make of you or anything else anymore.'

Will tried to calm her. 'It'll be okay.'

'Don't say that. How can it be okay if you won't tell me anything.'

If he told her, Will wanted to persuade Stuart to drive somewhere safe, but he feared that would only make things worse. 'I don't know where to start,' he said.

'Try.'

'He messed up. That's what happened,' complained Stuart. 'Tell her.'

'We didn't have a choice.'

'*You* did,' insisted Stuart.

'I couldn't leave her with him.'

'You should have gone to the police,' said Charlotte.

If Daz wasn't outside his flat yesterday, he would have. 'I was going to!'

'What were you doing at that pub?'

Will hesitated. 'We had to meet some guys who helped us find you.'

'But they weren't there?'

'No.'

Stuart muttered to himself.

Will said, 'Let's get you some clothes from your place. And then, before we do anything else, we go somewhere to think it through. Get our stories straight.'

'If you haven't done anything wrong, there's nothing to get straight, Will.'

'If we went to a hotel, we'd have space to take a step back.' He added, 'I'll pay.'

'I'm not going to a hotel.'

'So I'm still taking you to yours?' asked Stuart in frustration.

'Yes, to mine,' insisted Charlotte.

'Great.'

On the terraced street, they found a space close to Charlotte's digs. Her Golf was parked outside. The house appeared unaffected by events within. Leaflets protruded from the letter box, black bin bags were dotted along the road waiting to be collected. A weed grew from her front step, directly on the street.

Charlotte viewed the house cautiously. 'Will you go in for me?'

'If you want me to.'

'I haven't got my keys.'

Will hated himself for what she'd been through. 'What's the best way, Stu?'

Stuart huffed and climbed out. He approached the wooden front door with its frosted window and, after a quick scout around, jabbed his elbow into a bottom pane. It shattered with a brief clink. Stuart carefully reached through and unlocked the door from inside.

Will asked Charlotte, 'What do you want?'

'There's a biggish bag under the bed. Throw in some clothes from the wardrobe, some shoes and my jewellery box from beside the bed. My coats are hanging in the hall. Grab a light one. That'll be fine.'

Climbing behind the wheel, Stuart said, 'All yours.'

'Which one's your room?'

'Upstairs at the front.' Charlotte pointed.

'Okay.' Will opened the door and stepped down. 'Adam, come with, will you?'

Adam apologetically squeezed past Charlotte and followed Will into the narrow hallway that led to the living room. Will partly expected to find Wayne, or even Daz, waiting for him, but the room was empty. A knitted blanket hung off the couch. The TV played idly to the feminine space with its pastel-coloured cushions over cream throws. A noticeboard laden with pins and takeaway leaflets hung on one wall; two posters, one of a topless male model holding a kitten, the other of the Chippendales, hung on another. A staircase led up directly from the room, and a full-length mirror stood in the opposite corner. Will realised the room must have been exactly as it was when Wayne took Charlotte. 'Let's get this done,' he said, imagining them having to make a swift exit through the back door.

Charlotte's bedroom was very tidy. Beyond the double bed, a modern, white dresser was stacked with books on one side and beauty products on the other. Will could easily identify Charlotte's furniture because none of it matched the beige curtains, emerald green carpet and old teak wardrobe. He found the canvas bag beneath the iron bedstead and put the jewellery box inside. Adam watched as Will opened the wardrobe. 'You get the shoes, yeah?' Will pointed to the two rows at the bottom, and Adam stooped to collect them. Will grabbed underwear from a drawer and chucked them into the bag. Then he waited with an armful of clothes while Adam fussed getting the shoes in. Will folded the garments in half, dumped them on top, and zipped the bag shut. Adam waited for Will's instruction. 'Let's go,' said Will.

Following Adam along the hallway, Will said, 'Grab a coat.'

Adam removed a grey one and looked to Will for confirmation.

'Fine.'

Upon exiting the house, Charlotte called from the passenger window, 'Could you get my keys too. I think they're by the TV.' Will passed Adam the canvas bag before returning inside.

The request for her keys forced him to confront something he'd been trying to ignore, the fact that Charlotte may not want to know him any longer. She could barely contain her contempt asking him to fetch the keys, it was written all over her face.

It felt like a ginormous schism had opened between them. He tried to ignore his feelings since he wasn't able to talk to her about them right now. But beyond today, the outlook seemed bleak. Maybe he'd find the words to rescue them.

Will found the keys on the cabinet as she'd said. Since he was there, he switched off the TV. The silence was eerie, retreating through the room. Having seen for the first time Charlotte's home, he departed with a greater sense of her character.

Adam waited by the Golf hugging the bag. Charlotte was so relieved to see Will holding her keys, she couldn't help but smile and turned to open the van's passenger door, eager to get out of there.

In the same moment, the shrieking roar of an engine accelerating hard echoed along the street. The noise caused both Will and Adam to jump. Charlotte was startled, too, and searched for the source. It arrived at a breakneck pace, beyond the yellow Transit, the black, bulging saloon with its tinted windows. In the second it took Will to realise who it was, the Transit stuttered into life. Rattling from the kerb, it accelerated through the gap between the saloon and the Golf, leaving Will with a flash of Charlotte's startled face before he was in full view of his assailants.

The two guys with Daz were as surprised as Will to see the Transit leave. They turned to Will like it was his fault. The big one at the driver's door was the one from yesterday. The other, emerging from the rear door, had the appearance of an alcoholic street fighter with a scarred face and muscular frame. On both clenched fists, he wore knuckledusters.

Like a maniac, the one with the knuckledusters spread his arms wide and took exaggerated steps forward, raising his knees and hopping between steps like a bird of prey about to take off. 'Where you going?' he asked, revelling in his intimidating performance.

Will was frozen to the spot, stupefied by the rapid change in circumstance. The maniac pounced upon Adam, pushing him in a burst of motion that began with the straightening of his legs and ended with his outstretched palms launching into Adam's chest. It catapulted Adam into the brickwork between the front door and window of Charlotte's house, sending her bag into the air.

With the impact, Adam grunted and struggled with consciousness. The maniac hovered over his static form like a child over an ants' nest, choosing whether or not to stomp. Deciding against further violence, the maniac laid the full weight of his fury on Will, who fought a growing surge in his bladder.

☺

Charlotte was alarmed when the growling, shrieking car arrived at speed. She didn't like the look of the vicious thugs one bit. Neither did Stuart, judging by his actions, propelling them along the street as fast as the rust bucket's languid motor would allow.

'What, where are you going?' asked Charlotte feeling a degree of panic.

Stuart didn't reply. Foot to the floor, he took the junction at the end of her street with a daring that bordered on insane. Keeping it no slower than twenty, he took a chance on a break in traffic. He yanked the wheel sharply left and caused the tyres to shudder across the tarmac until they travelled straight along the next road.

'Are you nuts?' she yelled.

Terror etched across Stuart's face. For a large guy capable of protecting himself, reacting in this manner gave her the jitters. Who or what were they running from? She'd never seen them before and had no intention of introducing herself. Whatever caused it, she wanted out. None of it mattered anymore. Will, the sick creep from the club, this guy Stuart, they could rot. She was in good health and intended to keep it that way. As soon as the van stopped, she'd jump and run, pyjamas or not. But the van didn't stop. At the first sign of a delay, Stuart would take the next available turning. Left, right, the direction of travel didn't matter. All lanes were open to him. Keeping the van moving at all costs was his only intention. It would be a relief if the police pulled them over.

'Slow down,' she said. 'Where are you going?'

'Trust me,' said Stuart, scanning the road ahead for potential obstacles.

Further on, he confidently manoeuvred the van through a housing estate and onto a main road flanked by newly built offices and a leisure centre. Shaken by the rapid series of turns, Charlotte felt travel sick. Stuart followed the sweeping camber up past local shops towards another housing estate and a junction that served the dual carriageway. So far as she could be, Charlotte was relieved to see him take the dual carriageway, not wanting a repeat of the maze-like trip through the housing estate that left her feeling ill.

They cruised at fifty-five, the engine no longer straining like it might explode at any moment. She'd been seconds from claiming her car keys and speeding off to her parents' house, where she could begin to plan how to never have to see Will and his cronies ever again. What was going on with these people? The designer shopping bag held clues, but how far did she want to delve? It wasn't until Stuart sped through the housing estate, bouncing her around in her seat, that she'd spotted the rolls of banknotes popping out from the bag. That got her thinking. What if Will was planning to pay for her release? His parties made money. It wasn't impossible.

Charlotte took a moment to allow her heartbeat to settle,

carefully gauging Stuart before she spoke. He focussed intensely, presumably contemplating the situation they were in. Calmly, she asked, 'What's going on?'

His answer, when it came, was full of frustration. 'We're out,' he said, 'as far as we can. We're out.'

'*We*?' she asked but thought better of antagonising him further. 'I mean …'

'Those guys back there, they don't care.'

'I know,' she said, 'Try to calm down.'

Stuart shook his head, stifling an irritated laugh, like she'd insulted him. 'I tried to warn him.'

'When?'

'You don't get it, do you? You're from a different world. You don't know the people you're dealing with.'

'I thought you and Will were mates?'

'They'll stop at nothing. They're complete headcases. If I hadn't got us moving, who knows what would've happened. Especially to you.' Stuart nodded at her breasts.

Charlotte became aware of her flimsy attire. 'Really?' She adjusted her dressing gown.

'Too right. What do you think I was trying to explain to you earlier?'

Is that what that was, thought Charlotte. Disturbed by Stuart's version of reality, she pictured the three thugs approaching Will. 'If Will's in as much danger as you think he is, we can't leave him with them.'

'What else can we do?'

'Without wanting to sound like a broken record, what about the police?'

Stuart pursed his lips and shook his head.

'What are you afraid of?'

'Nothing.'

'Really?'

'Really. The thing is, I don't *really* know anything. I may know of those guys. But I've got nothing concrete on them.'

'The police don't know they have Will.'

'I know his name's Daz, and I know his phone number. That's about it. And let's be honest, a dealer named Daz ain't nothing special.'

'It depends what you mean by special.'

'Don't get all high and mighty. You're into the scene too.'

'Yeah, for the music.' She wondered how she was going to get out of this. 'What about the money?' she asked, 'In there.' Charlotte nudged the shopping bag with her foot.

Stuart hesitated. 'We stole it … Those guys, they wanted us to take it from the guy whose house you were at. Things got messed up.'

'Clearly.'

'Listen, I ain't stopping you do nothing you don't want to. But I ain't letting you go until I know you ain't going to ruin things.'

'Like how?'

'Bleating to the cops for a start. You do that, there's no way I can come back. I'm gone, proper underground.'

'And the money?'

'That's coming with me. That's all I've got.'

Charlotte couldn't believe the gall of this guy, abandoning his mates without a second thought. He wanted the money, nothing else, no matter how he dressed it up.

'Why don't you come with me,' said Stuart, 'I'll protect you.'

Charlotte couldn't believe what she was hearing.

'What else you going to do? The way those guys think, you took it from them as much as I did.'

Charlotte was indignant. 'I did not.'

Stuart's brow tightened. 'I'm telling you, you did. And don't think you can go giving it back. Will made that mistake. They'll own you before they let you go.'

'I don't know any of you,' said Charlotte, her voice rising. 'I don't know you. I don't know this Daz guy. Any of his scumbag mates. I barely know Will.'

'You're wrong. Trust me.' Stuart looked across at her, compelling her to believe him. 'They know you. That's the point. And they'll stop at nothing.'

Charlotte couldn't face him. He genuinely believed what he was saying.

'All I'm saying is think about it, the two of us. We need to stick together.'

15 / *Underground*

Will's attention was locked on the maniac who slowly stalked towards him.

Daz asked, 'Got what's mine?' He pulled a cigarette from a packet and lit it.

Will hoped a series of questions from Daz would deter the maniac, restraining him from further violence. 'It was in the van.'

'That's a shame, innit.'

The maniac sprang, grabbing Will with calloused hands and, after swinging him half-circle, released him into the Golf from close range. The keys flew from Will's grip. Winded, he felt a sharp sting in his ribs. Will tried to gather himself but, gasping for air, he was pulled backwards, terror sweeping over him. Pinning him against the metalwork, the snarling maniac used his forearm to snare Will at the neck. Barely able to raise his head, Will saw Daz stoop to retrieve the keys and compared their badge to the one on the tailgate.

'I'm having it,' said Daz, tossing the bunch to the massive guy who watched from the flank, preventing an escape on that side.

Daz indicated Adam. 'Get that one. Follow us.'

The maniac held Will while the massive guy swapped keys with Daz and lifted Adam as easily as Charlotte's bag of clothes.

'Showtime,' rasped the maniac, swinging Will off the bodywork and onto the rear seat. He climbed in next to Will and slammed the rear door. Daz got behind the wheel.

They rumbled through town. Will stayed flat, resisting any and all movement for fear of riling the maniac further. Slumped next to Will, he strained two cigarettes one after another in no more than a few drags each. Then, peering around the front seat, he talked to Daz in low, gruff whispers, incomprehensible to Will and enough to spike his paranoia.

He wondered what state Adam must be in. He imagined Charlotte's Golf following behind with Adam in a similar position and the wrecking ball at the wheel. Charlotte and Stuart were gone. The flash of surprise on Charlotte's face as Stuart pulled away told him Stuart must have reacted impulsively. If he knew of the maniac, Will didn't blame him. There was a faint hope he might return to get them out of this. It was all Will could cling to. He tried to ignore the tremor that ran through his body but it was inescapable.

The growling engine fell silent. Will felt a tight squeeze on his bicep.

'Get up,' barked the maniac.

Will obeyed, not wanting to give the maniac further cause for violence, but a sharp pain stabbed him in his ribs. He collapsed onto the rear seat.

The maniac showed no sympathy and dragged Will from the tinted cabin into glaring daylight. Will landed next to an unkempt front garden, overgrown, with brambles running through foot-long grass. Across the road were council semis painted in pale pastels. No saviours could be seen through the upstairs windows. Will passed into the shadow of the house. The Golf was nowhere to be seen. He jolted sideways, bumping over the doorstep, his body scraping the frame before the maniac dropped him onto a stinking, worn-thin carpet. Daz closed the windowless door behind him.

'Where?' asked the maniac.

'Basement.'

'He'd better not touch none of it.'

Daz stepped over Will. 'Give him a slap he does.'

The maniac's rancid hands were on Will again, lifting him, pulling him through a rank, squalid living room with ripped wallpaper and stained couches. A smaller, equally unhealthy version of the maniac lounged on the seat next to the TV. Confused by the scene, he chose to ignore it and returned to the inane gameshow.

Being dragged around a chair, Will gritted his teeth, suffering his stinging ribs. Above him, the scowling maniac kicked at a door with his heel. The next room was dark. Will thumped backwards down a flight of wooden stairs, his ribs getting hammered. As they descended, the environment became warm and sickly, and a drab glow emanated from beyond.

Released onto a dusty concrete floor, the maniac was back on Will, twisting him to face the radiant heat: a series of hot lamps above a crop of cannabis plants. The light reflected off tin foil taped over the brick walls and low ceiling.

'Don't you touch none of those,' barked the maniac before the knuckleduster wrapped across Will's face, and he landed heavily. Will lay still, listening to footsteps ascend the staircase, suffering the dust around his bleeding mouth and nostrils.

When the door above him clicked shut, removing all natural light, Will pushed up into a sitting position to relieve himself from the filth. He pinched the bridge of his nose and sent a trail of bloody snot onto the dirty floor, freeing his airways. Will wiped away the remaining residue with his sleeve.

Moments later, the door opened again. Will froze. In silhouette, the wrecking ball pulled Adam's slender frame into the gloom. With the sole of his boot, he stamped on Adam. 'Get in there,' his voice booming in the bare, underground cell. Without waiting for Adam to comply, he left, taking the light from above with him. Unsure if Adam could move of his own accord, Will waited.

He dared not make any more noise than necessary. Eventually, Will limped to the staircase, a simple wooden frame with no partition to prevent a drop to the concrete below.

Will found Adam staring blankly up at the ceiling. Upon contact, he jumped and took a moment to search Will's face but didn't show recognition. Will persuaded Adam to come down. He did so shellshocked, showing no understanding of where he was or what he was doing.

Sitting against the wall, Adam drew in his knees to his chest and rested his forehead on his arms. There was a lump where his head had made contact with the wall of Charlotte's house. Will suspected concussion and tried to reassure him, but not much Adam said in response made sense.

Waiting in the drab gloom, Will assessed his bruised ribs, contemplating the bleakness of his immediate future. Will wondered what Stuart would do now? What would Charlotte say to him? Would she make him come looking for them? As each second passed, this seemed increasingly unlikely, a delusion to help him get through it.

After some time, Daz and the maniac returned. Will huddled against the wall, unable to prevent them descending the stairs. When they reached the basement floor, Adam whimpered.

Without warning, the maniac tore across and stamped on Adam, sending him sideways with a sickening yelp.

'What you looking at?' he barked at Will.

Daz said to the maniac, 'They need to be with it.' Then he focussed on Will. 'They need to dig.'

Daz gripped Will's collar and brought his face close. 'When I tell you to do something, you do it. Understand?'

Will didn't have time to agree; Daz slapped him hard.

That was how it started. For how long the strikes continued, Will wasn't sure.

☺

They'd been travelling in silence for nearly an hour. Perversely, the time passed quickly because Charlotte was glad of the peace. She leaned against the passenger door with her arms folded. Stuart had taken them off the dual carriageway and onto the motorway, travelling north. She wondered if he actually believed she was considering his offer. Did he genuinely think she could be intimidated into a relationship? Because what else would it be if the two of them stayed together with the money, avoiding all trace of their previous lives. It was plausible. But really? Her with this guy? He was no different to the unsavoury types they'd left behind. Wayne was clearly deranged. With the number and types of people in his employ, it was an unlikely bluff that he could arrange a false alibi. She'd barely seen the three thugs that terrified Stuart. Let alone been seen by them. It seemed far-fetched that they'd want to pay her any attention, despite what Stuart conveniently believed. But if they did, without Stuart on her hip, they'd never find her. He was a burden if anything. Surplus to requirements.

Who knew what would happen to Will? She felt dull despair. Neither could do anything for the other. Although she'd try if she could. Will would certainly never be forgotten. But she suspected the memory of him would slowly reduce to that of a wild fling. The pleasure she shared with him, the thrill of excitement, pulling each other's clothes loose in an unfamiliar place. At that moment, she wanted him. He was charming. Their brief acquaintance provided a potential foundation. But that's how it should have ended: in sexual pleasure. Everything that followed was beyond her control. She became swept up by events. Carried along by emotion. Unable to see the situation for what it was, a fleeting bit of fun on a girls' night out. If she was regularly that way inclined, she'd have perhaps checked her behaviour. Because she wasn't, she'd become lost amidst raw emotions. As she was lost now. Only physically. Hurtling along a dual carriageway. Destination unknown. Compared to what she'd been through during the past few days, the outlook didn't appear too bad. All he had to do was stop. And boy was she going to give him grief when he did. That's how she felt. But she was unsure of its wisdom. Stuart clearly let his emotions fly when he wanted to. If she didn't play along, he might become violent. All the more reason to keep her distance.

She'd been keeping a subtle eye on the fuel gauge. The needle was in the red. She knew it wouldn't be long until he had to stop. They were twenty-three miles from the next motorway service station, half an hour at his current speed. If he stopped there, she'd be isolated from civilisation. Her choices would be limited to staying with him or running to the support of nearby strangers. The bedtime attire alone should be enough to convince them of her sincerity, if not her sanity. If Stuart possessed any sense, he'd abandon her at that point. She couldn't see him trying to reassure those she ran to, to try and take her back. If he stopped at the service station, she decided, she'd be better off remaining calm and staying with him. At least it would gain his trust. There were junctions in seventeen and thirty-two miles, both leading to towns. If Stuart chose to take either of these, she had an opportunity to escape with the money. If anyone deserved it, she did. What comparable torment could Stuart have been through for fate to let him have it? For all she knew, if she got him arrested, the money might be returned to Wayne. And there was no way on Earth she was going to let that happen. She'd rather burn it, however much was at stake. Granted, this she didn't know. But if Stuart was willing to abandon his old life, it must be a substantial amount. The rolls of notes appeared to fill most of the bag. The more she thought about it, the more it became impossible for her to see it any other way. One way or another, she'd escape this saga with the money. If she could get through the past few days with her sanity intact, she was pretty sure she could muster confidence when confidence was all she needed. She unfolded her arms and squeezed her thighs. It was time.

Telling herself to do it, her fists clenched, and she felt her fingernails scrape her thighs. Gently, hesitantly, she reached over to the gear lever, where Stuart's hand rested, and laid her sweaty palm on top. Preparing to look at him, she was nervous. But that was fine because that would be the case even if her intentions were genuine. When she did, he smiled to himself before glancing over. In his eyes, she saw victory.

'It'll be all right,' he said.

☺

Will came round in pitch black, cramped and constricted. Bumps and vibrations consumed his confined body and expelled a barrage of noise. His restricted movement and lack of sight made the experience extremely disorientating, like waking to find yourself rattling through outer space. A blocked nose denied his sense of smell and compounded his bewilderment. Further impacts assaulted his battered body and delayed the distinction between abstract and reality. He eventually determined he was in a car's boot.

Reaching forward, Will found a shinbone beneath the thin cloth of Adam's shell suit trousers. His clumpy trainers were close to Will's face. 'Adam,' Will whispered. But he didn't get a reply.

For how long they travelled, Will couldn't say. All sense of time evaded him. The constant whine dropped to a low groan, then the vehicle began rolling with the twists and turns of a varying camber. Being driven aggressively, Will sensed they'd arrived when they jerked to a stop immediately after making a sharp turn. His fears were confirmed when he heard the passenger climb out, and the dulled squeak of a gate swinging on its hinges.

The car's sporty suspension cracked and scraped as the driver covered the pitched ground, jolting Will around uncomfortably.

The pummelling finally stopped. Will waited. Through the boot lid, he heard a brief conversation, the maniac's gruff voice demanding a cigarette. While they smoked, Will caught the odd word or grunt, a short cackle of laughter.

Then they were coming for him. The two front doors opened and closed one after the other. The boot clicked open, cool air rushed in, and the metal lid angled to reveal stars. Will no longer saw the beauty in them. With Daz's sneering face passing between him and infinity, he felt the darkness was about to consume him. Adam's left eye and cheek were swollen, the skin red.

Will longed to be free and fought off a hand to climb out of his own volition.

'Watch it,' came a warning.

Stepping onto the uncut grass, the awareness that he was at the mercy of a villain haunted him. The night sky arched overhead, like a lens magnifying the entire universe onto his shoulders, his world confined to an anonymous field; its limits, a coarse border of brambles.

The big guy chucked two shovels onto the grass. With the implications, Will felt an urge to beg forgiveness.

Daz calmly lit a cigarette. 'Get digging.'

When neither moved, the wrecking ball stuck a boot on Adam and pushed him towards the shovels. 'Move.'

'Daz, man,' pleaded Will.

'Shut it,' Daz shouted.

Will and Adam picked up shovels and planted them into the

coarse grass. With each heavy load, Will felt increasingly lightheaded. Realising the action was his own, he clung to the importance of this like it was the only thing left in the world.

☺

Charlotte watched the white lines between lanes track by. Ahead, the road tunnelled into darkness. As every metre of tarmac, every sign, every road marking, every light disappeared behind them, Charlotte's plight remained. Her past fracturing from her future, these items of order and authority provided a constant. They ticked by like a steady beat, a metronome, offering stability and a reassuring link to humanity.

The first junction had long gone, miles behind on a different road entirely. Stuart didn't even appear to notice it. His attention remained fixed in their direction of travel with no care for the signs that guided them down Charlotte's imagined path to freedom. Perhaps he'd forgotten about petrol; difficult, given its necessity. The services were three miles away, and the next junction twelve. But Stuart showed no inclination for these options. Perhaps he had no plan at all and was driving until he decided on one. What was the idiot doing?

Now they were motoring along an obscure A-road. The van must be running on fumes, she thought. She'd been sitting so long her backside was uncomfortably numb. Charlotte shifted in her seat and folded her arms. Thankfully she hadn't held his workmanlike hand for too long. After his laughable reassurance, he appeared content to leave her be. Well, that was no problem at all. She shifted again and rested her elbow on the metal sill. It was a chore to stay composed.

'Shall we get a hotel?' asked Stuart.

God no, thought Charlotte. 'Let's keep going for a bit.'

'We need fuel.'

'Urgently?' asked Charlotte like she didn't want to hear it.

'We're pretty low.'

'Then I guess so.' She'd play along but let him know he wouldn't have it all his own way, 'I want a twin room tonight.' To which he looked affronted. Like his intentions were dishonourable. Oh, what an idiot.

'No bother,' he said.

Charlotte wondered about his mother. Did he have any women in his life? If he did, she didn't think they challenged him.

When the junction's countdown markers neared, Stuart indicated left. Ahead, a towering neon totem listed food outlets, as picture-perfect as the refreshments on offer. There was a hotel on site too. 'I don't want to stay here,' said Charlotte trying to sound casual about it.

Stuart looked over. 'But we need petrol.'

Charlotte preferred her idea a whole lot more. 'How badly? Can't you get it tomorrow?'

'In the morning?'

'Yeah, there's a town in a mile or so. We can find somewhere nicer there.'

'I thought Manchester would be good long term.'

'Stoke-on-Trent will do for now, won't it?' she said, reading from the sign. 'Do the gangsters know anyone there?'

Stuart thought it through then cancelled the indicator. He eased the van back onto the carriageway. 'You want someplace nice?'

'Can't we afford it?' Charlotte smiled nervously. He was going with it; hook, line and sinker.

Sanctuary neared like every metre was a mile. Unfamiliar with Stoke's geography, she'd need to discreetly pay attention. Ideally, they'd find a hotel near a commercial street or bars. Somewhere people gathered. She'd suggest it as soon as she saw one.

Charlotte's heart sank. It was a Tuesday, the week's dullest night. There would be no one about. Maybe one street with bars would be busy. She clung to this hope, remembering something distant about Stoke being famous for brewing beer. That would make any night popular. Maybe she was making that up. She knew it was renowned for pottery.

The dual carriageway passed through the city centre. Charlotte could see grand stone buildings to her left. Stuart took the first exit after the redbrick train station, turned right at the junction and followed the road to pass beneath a railway bridge.

Within seconds they were into the local infrastructure with its unique quirks. Newer office blocks were alongside redbrick buildings with terracotta trim. She saw signs for Staffordshire Polytechnic and her hopes for a throng of students piqued. Then a petrol station neared, a row of commercial properties opposite, and she spoke before intending to. 'That'll do.'

'Where?' asked Stuart.

'Petrol,' said Charlotte, pointing. 'May as well. You can ask them about a hotel if you want?' Eager to appear relaxed, she added calmly, 'Unless you know one?' She gave a little shrug.

'No,' said Stuart, indicating onto the petrol station's forecourt.

Under the strip lights, an empty hatchback was at a nearby pump, temporarily abandoned while its owner paid. The station's shop doubled as a local convenience store. Several cars were parked in bays, their owners inside among the aisles.

Across the road, a kebab house was open. Empty, a foreign worker busied himself, shaking the salad trays beneath the glass counter. Charlotte wondered about his grasp of English. He'd be no use if he couldn't understand her. Stuart exited the van without saying a word. Perhaps he'd mumbled some self-serving banality. It didn't matter.

She observed him in the driver's wing mirror, focussed on the pump's display until it clicked off, then, like a cheapskate, he spent way too long wresting dregs. Charlotte turned away to avoid getting caught spying. She'd watch him into the shop and, at the appropriate time, slide out through as narrow a gap as she could. When he paid, that would be the moment.

She was contemplating readying the bag of cash when the driver's door opened. Her nerves jumped. She urged herself to smile. 'Boo,' she said, instinctively trying to make a joke of her reaction. She expected another shy smile to reassure her in her hour of need.

'You've been through a lot,' he said, 'You'll settle down before long.'

'I guess.' She fixed on him, and he smiled shyly—there it was.

'You sure you don't want to grab a wedge and go?'

He had no idea. 'I don't think I want to go back there ever. Let alone right now.'

'Cool.' Stuart eyed the bag. 'Fancy chucking me some notes then?'

Charlotte retrieved the bag like it was no big deal. For the first time, she saw clearly the notes rolled along their long edge. All twenties, with perhaps twenty notes in each bundle. There were dozens of them.

Taking the top bunch, she removed the elastic band. 'How many do you want?' she asked, her gaze pinned to the stash.

'Five ought to do it.'

She rifled off five notes.

'How much is in there?'

She took a moment to decide, realising he was chancing his luck as much as her. She remained vague, said, 'A fair few thousand?' underestimating.

'Niiiiice.'

He was ecstatic. Charlotte couldn't help share in his enthusiasm handing the few notes over. She smiled and nodded to show she was on board, and, with that, he went merrily on his way across the forecourt. The wally didn't even look back.

☺

Yes, matey! A nice bit of cash and a lady along for the ride! Crossing the forecourt, Stuart was buzzing inside. He'd play it cool with Charlotte, let them get friendly, no rush. If he thought she liked anyone else, a gentle reminder of the dangers they faced would no doubt help her reconsider.

Stuart entered the shop, bummed by the short queue. He wanted to get back so they could begin their journey together. Look at her, calmly watching him from the passenger seat. A proper smart chick. He'd be firm but fair. Sometimes that was the only language people understood. But it would be for her own good. He knew Daz would've taken a piece of her if he hadn't gotten them out of there. Stuart felt justified doing what he did. He wasn't a mean guy. Sooner or later, that lot would end up in prison. He felt bad for Will, but his actions had caused all this. Charlotte was saved from a life not worth knowing. That was something he could be proud of.

Waiting impatiently for the dithering shop assistant to bag the guy in front's groceries, Stuart eyed the rows of chocolate bars. Nah, he'd get fit again. Get back into football, join a local pub league. Avoid the hooligan element this time. There was no need, especially with no affiliation to the Northern clubs.

She was worth getting on the straight and narrow for. The cash would help set them up. Especially up here. He had his trade. Heck, he still had Glitter's sound system in the van. That would be worth a bit. The cash was their nest egg. She'd come to see it that way over time. A reward for what they'd been put through.

Stuart didn't want to rob that guy. They were forced to do it.

Stuart knew how well connected Daz was. It was clear in his actions. If only Will saw it instead of making things worse. Maybe Daz would've brought them in on bigger scores. Pills were everywhere, and the scene showed no signs of slowing down. They could have made a mint. Will lost because he didn't know what he was doing. That was the difference between them right there.

'Sir?'

The young Asian lad called him forward as the guy with the groceries went by. There were loads of them up here. As many as in London, apparently. It didn't bother him. They seemed shy types, never on the terraces, getting lairy like the lads he used to ruck with. What did they do with their time?

Expecting fifteen change, Stuart whipped off two twenties and handed them over. The others he stuffed in his pocket. All good having a bit of cash on you. Then Stuart remembered the five grand stashed at his house, in a shoe box beneath his bed. He'd have to return for it. Not tonight, but soon. Stuart took the change from the cashier. Working through it, he figured the landlord would come knocking in three weeks once he missed his rent money. Not that Stuart would be there to pay him. At night his chance would come. Two minutes would be enough to go in and get it. He gave himself two weeks to do it. The rest of his stuff the landlord could keep to repay whatever he believed Stuart owed him. It'd be another sweetener for Charlotte.

Returning to the forecourt, Stuart stopped dead in his tracks. Where was she? The warm air hit him. His forehead drenched in sweat. He was compelled to run, hoping to all he knew she was leaning into the footwell, counting the money or something. It had to be that. Otherwise, he didn't know what he'd do.

Stuart wrenched the door handle to find the cabin empty. She was gone! With the money! There was no way she could run for long, not in a dressing gown and slippers. What was she thinking? She didn't know where she was. Stepping away from the van to see along the road in both directions, he wondered if following on foot would be easier. She couldn't have got far.

Stuart threw himself behind the wheel, slammed the door, and got the van going. He'd take the cash off her and go. Feeling stupid for believing in her, he thumped the steering wheel to vent his frustration. He should have chucked her out at the first set of lights. Adrenaline pumped as he stamped the accelerator and fishtailed through the forecourt to the exit.

Anxious to spot her fleeing figure, Stuart strained left then right, surveying the road both ways. What would she do? Get lost in the city centre then jump on a train, he decided. He'd hammer it around the nearby streets before staking out the train station. Stamping the accelerator, tyres squealed as Stuart hooked it right, leaving the petrol station in a cloud of smoke.

☺

Wayne watched rolling country roads swathe and sway in the headlight beams of Dan's Jag. They were guiding him towards redemption. Events had turned on a sixpence. From humiliation to revenge in a matter of hours. Before long, he'd be on top of this kid, Will, like a hundredweight.

Wayne would make it his business to determine if the kid played any part in stealing his sound equipment. Settle his doubts for good. It had to be him. The kid was mad, way out of his depth, with no clue who or what he was getting into. Wayne chewed over what was to come and saw the kid's sorry face as the interrogation began.

The way Wayne saw it, this kid lost the plot after his doormen gave him a shoeing for disrespecting the club. He couldn't have the punters doing all sorts in the toilets, could he? It would be bedlam in there. What did the kid expect? First, he robs him. Then he returns with a bottle. Then he's back to shoot up the club! And today, he goes stealing for the second time. Wayne thought the kid must have been stalking him to know where he'd be with the cash. He was unhinged.

Before he figured it all, Wayne was pacing his patio explaining to Daz why he hadn't showed, waiting for the plumber to finish, and trying to walk off his limp. Then Lew called, told him Daz was putting word out to find the kid; he was too. Wayne told him to stay on it and got hold of Dan to shore up his alibi. They talked through their story until they were confident it would match if questioned at a later date. He didn't trust the girl not to go blabbing to the cops. She was the one thing he couldn't understand. She didn't look the type to be with a guy like that. Maybe she was simple and didn't realise her man was mad. Grief was coming at him from all angles, but, thought Wayne, it was how you reacted that separated the men from the boys.

Once the plumber was done, Wayne hired a cleaner to scrub and tidy the upstairs room. There was no point in taking any chances. He remembered standing outside his house seeing the plumber off. A cop car showed, and the filth inside tried to poke their noses in. Now that was a nervy few moments. Wayne banged on about losing his keys at a party the previous night, watching the plumber's van disappear around the corner. 'Yes, a very heavy one officer. My mate there does locks.' What could they do? They didn't have a warrant. Wayne would've told them to sodding well get one if they wanted to go inside the house. He knew the girl was behind their visit.

While the cleaner cleaned, Wayne removed the bandage wrapped around his forehead. He left the two parallel strips of plaster uncovered. That was more like it. He had grazed palms from when he landed after the van hit him. The first time, it caught him on the backside and it was like he tripped. The second time, he was forced to turn as he fell and he landed on his hip and elbow. The third time, he was blinded by rage, otherwise he wouldn't have stood there, would he? He'd fallen the same way and landed on the same side. No wonder it had swollen up and given him his limp. Making his calls, he had to hold the phone in the opposite hand because of his elbow.

The next call Wayne received was from Daz again, the little delinquent, sitting atop his self-appointed perch. Over the line, Daz's tone was low and measured. Wayne was to meet him outside Ravisbourne with Dan and Lewis. A contact ratted on a kid called Will, apparently fuming after getting roughed up in Glitter. The kid's a dodgy music promoter, getting high and rich off a party scene that ate into Wayne's profits. The kid's got ambitions way above his station, thinks he can ruin Glitter chasing his own glory. Lewis was to be there to confirm the rat cause it was his turf. Wayne was to bring the seventy he owed, and they would split the stolen cash as and when it was found. That was the deal Wayne agreed to get his revenge. So far, Daz's crew had given Will a kicking and believed his story that the other robber stole the loot. Driven off with it, apparently, with the girl. His description matched the one who thought it was smart to run him over. Stuart. Wayne wouldn't forget that name in a hurry. It was lucky for Stuart he wouldn't be at the field. Wayne thought he might lose the plot as soon as he saw him. They knew where the girl lived, though, and this Stuart fella. They'd have to show their faces at some point, and Wayne would cause ructions when they did. Until then, Wayne having his way with Will would do to ease the humiliation.

Dan said, 'Won't be long, boss.'

Wayne thought Dan could probably spot his impatience by how he was shifting in his seat all the time, like his arse was wet—it was no thanks to the leather seats and all the grief!

The traffic cone they'd been told to look out for appeared at the verge. Dan braked and turned between two banks of rugged hedges, a metal gate in front. From the Jag's low headlights, the gate's long shadow stretched towards Daz's sports saloons. The white one looked especially out of place with mud splashed around its arches.

A guy crossed behind the gate, his scarred face screwed up in the bright headlights. With red, swollen hands, he unlocked the gate and swung it into the field. Miserable and wearing a dirty trench-coat, he struck Wayne as homeless. Wayne wondered if that was Daz's contact and, as they motored into the field, experienced a pleasant wave of anticipation.

☺

Will and Adam were confined to the backseat of the saloon. The grimy floor littered with crumbs and gravel added to the sense of waste Will's life had become. He leaned against the nearside door, trying to conserve whatever energy remained after their enforced dig. Towards the end, his limbs trembled with every shovel load. Adam mouthed an incomprehensible string of words, slumped against the opposite door. He'd collapsed to the ground towards the end of the dig. There was dried mud all over his face.

A car arrived. Its headlights reflected in the rear-view mirror and caused Will to squint. The flash of light stirred the big guy in the front seat from whatever murky depths he'd retreated to.

'It's time,' he said and shifted around to face them. His bulk shook the whole car. The exertion caused him to bare his teeth.

Lost in his own world, Adam continued to mumble to himself.

The big guy flung a rousing backhand at him. 'Wake up! Who you talking to?'

Adam kicked out like a terrified animal, flinging himself away from the big guy's swinging malice.

'Did you just kick me?' barked the big guy.

Shaking his head with tears welling, Adam let out a long, terrified wheeze.

'You're a mess you are.' The big guy cackled to himself. 'You won't feel a thing, kid.'

Through the driver's window, the big guy raised a hooked finger to Daz, who stepped from the other car. Will watched Daz pace off behind as much as his sore body would allow. The big guy raised a meaty fist and adjusted the rear-view mirror towards the action at the rear. The arriving headlights filled the compartment with light.

Thinking this might be the end of him cast a dark shadow across Will's psyche. Their innocent interest in music had led to this. All those shared cassette tapes and late night parties combined to form a series with a brutal ending. Even if they survived, Will doubted he'd ever listen to music with the same enthusiasm. What unfathomable melody could possibly raise him now?

Seeing his oldest friend sitting next to him in a blubbering stupor was painful enough. Their friendship had endured despite their parents' dislike of each other. Adam was too stupid for Will, and Will was, apparently, always leading Adam astray. Together they joked about it, but Will knew the sentiments took their toll. As a youngster, whenever Adam undertook the three-mile bike ride to visit Will, his cheerful manner was overcome by shyness at first sight of Will's parents. He wished he'd emboldened Adam instead of dismissing his views on anything other than a winning track. Real leaders supported their allies. He was ashamed of undermining him, but there was nothing he could do about it now. Maybe if he hadn't, Adam would have been the one to find the strength to rescue them. Unlike Will, who could do nothing but watch his life collapse, like he played no part in it.

Stuart was a crook of the lowest type. A weasel who looked out for no one but himself. Where was he? With the cash, that's where. Will couldn't believe he'd ever trusted the one-time hooligan. Look where it had landed him. Beaten and trapped in an unknown field. With a sensation of utter desolation, Will squeezed the door frame hard, like he might be able to break through it to freedom. No one would ever find them. Would they be remembered? Maybe their parties would. It was little comfort.

'You guys ready, 'cause this is it.'

Maybe they could make a run for it? Strain from the dig remained only in his arms. His legs felt capable. Adam would be no use. If Will was to escape, he'd have to behave like Stuart and go it alone. That was the harsh reality. Could he do it?

The big guy opened the rear door to extract them, causing Adam to tumble out. 'Easy,' he barked, roughly taking hold of Adam to hold him up. Pointing at Will, he demanded, 'Out.'

The aggression in the big guy's voice caused Will to cower inside, and all hopes of escape evaporated. Stepping onto the uneven turf, Will became lightheaded again. While he felt like he might faint, the big guy was upon him, pulling him upright, with Adam on the other side. Will found his balance compromised by his tied wrists and trembling limbs.

They werc frogmarched towards five silhouettes waiting beyond the hole they'd dug. Distant discussion floated through the night. Will tried to decipher their words, and wondered how he appeared to them. Did they understand remorse? Were they human? He could run now, left or right. Either way would do. Shake the big guy off, tear through the bushes and keep going.

Would they have the wherewithal to chase him?

The impact came across Will's back, ripped through his lungs, and sent a violent grunt into the sky. Like it wasn't happening, he found his floundering form falling into the hole. Landing in the wet mud, the walls concealed him from the horrors above. It was okay here, he told himself. The cold soil would numb his battered flesh. Overhead, he heard Adam yelp, then he landed heavily on Will's spine. The sharp pain in Will's ribs reignited, unbearably, before darkness covered him like a shroud.

16 / *Promotions*

Squinting in the headlights' glare, Daz approached Wayne's vehicle. Insects spun a mazy dance above the coarse grass. Hidden beyond the light, he found Lewis and Dan. Wayne joined them, lipping from the Jag like they'd done him proper. His face was still etched with amazement though. If only he knew what was about to hit him. It'd make earlier look like a breeze.

Daz revelled in his lies. Snaring Wayne, reeling him out here with the impression he was the guest of honour. What a coup. An opportunity Daz would seize to maximum advantage.

Somewhere behind, he heard Joe rousing the two from the Cosworth. Cal arrived after his trek from the gate. The scowl across his brow could have been caused by any number of irritants. His time to relieve them would come soon enough. Dan and Lewis were wary of Cal stepping a little too close, but Cal avoided their eye and neither wanted to make an issue of it.

Wayne was oblivious, full of self-indulgence, as he watched the two stumble from the Cosworth, arms bound. Their faces swollen enough, you couldn't read much on them. Dan held the sports bag ready. It was time for business.

'That the rat?' Daz asked Lewis.

Lewis nodded solemnly, transfixed by the kids, same as Wayne. 'That looks the one does those parties.'

'The money,' said Daz.

Dan carefully swung the bag, sent it arcing through the air to land beside Daz. Daz wished Wayne had put a hit on Will. An extra ten K in there would've been nice. 'Joe,' he called, his voice crisp in the still night air.

Joe left the two in front of the hole, retreated to a boot and returned clutching a spade. Without breaking stride, he swung it hard and fast against Will's back.

Will's blubbering face spewed a shapeless grunt going over into the hole. His scrawny mate went to pieces, buckling at the knees. Joe did well to stop him making a scene any more than necessary. He swung the spade to meet the scrawny one's backside, and the kid went head first into the hole.

Joe discarded the spade, reached inside his jacket, and removed the Colt. He angled the barrel low and put a quick-fire round into the hole. The gunshots echoed across the countryside. Calm as you like, Joe retrieved the spade and moseyed back to the Cosworth, his job done.

Wayne, with his mouth agape, was utterly transfixed by the scene before him. You didn't know we were going to do that, did you, thought Daz. He said, 'No snitches, no trouble, just us.' He could tell Wayne wasn't listening. 'You satisfied?' he asked regardless.

Daz thought Wayne's eyeballs would've been out on stalks burrowing into the shallow grave if it wasn't for those thick specs. Bored of waiting for Wayne to get with the programme, he yelled, 'Oi!'

Wayne's big eyes were vacant, like Daz didn't exist. His head honcho woke to the threat, puffing his chest and frowning at Daz like he ought to apologise for shouting at his boss. That was all the excuse Cal needed, spinning around and eagerly reaching for the shotgun hanging from a strap beneath his coat. From nought to a hundred in a split second, thought Daz.

Daz was supposed to give Wayne some lip about cheating him out of coke before Cal went berserk. But Cal couldn't wait any longer to have his day out. Struggling to control his enthusiasm, he took three attempts to grip the shotgun hanging from his shoulder. Daz thought the daft berk would do well not to blow Dan's head off.

Once the shotgun was in Cal's grip, it was up and swinging before Dan could react to the sudden change in events. The butt caught him square in the temple, dropping him to the ground in an instant. Cal watched him go and, revelling in the carnage, instinctively knew Dan wouldn't get to his feet. Who was next? Cal spun around with the shotgun, his fury switching to Lewis.

'Woah!' Lewis stepped back in surrender.

Cal hung at the point of attack, determining whether to accept the submission or not. His chest raised and fell heavily from the exertion. Dan pulled at the grass to drag himself away. Cal swung the shotgun between the two security guards, warding them off, before spinning around to train the shotgun on Wayne.

Daz felt his power swell. Wayne's defeat still hadn't sunk in, even though he stared down the barrel of a shotgun. 'I got your attention?' Daz asked.

Wayne's face slowly rotated to the source of the question. White and with glazed eyes, it was like he'd done an E. He didn't answer.

Keeping a wide stance, Cal circled Wayne, the shotgun aimed at the man's chubby face.

'Let him have it,' said Daz.

Cal stood tall and marched at Wayne. Raising the shotgun, he pressed the barrel into the nook between Wayne's nose and cheek.

'What's going on?' cried Wayne trying to look past the gun to Daz.

Cal forced Wayne backwards until the backs of Wayne's legs hit the Jag's bumper, and he toppled onto the bonnet.

'Who d'you think you're playing?'

'Playing?' stuttered Wayne before mustering some backbone. 'What you talking about?'

Daz didn't have to tell Cal what to do next. Cal leapt backwards, tearing Wayne from the car and throwing him to the floor. Pointing the gun at Wayne's forehead, Cal barked, 'Move,' flicking the barrel sideways to indicate the hole.

Wayne stared back in disbelief so Cal gave him a kick. 'Move!'

Wayne tried in vain to shield his face.

'Move,' yelled Cal, kicking Wayne in the direction he wanted him to go.

On his backside, Wayne scrabbled away from Cal and the hole. 'What, no, please!' he begged.

Training the gun on Wayne, Cal circled around and kicked him in the direction he wanted him to go.

'Please,' cried Wayne.

Panic set in. He rolled over and tried to crawl away, but Cal booted him on his backside, then circled around and booted him again while he scrambled on the turf.

'Get a move on,' said Daz.

With his blood up, Cal looked at Daz like he was about to take issue with how he'd been spoken to. But he held himself together and, instead, took an unshakeable grip of Wayne's collar.

With Cal dragging him across the grass, the closer Wayne got to the hole, the louder he spluttered and shrieked. Arriving at the edge, Cal pulled him roughly to his knees. The finality of Wayne's situation became overwhelming, and he began to blubber.

Daz paced forwards, offended by the teary, snotty face. He snatched the shotgun off Cal and aimed it at Wayne, who was now hyperventilating.

'Bite it,' said Daz, poking the barrel at Wayne's mouth.

With what was left of his courage, Wayne refused. Daz gave him a blunt kick to motivate him. Wayne grunted and doubled over, the wind knocked out of him.

Daz racked the chamber and lifted Wayne by his chin. He forced the barrel into his mouth.

'Do you wanna sell me the club, or do you wanna get buried here?'

The gun, and a growing quantity of mucus in Wayne's sinuses, hampered his breathing, causing him to splutter and choke.

'Answer me.' Daz was losing patience.

Wayne gathered some composure and defiantly shook his head.

'You think you can play me?'

Shaking his head rapidly, snot spurted from Wayne's nose.

Daz removed the barrel and placed it over Wayne's creased forehead. 'I'll blow your brains out.' He relished Wayne's misery. With the weapon hovering above him, Wayne collapsed around Daz's knees, begging for mercy.

Daz shook Wayne off. Stepping back, he took aim. On his knees, Wayne tried to cover his face, to shield himself, but his hands were shaking all over the place. Daz moved the gun to the side and pulled the trigger.

The booming shotgun recoiled heavily and, at point-blank range, Wayne's little finger exploded with a splatter of blood.

Wayne crumpled to the ground writhing in agony. 'It's yours! It's yours!' he cried, clutching his fist.

Daz watched him rolling about, savouring Wayne's capitulation. The plan that had been forming in his mind for weeks was finally coming to fruition. All thanks to his ability to spot opportunities.

Daz stooped next to Wayne, said, 'I ever hear a word from you again, I'll be after you. And I won't stop.'

To stand, Daz leaned on Wayne's head and pushed his face into the dirt. Bawling in pain, Wayne didn't even react.

'You.' Daz marched up to Dan, who lay dazed against the Jag, and kicked him.

'Get up.' Daz heaved at Dan, who'd covered his head. 'Take him home.'

Daz let go and Dan sagged to the grass. Daz aimed the shotgun and started counting backwards from three. He racked the chamber.

Dan raised his hands in surrender, struggled to his feet, and staggered over to Wayne. Pulling at his crying employer, he tried helplessly to get him to cooperate. Such was the difficulty in getting Wayne's attention, Daz wanted to storm over and do it himself, but a slight delay was the least of his worries.

Once they were up and moving, Daz pointed to Lewis with the gun. 'Your man there's my collateral. Until it's done.'

While Dan and Wayne clambered into the Jag, Daz lit a cigarette and smoked, pleased with himself. Cal came over and took two. Lewis pulled one of his own. They watched the car come to life and begin rolling across the field.

Daz retrieved the sports bag and said, 'Blubbering wreck.'

Lewis said, 'Wasn't pretty.'

'You gonna be my new head of security when we done.'

Lewis shrugged. 'You say so, boss.'

☺

Charlotte watched Stuart step up to the counter inside the petrol station. The moment had arrived. Her heart pounded harder than ever. Gripping the shopping bag, she unlatched the door and slipped through the gap, her attention trained on Stuart.

Out on the forecourt, she hunkered down and fled from the bright-yellow rust bucket as fast as she could. Her slippers flip-flapped noisily against the oily concrete floor, causing anxiety, but she didn't dare look back, no matter what. She just kept going, straightening to hurdle the low brick wall that marked the boundary.

Making the side street, lined with terraced houses and two rows of cars parked nose to tail, Charlotte couldn't help but steal a glance backwards, and saw Stuart at the till as the petrol station disappeared from sight.

Her slippers were unsuitable for running. She flicked them off to carry them. After about thirty metres of sprinting, she spotted a narrow lane, across the road, between a cash and carry and the next row of terraces. She crossed over and shot down the lane behind the houses. With a lack of direct street lighting, Charlotte dropped her pace for fear of tripping over unseen obstacles. The concrete was mossy and damp. She shoved on her slippers.

Wooden doors allowed access to the houses' rear gardens. Opposite them, beyond the concrete wall and overgrown vegetation, a freight yard served the railway line. Throughout the lane were patches of shallow, dried mud and piles of domestic waste.

The cover of night provided a moment to gather herself and organise the shopping bag. She tossed the two shirts over the concrete wall and removed four twenties, slipping them into her dressing gown pocket. Shaking the bag neat, she noticed a bulky object along one side. Sifting through the cash, Charlotte found a gun. Colour drained from her face. Pulling it out, she looked around comically, wondering what to do with it. Instinct told her to dispose of it, but what if Stuart found her? Would she have the fortitude to use it against him? The thought of Will carrying a gun appalled her. She suppressed the idea as though it insulted her view of him. She couldn't have been that wrong about his character. Without further delay, Charlotte hurriedly wiped the barrel clean and tossed it over the concrete wall. She levelled the notes and rolled the bag tight to leave a compact cylinder. She placed it behind the waistband of her pyjama bottoms, covered it with her top, and tied her dressing gown belt to secure it. It wasn't ideal but what else could she do?

Reaching the corner up ahead, Charlotte realised the lane returned her to the same street she'd fled along. She slowed, wary of Stuart. Listening carefully, the van's unmistakable rattle grew closer. Her heart rate kicked up. She retreated into the lane's shadows, squashing into a nook between a discarded washing machine and a pile of black bags dumped against a wall.

Charlotte listened for the van. It drew closer but then must have taken a turning because its noisy chug faded. Encouraged, Charlotte removed herself from the smell of rotting food and approached the street. Fretting about how many creepy crawlies might be on her, she couldn't help brush herself down.

Back on the street, Charlotte spotted the turning across the road and could hear the van rumbling away somewhere beyond. To the left, at the other end of this street, there was a park behind metal railings. She hung back for a minute or two to make sure Stuart wasn't travelling around the block.

Confident he'd gone and that she could hurdle the railing to hideout amongst the park's trees, Charlotte removed her slippers and sprinted the short distance towards it.

Arriving at the railing, Charlotte found a cemetery, not a park. She didn't fancy spending any part of her night among the gravestones. The road bordered the cemetery, and Charlotte worried Stuart might return along it at any moment. Tempted to retreat to the safety of the lane, she spotted a path beside the end terrace that led towards a footbridge.

Dashing over the railway lines, Charlotte felt vulnerable at such a high position. She couldn't get across quick enough. When she did, she found a canal with a footpath running along it. No roads were within sight, and it was unthinkable Stuart would choose to pursue her on foot. If he did, there was little chance he'd find himself near her anytime soon.

Charlotte tried to find her bearings. The city centre was left, it must be, the light above the buildings was so much brighter in that direction. Yes, definitely left. She could see the terraced houses she'd passed across the water. The central railway station was nearby, but Charlotte didn't like the idea of taking public transport in her current attire. She also feared Stuart might go there, thinking it was her quickest route out.

Charlotte paced along the murky waterway, estimating a ten-minute trek to civilisation. A taxi was her best option. She'd take a ride to the next town listed on the road signs: Newcastle-under-Lyme. It wasn't too far. A market town from what she remembered. Charlotte imagined quaint hotels and homely B&Bs, a world away from her current predicament. Any welcoming abode would do for the night. Gosh, it would be a luxury. But it was getting late. Finding one open might be troublesome.

Charlotte hurried to a trot. Considering her attire, she decided the taxi driver wouldn't complain if she waved the twenties and told him about a wild pyjama party. Getting into a hotel dressed like this might be a problem, though. Charlotte imagined a grilling from a standoffish receptionist wanting to protect the establishment's reputation. She tried not to stress. Worst-case scenario, she'd hide somewhere all night and buy a new outfit as soon as the shops opened. She felt a desire to get a haircut, too. A totally new style and colour. It would make her feel more secure. After that, who knew? She'd spend a week at her parents' house and think about it. No, it might bring trouble to her family. Charlotte told herself not to be silly. No way those thugs would venture anywhere near her folks' neighbourhood. No one of concern knew where they lived. She needed time for things to settle. She could do anything or go anywhere. With the previous few days' terror, the sudden realisation of freedom was overwhelming. Safety was within reach! A sense of liberation blossomed, causing her stomach to flutter. The additional bonus of the cash made her want to scream in glee, but she kept her desire in check. She could study for a PhD, take a year off—boy, did that appeal right now. There were so many more options than before. Maybe she could sneak back for the Golf and her belongings, then just drive. Charlotte wondered about the bag Will filled for her and realised it would likely be stolen. Wait! Everything could be; he had her keys. Her spirits dropped. Was it worth going back to check? Her car was the only thing of any real value. Hopefully, an insurance claim wouldn't involve returning to the premises. With the front door broken by Stuart, she could claim theft but didn't want to go back to finalise the details. Maybe the car was still there. The best thing would be to make an anonymous tip-off to the police, let them know everything. Then she'd take things as they came. Depending on her state of mind, she might stay in the hotel awhile and pamper herself. That sounded delightful. She could buy a new car. Or a motorbike—concealing her identity beneath a helmet appealed tremendously. She'd write to the girls and tell them about her period of reflection, about taking some time for herself, like Michaela going off to travel Europe. Maybe Charlotte could go and meet her. Did she need someone to confide in? Probably not. She decided she could tell no one what happened. Why risk losing what she'd gained? The cash needed to be kept safe at all times. She couldn't put it in a bank with no explanation of how it came into her possession, could she? Maybe she needed to get a job that paid tips and gradually deposit the money into her account. She quite fancied going abroad. Perhaps visit her father, wherever he was at the moment. Why couldn't she bag a racing driver and travel the world? That would be perfect. Charlotte reached down to feel the bulge against her belly. Time to move on from Will. There was definitely no going back.

17 / *3 a.m. Eternal*

Seven weeks after the terrifying night in the field, Will felt like he could still taste the cold, wet soil whenever he thought about it, as he did now, riding the train into town after visiting a guy he knew as Lines. Sometimes it was like he'd fallen into a dream world. Will could vividly remember being lifted from the hole, even though he was in a daze at the time. Did his imagination fill the gaps? Was it continuing to do so? Lately, moments would go by unnoticed. Was it a side effect of the stress he was put through? It could be a relief not having to contend with other people's every word.

After Adam landed heavily on top of him in the hole, he heard six loud shots but didn't feel anything. Was he dead already? A muffled conversation quickly became fiery. Will was too scared to move a muscle. Then the voices were near him, above him, and a single shot boomed, fiercer than the others. A harrowing scream pierced the air. Will started to pray it would all end soon. When there was finally movement, he didn't resist. The warm summer's air was a fleeting moment of relief compared to the cold soil and he spat the dirt from his mouth. The big guy dragged him to one of the cars, where he was slammed and pinned against the bodywork. Then Adam was there next to him, and Daz was in their faces, explaining how it would be from now on. How they'd have to work for him to pay their debt. All Will could feel was his aching body.

Becoming numb to unknown horrors, the two of them were thrown in the boot. Dumped outside Will's flat like bin bags, they gathered themselves and stumbled inside, the door showing signs of forced entry. Collapsing in heaps, the smiley-faced posters grinned down at them. Finding his TV stolen seemed trivial after what he'd been through. Will almost wanted to laugh. He was so happy to be alive. Stuart, Charlotte, Glitter, raving, they all disappeared in a swirl of joyous relief, enough to temporarily ease his woes. But his fatigue and his injuries were real, and they sapped his energy.

They were both badly bruised from their thighs up, a particularly bad one on his ribs. Will didn't think any bones were broken. The pain was mostly in his muscles and his joints when he moved. After getting over his beating at the hands of Glitter's bouncers, he would have to do it all over again. He would have taken a trip to hospital if he wasn't too scared. What would he tell them happened to him?

He and Adam stayed in the living room until the following evening, each to a chair, twenty-four hours of barely moving. Barely thinking. Barely talking, just staring at the walls with tired eyes and aching all over.

When Will did move, it was due to an urge to wash. In the shower, he let the water run over his body for a long while. Eventually, he broke down, with tears welling from deep within, sending him weak at the knees. After that, he was able to wash and removed the soil clumped in his hair and embedded under his nails. A retreat to the comfort of his bedroom was the only remedy. But, like the previous two nights, sleep refused to rescue him.

Adam faced the same waking nightmare. Too afraid to sleep at night, by morning, he was tormented by daylight. On the third day, he upturned the sofa and tried to sleep beneath it. Will didn't have the wherewithal to complain about the mess Adam was making of the living room.

That evening Will's appetite returned. He was grateful for the frozen meal he found buried in the freezer. Adam declined to share. While it cooked, Will cautiously broached the subject of their living arrangements. Adam seemed desperate to evade such talk. Preferring instead to cling to a dream of their next big party.

Although a party would provide an escape, it seemed an unlikely fantasy more than an imminent reality. Wondering what would happen next was a constant burden, stymied only by Charlotte and Stuart and what became of them. Were they together? Will felt empty thinking about it. The lack of sentiment Charlotte showed in wanting to leave him so soon after he rescued her hurt the most. Didn't she realise he'd done it for her? Could the speed and intensity of their relationship have ever made it anything more than a fleeting affair? Even so, it should have ended amicably, not plagued by resentment. He consoled himself by assuming she was safe and well. She'd be better off without Stuart.

Deep down, Will couldn't blame Stuart for running. After what had happened, Stuart's instinct appeared correct. Will was glad they hadn't tried to get in touch. Then again, maybe they did. At that time, Will was in no mood to answer the phone or speak to anyone. He simply didn't care for it.

Will saw Stuart in a new light now: his gruffness, mood swings, and negativity, Will put them down to excessive drug use, not only a tough life. Stuart rarely spoke about his parents, only once telling Will they were alkies who took no notice of him. At first, Will had been sympathetic to this. But looking back, there had to be more to why Stuart was so irritable and self-absorbed, and Will could see no other reason.

With all this turmoil constantly running through his mind, the days seemed to merge into one. Over time, the lack of sleep subtly affected Will's rationale without him realising, and he soon faced a new adversary: paranoia. Although his bruises were diminishing and his movement was back to normal, he worried some part of him might become infected. He'd heard how pus could lead to septicaemia. Regular trips to the bathroom to examine himself in the mirror gradually evolved into a fear of Daz returning to kill him. The need for support grew too great, consuming him entirely. Squatting against his bedroom wall, he peered behind the curtain. Remaining vigilant, to not be seen, he checked for anyone watching the flat. Perhaps Daz was keeping an eye on them until they were ready to do it?

It was too much. Will had to run.

While Adam festered in the living room, Will snuck into the paved rear garden and climbed over the wall. He repeated the action many times, travelling through successive neighbours' gardens until he reached the adjacent street without being seen. From there, Will dashed to the corner store and asked to phone a taxi. The storekeeper took one look at Will's dishevelled form and, presuming him to be homeless, refused. Will didn't have the energy for an argument and stumbled off up the street searching for solace elsewhere.

When a police car came rolling along a short while later, without intending to, Will stepped into the road, waving frantically to flag it down. The officers emerged to an incoherent ramble, a deluge of anxiety and woe, and kindly offered him a lift to hospital. Will accepted gratefully and, sitting in the back, felt safe, almost confident that normality would soon return. But the hospital Will was taken to was a secure unit, not A&E. Despite the soothing reassurances of the nurses, Will tried to explain a mistake had been made. They made sympathetic noises and showed him to a comfortable seat, where he was provided with a dose of Valium. This mollified his protests. Soon after, they gave him a tour. The unit appeared nicely maintained, clean, with social areas, a canteen, an outdoor courtyard and a games room stocked with board games. His concerns evaporated entirely, and once inside his own private room, he zonked out the second his head hit the pillow. His first sleep in over a week.

Waking the next day was like a bizarre hangover in that he had no idea where he was, but he felt as fresh as a daisy. His memory returned. Then his concerns, but they were manageable and he could see reason. His nerves no longer skittish; he felt ready for battle.

After a healthy breakfast, he took a stroll around the ward to find the exit and realised he was locked in. It was a secure ward. A burly porter came to find him at the end of a corridor and told Will he had an eleven o'clock appointment with the doctor. Will realised he was being watched on cameras.

The porter showed Will to the communal washroom so Will could freshen up. Once with the doctor, they measured Will's height and weight and took a blood sample. Asked about his concerns, he told the doctor he couldn't remember. What about the people he thought were 'after him'? Will knew there was still that to deal with, but he didn't want to get into it. He worried if he did, they'd keep him in even longer. Anyway, if Daz wanted him dead, it would have happened in the field. Will shrugged sheepishly and admitted to a particularly heavy weekend. 'Oh, really?' the doctor probed, more interested in this than his previous day's drivelling. Will enthusiastically told her all about his life and the music events he promoted, finding it nice to have someone take an interest in him.

'Well, it must be stressful if you have to arrange the parties as well,' she supposed.

Will explained he hadn't organised a party that particular weekend but felt emboldened enough to suggest smacky pills, perhaps laced with speed, as the cause of his sleep deprivation. It was a weekend carry-on gone wrong. The doctor was writing notes like a Nobel Prize might hang off the back of his hardcore antics. Will embellished some more, telling her all about the scene and what a riot it really was. She even laughed when he told her about getting stranded in Blackburn. At one point, after describing another three-day session, the doctor advised him how amphetamines were once prescribed for various health conditions. However, it wasn't done these days. A nurse interrupted after an hour or so to advise the next patient was waiting. The session was terminated with the doctor providing a quick summary: his lifestyle was reckless, and he'd thrown his circadian rhythms out of sync. He wouldn't be young forever, especially if he remained on his current path. He'd be kept in for observation for the next week to guard against side effects or relapses and to make sure his sleep cycle was restored.

So that's where Will stayed, watching TV and doing his best to keep out the way. The staff had enough of a job looking after the poor souls suffering from chronic mental illness. Most of them wandered around aimlessly without speaking. One unruly one kept trying to escape, another kept bursting into fits of rage and shouting at no one. He made several calls to his flat but each time received no answer. It was a worry he felt no need to share during subsequent sessions with the attractively curious shrink. Adam could look after himself.

A week later, Will talked his way out with a follow-up appointment arranged for the following Thursday and a prescription to keep him going until then.

Will returned to his flat, confident enough to enter via the street outside. Wary, but not afraid, of watching eyes, Will made a note to fix his front door. He soon found the repairs wouldn't stop there. In the living room, the cushions were all torn, their stuffing thrown over the floor. Reels of tape from his VHS collection littered the carpet. Black spray paint and obscenities covered the flyers. Across the mirror, was sprayed: U NO WERE, which Will took to mean: he knew where they would be. His bedroom door was kicked in and the doors also forced off his wardrobe. An unfamiliar object lay on the floor, taped around with paper. The curtains were ripped from the rail, and the heap of clothes dumped on top smelt of stale urine. Adam was nowhere to be seen. Surely he hadn't done this? Will picked up the object, which felt like a heavy metal ball, and went to the kitchen to take a Diazepam to calm himself down.

In the kitchen, he found every piece of crockery smashed across the tiles. The fridge freezer was tipped over, its door hanging loose, and the oven and the hob's four gas rings were left burning on maximum. Switching the gas off, Will imagined a gargantuan bill but found it preferable to a flat burnt through.

He swigged down the Diazepam and cut the tape to unravel the object. Beneath the first layer of paper, he was intrigued to find a fifty-pound note. Within the excess wrapping was a novelty cigarette lighter shaped like a grenade. Across the paper was scrawled: "When U comin clubbin Billz?" A disturbing indication of what was to come. Was Adam with them now? Will knew it wasn't finished until he faced up to it. All he could think of was the trip to Glitter he'd have to make and how he'd approach it.

Deferring the trip to the next day, Will began the clean-up, stuffing his clothes in the washing machine and finding a magazine to wrap the broken crockery. A soft knocking at the back door interrupted the wheel of frustration whirring away. Adam stood outside the backdoor, gaunt and frail. Will let him in and Adam told him he'd spent the day in the old coal shed. If anyone needed a week in rehab, it was him.

Will insisted Adam ate. Over takeaway fish and chips, which Will had to continually remind Adam to eat, Adam explained how a crew arrived to trash the flat the previous night. He'd only just started sleeping again and had been lucky to hear them coming, making his escape to the back garden in the nick of time. Will reassured Adam with his tale of the previous week and info he'd gleaned from the doctors. Maintaining the positive messages, he recommenced tidying. Adam suggested the two of them make a run for it, but Will knew that was no permanent solution.

In the morning, it took Will a moment to gain his bearings. The ransacked bedroom room appeared like an alien landscape. The day ahead seemed long and daunting, so he took another Diazepam. Having given one to Adam the previous night to help him sleep, Will left him in the flat and set off. He took a detour to Stuart's house and found the front door forced open. He didn't dare enter, picturing a scene similar to his own flat. At Charlotte's house, the front door was boarded up and the surrounding brickwork scorched by fire. He hoped she was okay. Glitter was shut when Will arrived. He tried the buzzer to no avail, then sat on a bench outside for an hour, but no one came.

Will returned to Glitter that evening after feeding Adam and providing him with a clean outfit. Two doormen were on duty. The railings arranged to organise the queue were devoid of customers. Will gave them his name and asked if Daz was there. After a curious exchange of looks, one retreated inside. The other ignored Will while he waited. Five minutes later, the doorman returned and told Will to come back with his mate, Sunday, two p.m. That was it. They resorted to looking up the street like Will wasn't there, so he left.

☺

As the train slowed for Will's stop, the platform coasted by through scratched windows. After five weeks of these errands, life wasn't so bad. He and Adam could do what they wanted so long as they came to Glitter whenever Daz instructed, usually on a Sunday. The work was to transport items to various locations. Daz never told them what was inside the cases, but Will knew it was money or drugs. Adam was made to wait at Glitter in case Will got any ideas of his own. It was where his oldest friend was now, as Will returned with a satchel from the man he knew as Lines.

Advertising hoardings came into view, the reality they promoted far removed from the world Will now knew. Promoting music started as an escape, but he'd become lost in a netherworld, living in a void where morality and compassion no longer existed. He longed for a new escape.

Will remembered the sleepless nights in his flat as being trapped in endless torment. After drifting into this new world, his only solace was that he was alive. That thought alone gave him strength. Where there was life, there were possibilities.

As usual, the one called Lewis escorted Will through the desolate club. A solitary bar served drinks to a small group, a far cry from the busy Sunday night a couple of months ago, the night he'd met Charlotte. He could see the spot where they kissed. How alive did he feel back then?

Lewis let Will into the office, and Will entered carrying the satchel. Adam waited miserably in a corner. Daz sat behind the desk of his new lair, watching the security monitor. Will placed the satchel down, and Daz took it.

'You know I been thinking,' said Daz.

Will was surprised to see him offer any form of conversation. They usually only got given instructions, short and sharp.

'That ex-piece of yours just about saved both your lives.'

Daz tossed a small cellophane bag onto the desk between them. Inside were four pink pills. Payment for Will's troubles.

'I ever see her again, I won't be firing blanks.' He mimicked a gun with his fingers.

Will held eye contact, waiting for whatever treat would come next.

'I'm joking, fella. You know what I really been wondering?'

When Daz didn't continue, Will enquired, 'What?' his voice tired.

'I been wondering whether Stuart's doin' her now.'

Will tried to remain indifferent to Daz's needling, show he didn't care either way. What did it matter? He couldn't go back. Without intending to, he noticed himself shrug slightly.

'There was this time,' said Daz, 'when some mad crazy shit was about to go off. Hooligan shit. Your man Stu bailed me out. He ever tell you about it?'

After a moment, Will shook his head.

'He didn't know it; I had a quarter mil cash on me that day.' Daz reflected briefly. 'You ever see Stuart again, you manage to keep those puny arms of yours down, you tell him he's the real reason you're alive. Out of respect for that. I'd like to know what he says.'

Will imagined the unlikely scene, him and Stuart shaking hands and making up. Will waited for whatever came next. He didn't believe a word of it.

Daz said, 'We're done.'

Walking from Glitter with Adam next to him, Will was glad to be physically healthy for the first time in months; since the night of their warehouse party. His follow up with the quack had gone without a hitch and his prescription was withdrawn. He and Adam had been teetotal since.

They'd spent their days visiting record shops, crate digging. It was all they could think to do and reminded them of being young and swapping mixtapes. Now there was more determination to their pursuit of music, like it had greater meaning and would help improve their futures. A lack of income prevented them from buying anything, but they listened for hours, day after day, until their fingers were raw from flicking through the vinyl's sleeves. They memorised the tracks they wanted to buy and promised to do so as soon as they could.

Will knew the arrangement with Daz was unsustainable. Aside from the legality, or lack of it, neither of them were getting paid. If he was to raise the subject, Will knew Daz wouldn't pay him. Will had four weeks of money left. He saw them getting evicted from his flat and Daz chucking them in a crack den somewhere. But after finding the courage to make that trip to Glitter, there were no more unknowns. Will's trauma was over, and there was order again. He had the measure of Daz.

When Mike from the Dance Inc. crew called the other week, asking if he knew where Stuart was, Will knew it was time. He let Mike know Stuart had run off with the sound system. Mike was surprised, but Will told him not to worry; he was making plans for a test event in Glitter. Will could tell Mike wanted to get involved, so Will told him to spread the word on the down low, keep the next few Sundays free.

Tonight was the night.

Like the others Will had received after each errand, he discarded the bag of pills in a roadside drain. Around the corner was an old red phone box. Will once visited it, like dozens of others, to advertise the 0898 phone number to call. Excitement ran through him for the first time in months. Will remembered the same sensation before the original Dominator party. All he wanted was to hear the music blasting loud. Nothing could beat it. If there was anything he'd enjoy again, it would be music.

'See that?'

Adam switched his gaze from his feet. 'See what?'

'The phone box.'

'Yeah?'

'That's all we need.'

'For what?'

'The greatest night of our lives.'

Will watched confusion turn to realisation as Adam said, 'No way.'

'What have we got to lose?'

Adam clutched his head. 'What are you saying, man.'

'Come on, I put word out weeks ago.'

'Noooooo …'

'Music sets us free.'

'Are you serious?'

'You want to stick with me for the ride or hang with that guy in Glitter?'

Adam was caught, his face blank.

'Do you trust me, brother?'

After a moment, Adam nodded.

'Come on then.'

'What is it? Where?'

Will said, 'Follow me.'

☺

Daz knelt at the safe and inserted the night's takings, along with some of his own cash. Tonight was a quiet one. Decent. Not too many punters to cause a mess. Fine by him. All he wanted was to write numbers down, add a zero here or there. What would it matter when the accounts were filed? No one would know the figures were contrived. He kept no record of attendance.

It would be a different story in a couple of weeks when the students returned. He could clean a load more cash, but the amount of work they'd have to do to keep the club in order would be a hassle. Maybe he needn't bother. That could deter the partying masses. Or he could get the boys on the door to get heavy on unwanted behaviour, like having too much fun. That might help thin attendances.

Closing the safe, Daz thought of Black Monday, when the pinstripes crashed the economy and rinsed all the joneses. Why play it straight? he thought. On paper, he was a director of two bona fide companies: Glitter nightclub and a chain of independent gaming arcades on the Essex coast. His other venture set up because the Europeans wouldn't do business without a front.

For years, his financial records showed a prudent lifestyle with minimal outgoings or extravagance—although a truck load of cash helped keep him topped up and enjoying life as he pleased. It was a job to play it straight for the authorities. He'd put enough away but to clinch Glitter, he persuaded his ma to remortgage and stuck her on the board for additional cover. She didn't want to know what he was doing; she'd never rat him out anyway. But it all worked towards keeping things looking legit.

He knew the opportunity would come to him eventually. It'd been gnawing away in the back of his mind for months: how to lean on Wayne to leverage his most prized asset. Then Will came along, and everything fell into place. He could have finished them all out in that field, left them buried, course he could, but it was messy business. Why bother when you had the clout to get them working for you.

Cal wanted a job on Glitter's door but scrap that for a laugh. You could forget looking legit if he was anywhere to be seen, especially front of house. Daz offered him ten grand and told him it'd be best to keep arrangements as they were, with Cal as head of special ops. Daz couldn't believe Cal fell for it. He only wanted to mug him off, hoping, as usual, he'd get pissed and forget, but, this time, the daft berk wouldn't shut up until Daz brought him the cash. When he finally did, Cal snatched it, shoved it behind the sofa, and fetched another beer. Dunce didn't even say thank you. At least Daz didn't hear any more about it.

Daz crossed Glitter's empty dance floor. His new domain gave him a sense of achievement. There as his own made man. Acquiring it helped chalk up a hundred grand. A fair price, he thought. Easily only a quarter market value thanks to Wayne running it on debt and pocketing the proceeds. Dozy old plank should have figured everything was going electronic. Even the poxy music. But Wayne couldn't argue. He was glad to get anything from the deal. Lewis reckoned he was losing the plot, jittery as anything these days. Reckoned he might even squeal. Daz liked that one. They both did. Wayne hauling the filth all the way out to that field to find nothing but dirt.

Will was his now, obedient as a toddler. No question after the night they gave him. Letting him know they could finish him whenever they wanted. Running roughshod was easy. Those he ran with were so wet, they fled at the first sign of trouble. Daz liked it when Will kept his mouth shut and did as he was told. He'd sooner bury the pair of them than ease up. Daz knew he gave away too much tonight, trying to get to Stuart. Next time would be business as usual. Daz sneered deviously. Soon Will and that Adam would believe anything he wanted. He only kept them alive in case Stuart or that piece Charlotte tried to get in touch. Will probably hoped he'd get a shot running one of his trendy discos at the club. But if Daz was going to do that, there were plenty of others he could work with. They'd probably be phoning and begging sooner or later. There were so many of them shady parties going on.

The real power was with the clubs, those who owned them and

those who controlled the door. And in Glitter, Daz did both. What did he need anyone else for? He was leader of an outfit that knew how to get what they wanted. His stock would rise when word got around. It wasn't the promoters you needed to go after; it was the club owners. Boys down in East London could learn a thing or two from him. No point fighting it out on the dance floor. If any firms tried that at Glitter, he might really have to put Cal on the door, but he doubted any would have the mettle.

Outside, Daz locked Glitter's front doors, dropped in the newly installed security bar, then inserted and fastened the heavy-duty padlock. He crossed the road to the waiting Cosworth, proud to be a legitimate businessman. No more arduous trips on public transport ferrying product or chopping powder in rundown hotel rooms. That life was gone forever. That life was Will's.

☺

While Will fetched some tools he'd stashed in a bush, he got Adam to hide in a doorway and make sure Daz left Glitter about eleven, as Will knew he usually did on a Sunday. Ten minutes later, in the shadowy alleyway, they were popping Glitter's fire door. The replacement wood splintered, but Daz had chained them from the inside.

Will couldn't accept defeat that easily. Tonight, he would finally extract himself from Daz's evil grip. Riding a wave of adrenaline, he and Adam pressed their weight against the bolt cutters and snicked through the chain. The job was done.

'Come on,' Will cheered. Glitter was cracked!

Adam remained outside while Will sprinted down the corridor. He barged through the internal doors. The distant alarm began wailing. Undeterred, he kept going. It was all theirs. Vacant, large, and soon to become a cathedral of acid house. 'Come on,' Will yelled through the hollow space. But he knew he wasn't done yet.

He went up the stairs and across the entrance hall to the alarm box, where Daz carelessly left the key. If Will hadn't spotted that the other week, his plan would've been impossible to achieve.

Will switched the alarm off. It was stopped in less than fifteen seconds. Hopefully, a false alert to anyone who may have heard it. Will covered his tracks, re-joining Adam outside, and retreated to the doorway out front until they were sure neither Daz nor the law were aware.

Twenty minutes later, they were sprinting to the phone box and barging each other to get in first. Will made it through and retrieved a ten pence piece. He held it above the pay slot. 'You ready?'

Adam started bouncing on the spot. 'Let's have it,' he roared, slamming his palm against the inside wall. It was a release for both of them.

Will inserted the coin, and it clunked down. Will said, 'We are going to smash this one to pieces,' like he'd never been more serious about anything in his life. He dialled the phone number he knew from memory.

Stuart's answerphone message from all those weeks ago played out over the line, but Will didn't dwell on it. He hit the hash key and entered the security PIN.

Adam shook Will enthusiastically. 'Play me some tracks, man.'

At the automated voice's instruction, riding a surge of adrenaline, Will announced, 'Ladies and gentlemen, boys and girls. Dominator, Part Two, is tonight, Sunday, August twentieth. Get your skates on, party people! The action starts at Glitter nightclub from midnight. Be round back in your coolest gear. You know the score, the secret party's finally here!'

Will slammed the receiver down, feeling a rush of excitement.

After calling Mike to confirm, Will got Rob on the phone. He was glad to hear his buddy's voice, even if he did sound tired.

'Are we on?' asked Rob.

'For sure.' Will could hear Rob stirring in bed and asked, 'You capable?'

'Of course I am.' He sounded like he was rubbing his face. 'Played a pukka gig last night. Guess where?'

'Where?'

'In a barn. With actual cows in there.'

'No way.'

'It got so hot, my vinyl melted.' Rob sounded like he still couldn't believe it.

Will laughed.

'No joke, they opened the doors, and I played half-hour with cassettes until the place cooled down.'

'Nuts, man.'

'The *cows* escaped.'

Will laughed.

'Seriously, the scene is getting proper hardcore these days. Police got it on lockdown. You've done well to keep a low profile.'

'Needs must, mate.'

'So, where's this secret party of yours then?'

'Glitter.'

'Glitter!'

'Yep.'

'How'd you organise that?'

'I'll tell you later.'

Rob sounded like he jumped right out of bed. 'I'm gonna play an actual club.'

'Right now,' said Will, deadly serious, 'see you round back. A-S-A-P.'

Back inside Glitter, Will and Adam cut the chains from the

other fire doors for safety and to provide an escape. The second room was opened so the crowd could use it as a space to chill. The bars were secured behind newly added metal shutters, but they wouldn't need them.

Once the DJ booth was powered up and tested, they were pretty much ready to go. No turntables to wire in, no lights to rig, no heavy-duty sound system to wheel through. It was all there, ready and waiting. Man, did Will want to own a club. A constant trickle of excitement buzzed through him.

The lighting desk sat below the decks. They took time to program it, deciding on a lighting arrangement of pink and blue spots, which looked awesome, spinning and flashing together. Glitter had a smoke machine, but it only wafted smoke instead of blasting it out. After briefly considering Wayne's whereabouts, Will decided he didn't care one bit.

With nothing else to do but turn on the lights in the toilets, Will and Adam returned outside to hang by the fire doors. With a clear view along the alleyway, they passed the time naming tracks they wanted Rob to play. Their list went back and forth casually, without much thought.

Initially, Will worried the night in the field would affect Adam permanently. Beyond bouts of immaturity, he was a delicate soul who longed to be popular. When they were young, he was always fun-loving and kind to others. As an adult, downtrodden by his lack of good grades and the strains of earning a living, the party life must have offered the easy escape his fragile psyche craved. But over these past few weeks of sobriety, Adam had slowly rekindled his old self.

True to his word, Rob arrived ten before midnight with a pleased-to-be-there spring in his step until he noticed their virtually healed faces. 'What happened to you two?'

Will didn't want to get into events that were best forgotten. 'I'll tell you later.' He took hold of Rob's shoulders. 'Are you ready to rock it, my man?'

'Always.' Rob laughed and shook both their hands. 'What's the score then?'

'We wait until the crowd arrives, then get it on. Okay with you?'

'What about inside?

'Good to go.'

'Nice, nice.' Rob studied Will's face like the faint marks would provide answers. He said, 'Police been getting their batons out lately. You seen much of that?'

'Everyone's having a pop,' said Will, trying to be evasive.

'Yeah, heavy.' Rob persisted, 'You both definitely okay?'

Will nodded. 'Yep.'

'Yeah,' droned Adam.

Rob reluctantly accepted their answers and looked over Glitter's exterior. 'Hey, I'm happy it's not a barn.' Rob grinned. 'I hope they bought a decent replacement.'

'It sounds good, mate.'

'Tracks on at twelve then.' Rob nodded to them and went inside.

The first revellers arrived moments later, dancing into the alleyway in their baggy outfits. Will could see their smiles from thirty paces. He called down the corridor to Rob, and by the time their guests were at the doors, Will could hear the first beats thumping out. 'Fives, please.' Will smiled. 'Notes only.'

Soon another group arrived, then another, until they swarmed from both directions. A hatchback turned into the alleyway with people pitched through the sunroof. Its headlights illuminated a steady stream of revellers, dancing along, eager to be inside.

A swarm huddled around Will and Adam, waiting for their notes to be taken. If anyone held coins, they'd be enthusiastically directed to the cash machine around the corner. Their inconvenience was an unfortunate necessity, but not many complained. When Dance Inc. arrived, Will shook their hands and let them in for free.

Taking the money and stuffing it into his pockets, Will buzzed with excitement. More and more cars rolled up alongside brightly dressed people, wending through on foot. Horns beeped, headlights flashed, and revellers whooped and cheered to an assortment of lively beats blasting from car stereos. A fair number carried glowsticks, more than he remembered at the first Dominator party. Maybe it was a new trend.

The pals they made on their night out in Blackburn arrived, hollering greetings from the back of the huddle, laughing and joking with everyone until they were inside.

By the time Will's pockets were full of notes, a line of parked cars filled the alleyway. His headcount tottered around a thousand. He didn't want to push capacity too close.

'Roadblock,' yelled Adam, his excitement as wild as Will's.

'Big time.'

Once everyone was in, Will and Adam retreated inside to join the party. Heading down the corridor, Will was reminded of a visit to The Project in Streatham, when those wanting to hear the music no one else played were let in through the back doors after the regular crowd left at two a.m.

Diving into the main room, they were hit by an invisible wall of heat and a doubling of noise. Flashing pink and blue light swirled through drifting smoke. On every level, people danced with unadulterated passion, like one giant organism rippling in the soundwaves.

Across the dance floor, raised up, Rob held an arm in the air as Paris Brightledge sang, "It's All Right", about hope and a better world, telling everyone what the music was about. The whole crowd went wild to the rumbling bass and uplifting piano chords.

Rob flicked his wrist over the controls, and a breakbeat kicked in, the next track on its way. The kick drum's thump encouraged a roar of appreciation, and a wave of silhouetted hands started punching the air. Will and Adam did too.

Taking a wander to check everything out, those who recognised them from the door shared beaming smiles. Sometimes they received a friendly pat or a thumbs up. One girl stopped them and offered puckered lips with exaggerated affection. Will knew she was high and responded by theatrically kissing each of her cheeks. Another flung her damp arms around Will and affectionately kissed his lips. He could feel her body heat radiating through his T-shirt. Will shared her beaming smile. 'Having fun?' he asked, but she was too taken by her buzz to reply. She kissed him again and danced off into the crowd.

Entering the second room, a carpet of guests covered the floor. Chatter fluttered into the air to merge with the music somewhere overhead, like the basement at Hedonism. Among them were two girls who were applying DayGlo face paint for a pound per person.

The atmosphere was the same in the diner, where chrome-trimmed booths burst with people enjoying themselves. On the stairs to the front doors, every step bubbled with two or three private conversations. The many bodies would hinder any coppers wishing to halt festivities, as would the cars filling the alleyway.

'Let's get back on it,' called Adam, dancing off into the crowd.

'Right on, brother.' Will bounced after him with a reinvigorated dance step amidst the smoke and flashing lights.

Will felt alive again. The dance floor's wooden boards buckled and bounced. The night still young, Will and Adam danced like they were in competition. Everybody shared the same intensity and desire. The room was peppered with specks of multicoloured light, like a sea of stars, caused by hundreds of glowsticks held aloft. Darting beams of coloured light traced over the intense crowd. Will would stay amongst the hot, smiling faces and most amazing music for as long as he could.

Will revelled in the bedlam, a release from weeks of pent-up frustrations, being hustled by a devious crook. He'd be damned if he let Daz hijack the music scene he loved so much. Didn't Daz realise Will was a king? No one could get in his way. He made this night—he made all the nights!

Rob's mixing drew another roar of appreciation, and Will cheered like the rest of them. Rob seemed to control the crowd's every move, like a conductor in front of his orchestra. Every flick of his wrist altered the sound, and the revellers reacted with glee. Look at him, thought Will, watching as Rob flipped the record before placing it on the turntable. He was a master at work, and he held the crowd in the palm of his hand. Their admiration made Will want to buy a set of decks. He would one day. But that dream was for another time. For now, he wanted to experience everything Glitter offered. The most incredible tracks. The friendliest of people—beautiful people. Everyone looked beautiful when they smiled. The lights were mesmerising, their bold, translucent colour cutting through wisps of smoke that drifted over the rapturous party. Even compared to their warehouse gig, the atmosphere was intense.

The beat thumped through Will's chest, lifting him. 'Come on!' he cheered, throwing his arms in the air, bouncing and stepping to the new rhythms. The hi-hats and horns, toms and percussion, they sounded so good on a permanent sound system. This was forever music, turning days into night and nights into day. Look at all these people, free from their jobs, celebrating the weekend like it was all that mattered. It *was* all that mattered. This was where Will belonged. Among them. Among this sonic heaven, this audio elixir, looping out every four bars, beat by beat, driving him on, driving all of them on. This was their time, unstoppable, immovable, relentless. He was going to find a club and make it his own. Anything was possible now. Nothing was off limits. If it could be conceived, it could be achieved, like life and ambition and your own personal drive to be who you wanted to be. Will would do it, sell up and do it all over again if he had to. No one could stop him. Who among them could resist its appeal? Together we dance, my friends. Until the soles of our shoes fade and our limbs go weak. Together we dance.

Rob introduced another track. The thump of a kick drum gradually gaining momentum, pounding over and over, four-to-the-floor. A crescendo of cheers rang out, and the multicoloured stars in Will's universe began to dance. A speaker crackled as it buckled under its own pounding vibrations, like every input was set to maximum. Everyone was in a state of rapturous joy. Will didn't want it to end. He'd enjoy every second, for he knew they might not have much time.

☺

As the track broke into a luscious harmony, Rob felt the crowd's cheers reverberating through him. Their passion and enthusiasm made them reach out like they wanted to touch him. He was being worshipped like a god. This is where the DJ belonged, he thought, in a nightclub, not a barn! Then the musical world would belong to them. A new breed. No longer an afterthought. The person who operated the sound system, promoted drinks offers and took requests. Without a doubt, it was their moment.

Soaking up the adulation, Rob remembered his trip to New York and the musical auteur who took him on a journey across an audio soundscape emotive beyond words. With the world's best sound system, Paradise Garage was a sonic temple of hedonism. A few blocks over, Tracks wasn't as slick. But with David DePino behind the decks, it really didn't matter. Playing the freshest of house tracks, the atmosphere was electrifying, and Rob came away convinced it was the future of music.

The UK had trailblazers bringing Chicago labels like Trax and Prelude to the fore, but house didn't really ignite until Hedonism. When a derelict warehouse near Hanger Lane pulled a bigger crowd than a West End super-club, that's when Rob knew things had changed. House music all night long, baby! E might have been the catalyst, but house music was bigger and better than a cheap thrill, one the acid teds latched onto because it was the latest craze.

When the beat kicked in, Rob turned the dial to increase the low-range, and it was like the dancers' energy increased with it. Their smiles lit up and the ripple of bodies amplified in intensity, like a digital equaliser bouncing towards maximum. He didn't want to turn away. The smiling faces were too infectious. But he needed to select the next record, so together they could go again.

Rifling through his case, Rob decided on the next track, "Lack Of Love". Flipping the twelve-inch over, he laid it down and set the needle to drop. He matched the gains and the two records' speeds within a bar of sixteen. Wanting to cue the track from the beginning, he waited for the moment to introduce it. In the corner of his vision, a flurry of activity distracted him, a police line pushing forward onto the dance floor. With the party ecstatic, guys and gals were reaching out to hug them, and the stern-faced bobbies fought to maintain possession of their helmets as well as their dignity.

Rob tried not to let the law's presence dishearten him. All good things must come to an end. It was gone four a.m. and he'd spun a prime set. There would be no running this time. He'd play to the end and suffer the consequences.

As soon as the next breakdown landed, Rob released the record from his fingertips and allowed the introductory beats to skip over the warm harmonies. He'd practised this mix many times and knew once the breakdown ended, the vocals would begin. Rob first heard the track at the Hacienda. The crowd went wild, like he hoped they would tonight. He looked up to see a wave of arms reaching towards him through the light beams.

The police persisted into the crowd, their faces red, their shirts drenched in sweat. To distract himself, Rob whipped the volume up and down to cause the breakdown's solid harmony to pulse. Not long now. He adjusted the first channel's volume control and matched it with the second. Gradually he tweaked the trebles and midranges. With one bar of four left, he cut the bass on both channels and reset the levels. As the breakdown ended, he released the bass. With the acid drop and the tribal beats dancing beneath it, the whole club shuddered under the speakers' vibrations. The crowd erupted with unbridled joy, a mass of raging ecstasy. Rob checked for the bobbies and thought a couple of them were so surprised by the increased enthusiasm they'd stumbled sideways.

How would he top that last mix? He rifled through his vinyl and found a heavy white label, one that banged within sixteen. He'd fade from this one when the vocals ended and the distorted bassline began, then keep the remaining tracks slamming and the energy levels high. There was no way he was going to give the bobbies an easy time on their way through. And you never know, thought Rob, his best selections were still to come; he might even win a few of them over.

18 / *Paradise*

Will and Adam stepped off the bus, each carrying a small rucksack. Will looked over their destination, safe in the knowledge nobody except Rob knew where they were.

They'd slipped out of Glitter via the fire escape as soon as they'd clocked the flashing blues and the flurry of guests returning to the main room from the front stairway. Stepping into the alleyway, a gaggle of revellers danced around cars, enjoying beats pumping from stereos. It was easy to dance past them incognito and catch a taxi.

Walking along from the coach, the dawn sun peeked above the spinning airport control tower. A morning mist settled over the runway. Construction work was being undertaken, and Will and Adam followed the temporary metal railings from the bus stop to the terminal building.

'A couple of grand in your pants ain't as cosy as I thought it'd be, man.' Adam reached down for a scratch and a readjustment.

'Watch it.' Will looked around cautiously.

'I'm just saying.' Adam flung an arm around Will's shoulders. 'I haven't slept, bro.'

'Neither have I.' Will shook himself free. 'Be cool.'

'I am.'

'Sure you are.'

Passing through the automatic doors towards check-in, Will saw IBIZA flashing on the screens behind the desks. He couldn't wait to board the plane.

It was two years since their last trip. Back when they were both still innocent. Invited out by Adam's older brother, a hotel manager on the island's west coast, they could only guess what the holiday would have in store for them. San Antonio was full of cheesy discotheques selling cheap beer and spinning tacky holiday records. But one bar catered for Brits keen to get away from the southern soul scene as much as the weather. Will and Adam soon found themselves in Amnesia, an open-air club, where millionaire yacht owners cavorted alongside flamboyant drag queens, pop stars and famous actors. The decor mirrored the clientele's own exotic tastes with fountains, palm trees and plush alcoves. Will was in awe of it all. Not just the toned, affluent clientele, who were happy for him to join them, but with the club's production design. They were a million miles from the sticky carpets and garish lights of UK nightspots. The music was as sophisticated as the crowd and the DJs mixed up-tempo reggae with soul, funk, electro-pop and Chicago house in a manner that encapsulated the venue's magic. Hearing "Imagine" one morning under the dawn sun, Will was convinced he'd found the heart of egalitarian culture.

Their rucksacks travelled along the conveyor belt and through the plastic strips hanging in front of the hatch. They took their tickets from the airline's staff member, who watched them depart with an efficient smile.

In a celebratory mood, Adam wanted a Lucozade to help him cope with the lack of sleep. Will left him to it and headed for the departure lounge. He was anxious approaching security but knew his tiredness would provide cover if airport staff quizzed him.

He scooted through the X-ray machine with a polite smile and took his items from the tray. Travel advertisements led to the rows of seating surrounded by chain restaurants and fast food outlets. TVs were fixed in pairs, attached to frames above the seating. One TV displayed a constant rotation of departure times while the other screened the morning news with subtitles. Will took a seat near one of these and waited for the gate to be announced.

Through the wall of glass overlooking the runway, Will watched aircraft taxiing for take-off. Will was keen to see what Ibiza would offer and planned to make something happen. Who knew what lay ahead? There would be plenty of bars to approach. He couldn't wait to fly Rob out as one of his resident DJs. Adam's brother still worked out there and could hook them up if necessary. Ibiza seemed like the right place at the right time.

Will remembered when he and Adam would head out Saturday afternoons, hit Oxford Street and listen for Kiss FM. All the trendy stores played it. They'd shop until the locations of the night's warehouse parties were announced, then head off to get ready. Despite the dodgy venues, there was never any trouble. On Sundays, house-heads would congregate on Clapham Common to chill for the day. You could tell everyone was on one, crashed out listening to ghetto blasters, wearing the same bright clothes from the previous night. Over the weeks, word got around, and the crowd grew from tens to hundreds. By the end, you'd have to get there early if you wanted to arrive before the police cordon. The only other grief you would get was someone accidentally kicking over your Lucozade.

Ever since Will could remember, music got a hard time from the law. Growing up, tuning in to Radio Caroline was a thrill, like he'd joined a club that didn't care what the authorities thought. How terribly the youth might turn out if they heard rock and roll! Now house music signalled the demise of society.

People needed an escape from the humdrum, and Will would do his best to make Ibiza *the* place to go. The Balearic vibe helped create the UK scene. Now it was time to take it back. Will had a new lease of life, and he'd make it the heart and soul of the party.

Everyone wanted to be part of something. There would be no issues. He'd do his best to make it a paradise for partygoers from all over the world. That was how he saw it, and he looked forward to what the nineties would hold.

There was a moment, he remembered, that permanently changed his musical tastes. "Planet Rock" by Afrika Bambaataa. That track ruled his world. For months he couldn't get enough of it. An electronic drum machine had created his future. Its infinite beats transporting him to a world of freedom. Just like the island he was visiting now.

Sleep deprivation made Will smile inanely to himself. He needed shuteye but didn't want to miss the flight. Keeping a lookout for Adam, Will swapped the TV news for the holidaymakers who meandered through. He tried to guess whether they were departing for a trip or returning home by how troubled they seemed. He was heading to a world free of trouble. An island where reality ceased for the duration of its guests' visit. Anything was possible out there.

Drifting back to the TV, Will recognised the local newsreader, who received his few minutes every half hour. Looking closer, the image of Glitter nightclub hooked him. He read the subtitles passing across the screen:

… *Police arrived at an unlicensed party* …

… *held at Glitter nightclub* …

… *in the early hours of this morning.* …

… *We join our reporter live on the scene.* …

Will thought last night's gig deserved some press. He did call them, after all.

The news studio cut to a female reporter, outside Glitter, surrounded by dozens of brightly dressed partygoers who revelled in the attention. A blue light flashed over them all, indicating the off-screen police presence. The reporter presented to camera, her words as subtitles:

… *The nightclub has recently been* …

… *under scrutiny from senior officers* …

… *after a number of violent incidents.* …

… *This morning, as the party continues* …

… *outside, it is understood police are* …

… *seeking to have the club closed down* …

… *by court order.* …

Will jumped up. 'Come on!'

Everyone in departures turned in his direction. He lifted his hood and, with no apology, ducked into his seat.

On screen, overenthusiastic celebrations distracted the reporter. She politely acknowledged the partygoers before returning to her notes:

… *One officer told me they are* …

… *seeking the permanent revocation* …

… *of Glitter nightclub's entertainment* …

… *licence.* …

Will watched smiling revellers dancing around, the dawn sky brightening behind them. To camera, the reporter said:

… *No one was arrested in connection* …

… *with the unlicensed rave.* …

… *Leaving police reluctant to admit* …

… *this is yet another case where the* …

… *acid house protagonists* …

… *and their whereabouts* …

… *remain unknown* …

Printed in Great Britain
by Amazon

87882783R00163